Cut–Through Valley

Dean Feldmeyer

SILVER DAGGER

M Y S T E R I E S

This book is a work of fiction. All names, characters, and events are the product of the author's imagination. Places are either the product of the author's imagination or are used fictitiously. Any resemblance to actual events or persons, living or dead, is entirely coincidental and beyond the intent of either the author or the publisher.

Hardcover ISBN 1-57072-121-1
Trade Paper ISBN 1-57072-137-8
Copyright © 2000 by Dean Feldmeyer
Printed in the United States of America
All Rights Reserved

1 2 3 4 5 6 7 8 9 0

In memory of Marvin E. Feldmeyer, my dad.

CHAPTER 1

ERASMUS WISHBONE HAINES DIED on the Monday after my first Easter in Baird, Kentucky.

I have, in my pastoral career, presided over more than a hundred funerals—said the words of comfort, read the Twenty-third Psalm, preached homilies, and prayed for words that are supposed to give meaning to grief—and, if I think hard, I can remember maybe a dozen of the names of those I've buried.

I'll probably stand beside a hundred more graves before the bishop puts me out to pasture, and by that time the number of names I can recall will, no doubt, be down to half a dozen: Lori P., a two-year-old who was shaken to death by her stepfather; Ronald I., who was sixteen years old and the captain of his football team and got drunk and drove into a telephone pole with a car full of his buddies; Karl D., who was over seventy, his nose and mouth eaten away by skin cancer; Pete M., whose mistress showed up at the funeral and caused a scandal. A few others.

For most of my funerals, however, I have been just another prop along with the flowers and the casket and the hearse. Part of the ritual of death, American style: The minister in his black suit and cleric with his little black book of magic words tucked under his arm. As anonymous to them as they were to me, even when they were members of my church.

Some of that changed when I came to Baird, Kentucky. I lost the black suit and the cleric. In Appalachia such clothing are considered "too Catholic" and not appropriate for a Methodist minister. I do my preaching here in a tan, wash-and-wear, cotton suit in the summer. In October I switch to a gray, wool, herringbone jacket and black slacks. The shirts are always white. The ties are forgettable. On weekdays my uniform is blue jeans, plaid shirts, and sneakers. Appalachian chic.

My church here is smaller. Much smaller than my former, suburban cathedral. I know all one hundred ten of the members, and the thirty or so who show up on Sunday morning for the worship service I call by their first names. They address me as "Dan" or "Reverend Thompson" or "Rev'r'nt," or sometimes "preacher" as they shake my hand and pass through the door of the sanctuary after the service.

I had never shaken the hand of Erasmus Wishbone Haines, though. He'd never been in my church.

So why do I still I remember his name?

Perhaps it was the violent nature of his death. Ras Haines had been murdered—beaten and kicked to death, his body left in a bloody, broken pile just a few feet from the place on the front porch of the farmhouse where he passed most of his evenings. It's the violent and untimely deaths that stick in your mind. Death is supposed to come at the end of life, in old age, in bed at home or in a hospital or nursing home. God's plan does not call for early and violent death; that's a twist we lesser beings have interjected into the scheme of things.

Or maybe it was the timing—the day after Easter.

American culture has declared Christmas the highest holiday of the year, and we in the church have pretty much fallen into line with our pageants and decorations and carols and parties. But, in fact, Easter is still the highest, holiest day of the Christian calendar. It is the day when we affirm, once again, that death is not the end of life. In ancient and pagan cultures the celebration we call Easter was a celebration of spring and the return of life after the long death of winter. It's not much different today. We've simply lifted what is obvious in nature to theological significance. Easter reminds us that life is triumphant.

It's a pretty big deal.

The year Ras Haines died, Easter fell on the first weekend of April and spring was in mid-stride. The dogwoods and redbuds were starting to show color, the crocus had come and gone, and the daffodils were just opening.

My son and daughter had made the trip from California, where they lived with their mother (my ex) and their stepfather (a lawyer) to spend holy week with me. We had gotten up early on Sunday and opened the church for the sunrise service, then gone to the Baird Diner for breakfast.

Upon returning to the church, we found it nearly full of people with new clothes and scrubbed faces. The singing was robust and my preaching was inspired. Dora Musgrove didn't hit a single clinker on the out-of-tune piano as she accompanied the hymns.

After the sunrise service we all gathered in the basement of the church for coffee and hot cross buns and then went back upstairs and did it all again. New hymns, new sermon, same new clothes and scrubbed faces. Halfway through the first hymn, my mother walked through the back door, beaming and waving, and made everyone slide down so she could sit in the pew next to Naomi Taylor, the love of my life, and May June Hall. May June's husband, Ray, the township constable and postmaster, had even put on a suit and come in to sit in a pew instead of out on the front stoop where he usually sat so he could smoke his Camels and drink coffee while he listened to the sermon and choir anthem.

After the second worship service Mom took us all to Perry for Easter dinner. Since we didn't have a reservation at any of the American restaurants in the county seat, we ended up eating at the Red Dragon, a Chinese restaurant run by a Vietnamese family. We ate and laughed and had a wonderful time.

After dinner we went to the town hall and watched the Easter egg hunt on the lawn. My kids were too old to join the battle for the prize eggs, but they laughed like hyenas, watching the little kids scramble around the courthouse green, falling and pushing and scrapping for the Easter Bunny's treasures, one of which was reportedly worth a five-dollar prize.

After the Easter egg hunt we drove back to Baird and sat around my parsonage and talked and smoked and napped.

It was a wonderful day; then it ended.

Mom hugged me and left, taking my kids back to the airport in Lexington. Naomi kissed me and left to drive back to Perry where she was working temporarily for Percy Mills, the oldest and richest lawyer in Durel County, preparing income tax returns for his clients. Ray and May June left arm in arm, to go back to the diner and their apartment on the second floor. No kiss or hug from either of them.

After everyone left, I sat by myself in the living room of the parsonage and tried to get interested in something on television. Easter night Hollywood Bible epics were on all the networks and everything else was showing reruns. I nuked some fried rice that was leftover from lunch and cracked a Budweiser, but neither of them tasted right. I tried to get re-interested in a book I was reading before the kids had arrived the week before—something about the Civil War—but my mind wouldn't absorb the words. I would read them but they would just stick there on the page, refusing to fly up into my brain.

Too early to go to bed, I put Leo Kottke on the stereo. Steel string acoustic guitar, instrumentals only—an Easter present from my daughter. Lit my pipe with the Zippo my son had brought for me and fell into a perfect blue funk.

Self-pity, loneliness, and guilt. These three are the horsemen of the mental health apocalypse. Jewish mothers have nothing on teenage kids when it comes to guilt. How dare those kids be so bright and well-adjusted and happy and marvelous while living with a lawyer in California, for the love of Mike.

I threw the fried rice away and drank the Budweiser. Then I drank another. Then another and another.

Then I fell asleep on the threadbare nylon couch in my living room.

The next morning the loneliness, self-pity, and guilt were still present. Hangover had ridden up to join them. And behold, a pale horse, and the name of him that rode on it was Headache, and Nausea rode with him.

That Monday, like all others, was supposed to be my day off. It wasn't the kind of day upon which I wanted to be told about a violent death and asked to be the presiding minister at a funeral. So maybe it was the timing of the thing that makes it stick so securely in my memory. But probably not.

No, there was one other item about this whole affair that lifts it up above all the deaths I've attended and makes it stand out like a single dandelion in the green garden of my recollection. It was sort of odd and sick and silly and sad at the same time, and when I heard it, I didn't know whether to laugh at the absurdity or cry at the tragedy of the thing.

Erasmus Wishbone Haines was a dog.

Calvin Haines wanted me to say a funeral service for his prize beagle. Not just a prayer, mind you. He wanted the whole nine yards. The words of comfort, the Twenty-third Psalm, the sermon, the prayers—the whole shebang.

"We'll be doin' it at my place," he said. "So there don't have to be no music." Then he thought for a moment and added. "'Lest you think I should play my guitar." He pronounced it GIT-tar.

Had I not been so miserably under the influence of the four horsemen that morning, I might have thrown him out of the little room between the church and the parsonage that passes for my office. But I was feeling so low, so sad, so depressed that I couldn't help but feel sorry for the poor guy.

He was in his early sixties with a completely bald head, the top of which was snow white, where his ever-present hat protected it from the sun. Somehow, in spite of the hat, his oval face was already starting to show sunburn from working outdoors in the clean air and sunshine. His nose was starting to peel and there was electric razor burn on his throat. He had cleaned up to come into town and talk to the preacher. His bib overalls were brand new, dark and stiff. His plaid shirt was a little frayed at the collar but clean and pressed, and the tie around his neck had probably belonged to his father. He held a brown felt fedora in his hands, letting it hang between his knees, running the brim through his fingers as he talked.

Calvin was a man clearly uncomfortable with words. He stammered and he stuttered and he cried. Big round tears rolled down his cheeks and he sniffed and wiped his nose with a red bandanna. "I found 'im this mornin' when I went to do my chores," he said, folding the bandanna back into his breast pocket. "Who'd do a thing like that?"

I shook my head. Nothing to say. Now I felt like crying with him.

He stared at the floor in front of him and went on: "Person'd do that hates with cruel hatred, I'm tellin' ya."

We sat silently for a few moments until I couldn't stand it anymore and agreed to do the funeral. What the heck. Man loves a dog that much it must have a soul, right? I wondered if anyone would cry that hard for me when I went.

Calvin took a long breath and spoke softly. "He had the sweetest face. Just look up at you with those big brown eyes and melt your heart, he could. Weren't no account as a watchdog. He just naturally loved folks. Loved bein' around people. Anytime someone come to the house he was just sure they come to see him.

"An' sing? My, but that dog had a voice on 'im. I could hear 'im on summer nights chasin' rabbits out behind the woods. And then, directly, he'd come up on the house and lay down on his spot and just take him a nap there, snuggled up to my foot.

"Lord, Reverend, I don't know what I'm gonna do without ol' Ras around." And then he wept. Huge, wracking sobs that shook his whole body. He was a big man, maybe six feet or more, and it was a big cry. I came around my desk and put my arm over his shoulders and he leaned into me.

And then I cried, too.

Okay, so I'm a crier. I was hungover and lonely and miserable and I didn't know a damn thing about Erasmus Wishbone Haines, but I knew what loss was like. Hadn't I just said good-bye to my own children the day before and sent them off to live a thousand miles away with a man I didn't even know? And wasn't it my own fault? Hadn't I thrown them away with my marriage and my career and everything else that was dear to me when I decided to take a roll in the hay with a Sunday School teacher three years ago?

So, yeah, I cried, too.

For three or four minutes we just sat there and cried like a couple of homesick kids at camp, and then we straightened up and Calvin put his bandanna away and ran his hand through the place where his hair used to be and he stood up to leave.

"Ray can show you how to get to my place. 'Bout ten o'clock be okay?"

I said that it would.

"Okay, then. I guess I got some things to do."

And he slumped from my office, waiting to put his hat back on until he was outside the church. Old world manners.

A person who would do a thing like that hates with cruel hatred, he had said. It sounded Biblical to me so I looked it up. I found it in the Psalms. Number twenty-five: "Consider how many are my foes, and how they hate me with cruel hatred."

I never did do that funeral for ol' Ras.

As it turned out, sweet sad old Calvin Haines had quoted a more accurate verse than he could have realized.

CHAPTER 2

IN BIG, SUCCESSFUL, THRIVING CHURCHES there are four Sundays each year that are unofficially known as "Associate Pastor Sundays." These are the days when worship attendance is so predictably low that the senior pastor takes the day off and gives the pulpit to the younger, less experienced associate pastor.

The traditional Associate Pastor Sundays are the Sunday after Christmas, the Sunday before the Memorial Day holiday, the Sunday closest to Independence Day, and the Sunday after Easter.

Earlier in my career, when I was the rising star of the conference, destined for greatness and/or the episcopacy and/or both, I was a senior pastor. After I was kicked out of the ministry I spent two years teaching school before I applied to have my ordination reinstated.

The August previous to Erasmus Haines's passing, I had arrived in Baird, Kentucky, as the pastor of a church most seminary students would have turned up their noses at as being beneath their ability and station. The bishop called it a "probationary appointment," but I knew that I would probably grow old and die in Baird before he would move me to a church that I could do any real damage to.

By the following April, when Ras Haines died, I had been back in the pulpit for exactly eight months and I was preparing to preach my first Sunday-after-Easter sermon in over fifteen years. Now I knew why I had always turned that day over to my associate pastor. I felt empty. Drained. I had shot up my entire homiletical magazine on Easter morning and I could find nothing worth saying for the following week.

I read the lectionary selections for the first Sunday after Easter and they were about as inspiring as plain yogurt. I looked back through some old sermons with the thought of reworking one of them and I felt embarrassed at how shallow and dull they seemed. I even thought of lifting something from one of the greats. Maybe Karl Barth or E. F. Tittle or Martin Luther King had said something that I could rework in a pinch—always citing my sources, of course.

Nothing.

My cry with Calvin Haines seemed to have soothed some of the blues I was feeling to a dull ache, but the hangover was still there, pounding on my skull and making my stomach roll like a tidal wave every time I thought of food.

I tried calling Naomi at her temporary office in Perry, but Percy Mills's secretary and son, David, told me she was with a client and couldn't be disturbed. "Would you like me to ask her to give you a ring, Reverend? She shall have concluded her work in about an hour, I believe."

I told him I'd try back again later or call her apartment that evening. Prissy little twerp. Sixty-six, maybe sixty-seven years old, single, and still working for his father. His accent was more Savannah than Kentucky, and it always seemed to me that it set him aside as some kind of aristocracy—or he acted like it did. Also, I think he was gay—a tough way to be in Perry, Kentucky. Walked like his shoes were too tight, or maybe his underwear. His father was a proper man and neat about his appearance, but next to David he looked like a lumberjack.

Anyway, I didn't really want to talk to Naomi over the phone. What I wanted to do was go up to her cabin on Mt. Devoux and sit in the hot tub with her and tell her how much I missed her and my kids and how I wanted to get married and hold hands and make love in the afternoon on her deck overlooking those beautiful, foggy Appalachian mountains.

But Naomi wasn't at her cabin. She was renting an apartment in Perry so she could be closer to her work, and she would be there until April fifteenth, two weeks hence. And she had made it clear that she wasn't going to marry me until her mean, hateful daddy died, which could be the next day or fifteen years in the future depending on how he handled the black lung disease that was turning his chest to stone.

I popped four generic ibuprofen, slipped on a windbreaker, and let the screen door slam behind me. The Baird Diner sits about a hundred yards down the road from my church and attached parsonage, so I walked. The Mountain Baptist Children's Home across the road was quiet. The kids who stayed there were back in school. Years ago the M.B.C.H. had housed close to a hundred school-age kids. Now, in the age of mainstreaming and foster care, it never had more than twenty or so—and these were the ones who were so mean, incorrigible, or just lost that the county couldn't place them in foster homes. I had never seen kids as sad as these, and I taught for two years in the inner-city.

Aunt-tiques, a store that has never been open, still wasn't. No one was outside doing anything. A couple of cars passed me on the road, and one honked a horn in greeting. I waved hello but I didn't see who it was.

The lunch rush was over when I got to the diner, and May June was washing dishes and humming a hymn. She is a little round lady who looks to be in her sixties, but I'm not very good at guessing the ages of people who are a generation older or younger than I. She and Ray could be anywhere from fifty-five to seventy and they'd look like mid-sixties to me. They've never told me how old they are and I've never asked.

Her clothing varies only in color—house dress duster and running shoes with sweat socks. She wears her salt-and-pepper hair in a bun.

She is the sole proprietor and employee of the Baird Diner and the Baird Store, which is just another room off the diner. The store sells magazines, cigarettes, candy bars, and soda. A few canned goods and disposable diapers are available for emergencies. Lately she'd begun selling single condoms on a cardboard dispenser by the checkout counter.

The diner sells hamburgers, fried bologna sandwiches, country heart-attack breakfasts, and a different blue plate special every day. May June is cook, manager, hostess, and waitress. The diner seats twenty—twelve at three card tables and eight at the counter—but I've never seen more than six in the place at one time.

When I came in, May June was ringing up some Marlboro Reds and Pepsis for a couple of guys in worn bib overalls and dirty T-shirts. When they left she waddled down the counter to where I had flopped down on a stool.

"Well, look who's here," she said, smiling and wiping the counter. "How nice. The handsome, young preacher decides to spend his day off with the poor old lady."

"I spend all my days off here," I said. It was only a slight exaggeration, and I might have even shown something of a smile.

"You do unless Naomi's around. If that girl's anywhere near, you're off chasing her and you couldn't care less about a fat old granny woman," she teased.

I shrugged. "It's a fearsome power that girl has over me, May June. That's a fact."

May June reached across the counter and patted my hand. "You miss her, don't you?" She paused for just a beat, then added, "But I think it's them children o' your'n that you miss the most."

A lump the size of an apple leaped into my throat and nearly choked me. I couldn't breathe. I couldn't talk. I desperately wanted to bury my face in her big bosom and just cry like I had cried on my mother's breast when I was a little boy and only she could make the hurt go away. I squeezed the tears back down behind my eyes and swallowed hard and managed to say, "They're so great, May June."

She just nodded and patted my hand again.

"They're so smart and bright and good and . . . and just every damned thing. And they're all those things without me. Danny's going to get his license in September, and who's going to teach him to drive? Some California lawyer with a tan and a Rolex and capped teeth.

"When Suzanne was little she wanted to be a minister just like her daddy. Now she wants to be a screenwriter. She's got braces and I wasn't there with her when she had headaches and her mouth was too sore to eat. It should have been me that made her those milk shakes, not him." The lump was back in my throat and it was hard to breathe again.

"You got a right smart of anger for that man, don't ya?" May June turned and poured me a cup of coffee from the percolator she kept on the counter for herself and Ray.

I swallowed the lump again. "I guess I do. I don't hate him, really. I don't even know him. I've talked to him on the phone a couple of times and he seems like a nice enough guy. I don't even know if he has a Rolex and capped teeth. It's just that. . . ." I sighed a sigh that had been building up for about twelve hours. "I don't know."

"It's just that you miss your kids and you feel guilty because they don't live with you anymore. And you're afraid you're losin' 'em."

I stared into my coffee and nodded.

May June opened a Sweet'n Low packet and dumped it in my cup. Stirred it. "They love you, Dan. It don't take a psychologist to see that. They hang on your every word and they miss you as much as you miss them."

I knew that. I think that's why it was so painful to say good-bye to them every time they went home. Hell, if they showed up dressed in black with their hair in spikes and dyed green, I'd be glad to see them go. It wouldn't be painful at all and I'd be able to say to myself, "See! They can't get along without me!" But they could. Yes, they loved me and I loved them. The difference was that I needed them. I wasn't sure they needed me anymore.

As if reading my mind, May June said, "They would have moved away from you eventually, anyway, you know. You might give a moment to thankin' the Lord that they're the kind of kids you can be proud of. And you might give them a call an' say as much."

Then she tiptoed so she could reach over the counter and she patted me on the cheek just like my mother had done when I was a kid. The pain and guilt and loneliness didn't disappear, but they receded a few inches into a dark place in the back of my mind where I could ignore them. Until the next time.

"You eat?" May June asked.

I shook my head, guiltily.

She tsked and shook her head. "Well, it's no wonder you're feelin' so poorly. You just need somethin' made with love to fill that hollow place in your gut. What would you say to a bowl of my vegetable soup, some peanut butter and strawberry preserves on hot sourdough bread, and a piece of coconut cream pie?"

The screen door slammed. "I'd say that sounds just about right," Ray said as he walked through the diner to his office, sorting a big handful of mail as he went. He acknowledge my presence as he went by, without looking up from the envelopes. "Hey, Dan." He was wearing his everyday uniform: gray Sears work clothing and black, size-fourteen work oxfords. Ray stands about three inches taller than my six feet, and his steel gray hair was starting to show white around his ears.

"Hey, Ray," I said.

"Kids gone back home?" he called from the little post office.

"Left last night," I called to him as May June slid a quart-size bowl of homemade vegetable soup in front of me. "Mom took them to Lexington to catch their plane back to L.A."

He came out of the post office and poured a mug of coffee the size of a beer stein for himself. "They're good kids. You can be proud of 'em."

"We done been through all that, Dad," May June said, sliding a plate down next to my soup. Two inch-thick slices of sourdough bread as big as my hand lay on the plate. She had warmed them on the griddle with melted butter and then slathered peanut butter on each piece. As the peanut butter melted she plopped a tablespoon of homemade strawberry preserves into the middle of each piece and stirred it around. A cold can of Diet Pepsi went next to my coffee mug.

"Where's mine?" Ray asked, looking up at May June. He winked at me.

May June opened the cooler and took out two pieces of coconut cream pie. "You done e't your lunch, ol' man. You pack away any more and you'll be big as a house. Here's some pie. Now sit down and hush."

The pieces of pie were maybe five inches across at the crust, and the meringue stood up three inches above the filling. Brown coconut shavings clung as thick as bluegrass to the meringue.

Ray dug into his pie while I slurped soup and gnawed at my PB&J.

"Cal Haines stopped by this mornin'," he said around a mouthful of pie. "Said he come into town to talk to you."

I swallowed some bread, used my tongue to scrape the peanut butter off the roof of my mouth, and nodded. "Yeah, his dog died. He's pretty beat up over it."

Ray and May June both stopped what they were doing and stared at me. "Which dog is that?" Ray asked.

"He said his name was Erasmus." I dipped the second piece of bread into the soup broth.

May June gasped. "Erasmus Wishbone? Erasmus is dead?" She held her dish towel over her breast.

"Well, I'll be damned," Ray said, shaking his head. He pushed the crust of his pie away and sighed at mine. "How'd he die?"

"Someone killed him," I said. "Sounded like kids. Calvin said he found him in the front yard this morning."

"Someone killed Erasmus Wishbone?" May June again. Still in shock.

I finished my soup and was too full for pie, but I pulled it in front of me anyway. "Yeah, Calvin said someone beat and kicked him to death."

"Oh, my lord," May June said and went back to her sink of dirty dishes, shaking her head.

"Dirty shame," Ray said. He was still looking at my pie, but I think he was talking about the dog. "Ol' Cal must be pretty shook up."

The pie was delicious. "Ray," I said, between bites. "I've never seen a person so shook up over the death of a pet. Calvin's a mess."

Ray sighed and shook his head again. He started his cigarette ritual, which meant he was thinking or about to tell a story or both: Take metal cigarette pack out of shirt pocket, open pack, take out cigarette, close pack, tap cigarette on pack, put pack back into shirt pocket and take disposable lighter out of pocket while laying cigarette on lip, light cigarette, and take a deep drag while replacing lighter in pocket. Finally he spoke.

"Preacher," he said. (Yes, this was going to be a story.) "One time a couple o' years ago, Mother and me was down in Gatlinburg takin' in the sights. We stopped on the street there at one o' them frozen yogurt places they got on account of no one sells ice cream anymore, 'less it's got a Dutch name and the whole garden mixed into it." He looked over at May June, bent over the dishwater. "You remember, Mother?" She nodded.

"Well, we got our cones and sat down on a bench in this little park-kinda place and along comes this little old lady—ain't nothin' but a wisp of a thing—and she's got this-here little curly haired dog with ribbons on its ears tucked under her arm. She goes up to the yogurt place and she gets herself a hot fudge sundae and she sits down across from us on another bench, and you know what she done?"

"Ate her hot fudge sundae?"

"Oh, yeah, she done that. But while she's doin' it she's talkin' to that dog the whole time like it's a human bein', see. 'Well,' she says. 'I think we've seen all the Precious Moments they have in this town, Diana.' Stuff like that. And the whole time she's talkin' to that dog like it's been shoppin' with her, carryin' a purse of its own an' what-have-you, she's feedin' that dog bites of her hot fudge sundae." He looked at me for a moment, then added: "Off the same spoon! One bite for her, then one bite for the dog, then one bite for her, and on and on."

I didn't know what to say, so I said, "Huh."

"The point is," he said, since I obviously had missed the point, "that little curly haired dog with the ribbons on its ears was a pet. Erasmus Wishbone Haines weren't no pet. He was a dog."

I almost said "Huh" again but May June had made her way back to where we were sitting, wiping her hands on her towel. "Folks up in the hills can't afford pets, Dan," she said. "They got cats to kill mice and they got king snakes to kill copperheads and they got dogs to hunt. You'd live in these parts the rest of your life before you saw anyone feedin' a dog off'n the same spoon they ate with. Dogs is dogs, and people is people."

I thought about it for a moment and decided that as broken up as Calvin Haines was over the death of his dog, it wouldn't have surprised me a bit to see him sharing his hot fudge sundac with it. "But why—"

"Erasmus Wishbone Haines," Ray said, as though announcing the dog's arrival. "He was sired by Alexander Erasmus Pride out of Leontine Wishbone Lewis. The bitch's daddy was Wishbone Stew, the huntin'est dog this state has ever known."

May June jumped in. "Erasmus was state grand champion three times in show and five years running in hunting competition. He was sired to Marietta Trueblood and his pups were expected to be state champions, too."

All I could do was shake my head in disbelief. "He didn't say anything about any of that."

"Not his way," Ray said. "Cal's hill people. Wouldn't do to be braggin' about somethin' the Lord done. And it was the Lord created them dogs. All we do is feed and train 'em. Oh, he loved that dog, don't think he didn't. That dog was like family to ol' Cal. It's just that he didn't love it like a person. That's all I'm tryin' to say."

"He said something about Erasmus singing," I said, still confused.

"It's beagle talk," Ray said. "Beagles bay when they're on chase. See, you probably think of a huntin' dog as a setter or a pointer. Bird dogs. They find a bird and point to it or flush it out for the hunter. A retriever goes and gets it after it's been shot. Beagles ain't no account as bird dogs, though. They're hounds. They give chase."

Ray stubbed out his cigarette and broke off a piece of his discarded piecrust and nibbled it as he talked. "A well-trained beagle will either chase the prey in a circle or corner it and hold it. The hunter stands in one place and listens to the dog's bayin' to know where it is." He tilted his head back and gave an admirable imitation of what must have been a beagle giving chase. "Ow-oo, Ow-oo! If the dog is chasin', all the hunter has to do is stand and wait and the dog'll bring the game around to him. If the dog isn't movin', it means he has the prey cornered or treed. The hunter just follows the sound of the dog's voice. Beagle boys call the dog's barking his voice or throat. It's called singing 'cause it's music to a hunter's ears."

"Erasmus had one of the best throats I ever heard," May June said. "You could hear him nearly a half mile away, dependin' on the weather."

"Well, if ever a dog deserved a funeral, I guess it's that one," I said, resigning myself to the inevitable. "Calvin asked me to come up to his house and say a funeral for Erasmus."

Ray and May June just nodded their heads. Perfectly understandable to them. You wouldn't share your hot fudge sundae with a dog because that would be silly and wasteful. But it was perfectly sensible that you would want to do a funeral for one, complete with psalms and sermon and GIT-tar music.

"Calvin said you could show me how to get to his place," I said to Ray. "You know where it is?"

Ray nodded and stood up. "I'll show you on the map. He's up over Mt. Devoux at Cut-Through Valley." I followed Ray into his constable's office.

A few minutes later I emerged with a hand-drawn map in my pocket and a little more knowledge about beagles in my brain. Ray took his seat at the counter and I picked up a pack of pipe tobacco in the store. As I attempted to pay for the tobacco and May June attempted to ignore me, Ray asked what time the funeral was the next day.

"He said around ten o'clock," I said.

Ray nodded and lit another cigarette. "Maybe I'll go up there tomorrow afternoon. Pay my respects. Knock back a couple with Calvin."

"Might be a good idea," I allowed. "Calvin could use a friend right now."

"Well, I don't want to intrude on his grief, but I reckon you'll be done with the funeral by lunchtime. Maybe he and I could talk."

I started out of the diner and then something occurred to me. I turned back. "What are you thinking, Ray?"

He shrugged. "In the past six or seven years ol' Ras has won near $25,000 in prize money. Could be some folks is tired of seeing him walk off with the trophy every year."

"You don't think it was kids?"

He shrugged again. "Don't know. Can't hurt to talk."

CHAPTER 3

MAY JUNE PUSHED ANOTHER QUART of vegetable soup at me, sealed up in Tupperware, so I didn't have to worry about supper that night. I spent the rest of the afternoon wondering what the hell I was going to say at a dog funeral the next morning.

I never had a dog.

My mother is a cat person. We had a big old black-and-tan tom named Tom Jones, who spent as much time away from us as he did with us, coming home only when he had lost a fight. Mom said she had known men like that.

We also had a house cat that was part Siamese, named Cleopatra, who thought she was doing us a favor by living with us and letting us feed and take care of her. She never came when we called her and was constantly underfoot when we didn't want her around. The only time I can remember her ever showing me anything remotely resembling affection was when I was helping my Uncle Dave carry Mom's new queen-size mattress up the stairs to her bedroom. Cleopatra just couldn't get close enough to me that day and I nearly broke my neck on the stairs trying not to step on her. Once the mattress was in place, Cleo was interested only in my mother's lap.

"You get a dog, you might as well have a child," Mom always said. "They're clingy and utterly dependent. Cats, on the other hand, can take care of themselves."

There was no arguing with her on the subject. Whenever one of my friends would bring home a new puppy and I would come home full of stories about how cute and wonderful it was, Mom would just close her eyes, frown, and shake her head.

"They're clingy and utterly dependent," she would say. "Play with Cleo if you're in such a hurry to have a pet. Then, after you're done playing with her, clean out her litter box, take her to the vet, feed and water her twice a day, and make sure she gets her hairball medicine."

I would look at her in dismay and she would pat my face and say, "Having a pet is a big responsibility, Daniel. When you're an adult you can have all the dogs you want and they'll be your responsibility. If you get one now it will be my responsibility. And, to tell you the truth, you and Cleopatra are just about all the responsibility I can handle at this point in my life."

So I never had a dog.

Once I got to be an adult I had kids of my own and I used exactly the same arguments on them. Our cat was named Ferd, and my ex-wife got him in the divorce settlement—with the kids and everything else we had.

Well, she was welcome to him. My daughter, Suzanne, said Ferd had peed all over their Los Angeles house when they moved in with the lawyer. I told her cats sprayed their territory to identify it and I didn't think it was pee, but she said that whatever it was, it smelled just as bad. Take that, Mr. Rolex.

Anyway, my Bibles and commentaries offered no help in preparing the funeral. Nothing about dogs seemed to work. The Bible doesn't have much good to say about dogs. Mostly they are pictured as scavengers and wild animals. So I settled on some generic passages about friendship and faithfulness and loyalty. I had no idea if they would work or not, but it was the best I could do on short notice.

I skipped supper in deference to the ten pounds I had gained over the winter and settled for a couple of cups of coffee and my pipe. Watched the late news on a Corbin station and caught the first half-hour of Letterman. Went to bed after the "Top Ten List." It didn't seem very funny and even Letterman seemed to know it, rushing through it and on to the first guest. Of course, nothing seemed very funny to me that night. I guess the depression wasn't buried as deep as I had thought.

The Big Ben alarm clock next to my bed said 6:50 when I woke up the next morning. It hadn't rung yet, so I turned it off before it had a chance. I lay in bed for a few minutes thinking about Naomi and realized that I had forgotten to call her back the day before.

At twenty-four, Naomi Taylor was sixteen years younger than I and the most beautiful, sought-after woman in Durel County. And she was the love of my life, my infatuation, my obsession. Mom says I am sickeningly in love with that girl—and she is probably right.

The only saving grace to my pitiful state was that Naomi happened to be in love with me. Love handles, gray sidewalls, shady past, and all, she didn't care. She didn't even seem to notice. She loved me. Go figure.

To be loved unconditionally is a thing rare and wonderful, indeed. It is, I think, the closest we can actually come to the divine in our mortal lives. That Naomi Taylor was capable of such a love for me, of all people, says nothing about me. It says volumes about her.

But, honestly, it wasn't that sweet, angelic, loving side of Naomi

I was thinking about that Tuesday morning as I lay abed. It was, rather, the lusty, passionate, physical Naomi which occupied my thoughts and fantasies. I'm male, after all, and it was morning. So cut me some slack.

I answered nature's demands and allowed the two mugs of coffee from the previous evening to make egress, then I crawled back into bed and called her on the phone.

"M-m-m-ello."

"Did I wake you up?" I propped myself up on two pillows.

"M-m-m. Hi."

"How you doing?"

"'Kay. Schedule C's are on the shelf next to the mchapdh."

"Naomi? Hello? Hey, are you awake?"

"Dan?" She was awake, now. "What time . . . it's seven o'clock!"

"Sorry."

She sighed. "Oh, it's okay. It's just that I didn't get to bed until three o'clock this morning. You wouldn't believe the mess some of these people's financial lives are in."

"Tough day, yesterday?"

"I worked for twelve hours on Carlisle Pettibone's taxes. He brought all of his receipts and papers piled in four beer-case boxes. It was a mess."

"Worse than mine?"

"Yours was tic-tac-toe. His was three-dimensional chess. My head still hurts."

"Why don't you take a long lunch hour today?" I suggested. "I could drive into Perry and we could fool around for a couple of hours."

"Oh, Dan, I can't. I've got Meyer Perlstein coming over at eleven and I'm supposed to do—"

"Meyer Perlstein? Is there a Jew in Perry?"

"He's the only one I know of. Him and his family. They own Perl's Furniture Store. I'm doing his business and personal taxes. It's gonna be a killer."

"Where's he go to worship?"

"Dan, did you call to talk to me about Mr. Perlstein's religious practices?" She was sounding tired again. Not mad, just exasperated.

"No, I called to talk dirty. About sex, you know? You wanna? Forget about your 10W40's and get sweaty?"

"Dan, 10W40 is a kind of oil."

"Sounds good to me."

"It's less than two weeks to the fifteenth. I'm gonna be workin' fourteen hours a day till then. I'm sorry, hon, but this is what I do. I'll make it up to you, I promise."

"I like smart women," I said. "Do what you have to do. I'll be waiting right here." There was something in my tone that I didn't intend to be there. As soon as I said it I knew that she would think I was feeling sorry for myself, which I was. But I didn't blame her. I *do* like smart women. "I'm not upset," I lied. "Just lonely."

"Yeah, me too."

"Yeah," I said. All of a sudden, it seemed, neither of us had much to say. After one of those long, long pauses I said: "When will I see you?"

"Maybe you could drive into town and I could take a break for a sandwich or something. Tomorrow?"

"Sure. Sounds good," I lied again. Oh, well. A sandwich was better than nothing. "I'll bring the 10W40," I said, a la Groucho.

"Oh, Dan." That was all she said. Just two words. Then she hung up. And it wasn't, "Oh, Dan, you silly thing." It was, "Oh, Dan, you pain in the ass." The giggle I had hoped to elicit wasn't there. Just fatigue.

Oh, well. She was probably just tired. Four hours of sleep and then another day of punching numbers. How could such an exciting, enticing, perceptive, with-it woman be so interested in numbers? When she wasn't doing taxes for Percy Mills, she was balancing the books for her father's several business interests over, under, around, and through Clark Mountain. He was into coal, mostly, but he also did some logging and some farming and land-lording. He owned almost the entire mountain—above and below the surface. Her degree was from U.T. Knoxville in finance or economics. I could never remember which.

Tomorrow I'd cheer her up. I'd drag her away from the office and the calculator and we'd go over to the Box Car Diner for burgers and shakes. And then we'd hold hands on the courthouse lawn. That'd be nice. I guess.

I showered, shaved, dressed in my tan suit, ate a hard-boiled egg, drank a glass of juice and two cups of coffee, and headed up State Route 3 across Mt. Devoux to Cut-Through Valley and Erasmus Wishbone's funeral. My little black book of magic words was on the seat next to me as my old VW Superbeetle coughed to life. Ray's map was tucked into the cover of my book.

It took nearly an hour to get to Calvin Haines's place. I had to wind up over the mountain on what passes for roads in Appalachia. The winter had managed to leave them in even worse shape than they were before the cold set in, and my kidneys and teeth were well rattled by the time I got there. The weather was mild and sunny—perfect spring. The sun made it too hot to keep the windows up, and the cool mountain air made it too cold to roll them down, so I just cracked them a little and let the wind mess up my hair. Calvin didn't strike me as a man who would worry about a messy widow's peak, and Erasmus was in no shape to care.

Speaking of peaks: Mountains don't peak in Appalachia like they do in the Rockies. Millions of years of erosion have worn the peaks away and left rolling crests in their places. Cut-Through Valley sat neatly down in between two or three of those crests only about twenty miles from Baird, as the crow flies.

Ray had told me that the Haines farm had once been one of the best in the county. There were even a couple of old coal mines, long since played out, hidden in Calvin's two hundred acres of undulating pasture and cornfields and forest. According to Ray, the name of the valley had come from sometime in the forgotten past when people had cut through where the Haines farm now sat to get from the little burg of Mt. Devoux to the equally little burg of Baird instead of taking the longer road that would later become State Route 3.

The road that led off Route 3 to the farm had no name and it circled around Cut-Through Valley and met itself at a fork just a half mile off the Treadwater Trace, which ran on up the mountain and petered out into a hundred little tracks and lanes.

Calvin's house, barn, and outbuildings sat about fifty yards back from the road in the middle of the fork. Everything was old but immaculate. The two-story house was white with red trim, the lap-siding painstakingly painted. The barn and all the buildings were red with white trim. The yard was full of dandelions and wild strawberries, and a quarter acre of garden had been plowed and tilled behind the house, waiting for weather warm enough to plant. A few tomatoes were already in the ground, covered with big glass jars to protect them from any late frosts. The half-ton GMC pickup truck parked by the barn was old but well cared for, the snow tires still on it, the bed full of sand for winter traction.

I parked where the tire-track driveway ended next to the house and walked up onto the porch to knock on the door. A heavy rocking chair sat empty with an old hook rug next to it. Erasmus's rug.

I knocked a couple of times and the wooden screen door rattled against the frame. Birds sang in an oak tree in the front lawn and a squirrel chattered in one of the trees around the side of the house.

No answer.

I tried again. A baby rabbit ran from under the porch, stumbled, fell over its own feet, got up, and ran off toward what looked like a henhouse.

Still no answer.

Maybe he was in the barn or around back, digging the grave. I called out as I stepped off the end of the porch and walked around the house. "Calvin? Mr. Haines? Anybody home?"

Nothing.

A shovel was stuck in a pile of loose earth beside the small grave, next to the garden. The little bundle wrapped in a handmade quilt must have been Ras. He was laid out next to the grave. There was no sign of Calvin.

There were four outbuildings besides the barn. The building that looked like a henhouse was just that, only empty. No chickens—or people—had been there for a long time. Another was a toolshed, well-stocked and ordered, everything neat as a pin and not so much as a padlock on the door. The third was what used to be a smokehouse, now used for storage. As I got closer I realized that the paint on this building was darker and thicker than on the others. The wood was probably a hundred years old and it smelled of smoke and ashes. I never did discover what was in the fourth outbuilding. I found Calvin in the barn.

His body was hanging between the two haylofts, his feet about even with my eyes. The rope ran from his neck, over one of the rafter beams, and down to one of the posts on the right that held up the loft. The knot behind his head was a traditional hangman's noose.

My first reaction was panic. I said something aloud, but I don't remember what it was. "Oh, my God!" Something like that. I ran to him with the thought of getting him down, somehow. The smell brought me back to reality. He had evacuated his bowels and bladder in death. Now I realized that his face was swollen and purple, his tongue bloated and bulging out of his mouth. I looked around desperately trying to find something to cut him down with when I saw the dog. It was a female. Dead and bloody. She looked like every bone in her body had been broken. Her nipples were swollen and distended. She had been nursing pups.

I don't know why, but I think it was the dog that got to me. Maybe it was a cumulative thing; I don't know. But I started to see little silver specks in front of my eyes, and my ears started to ring, and I could feel cold sweat popping out on my face.

I stumbled outside and sat down on the ground, leaning up against the barn door. I rummaged through my jacket pocket until I found a smelling salts capsule, broke it open, and passed it gently back and forth under my nose.

Normally my head clears immediately when I use the salts. My faints are brought on by a minor heart thing called mitral valve prolapse and it's nothing serious. Just embarrassing. Usually a little whiff of ammonia takes care of it.

But I was still pumping on adrenaline and my pulse was racing. So I took another hit and managed to bring my brainstem down to absolute zero. It woke me up, though. I managed to pick myself up and drag myself to the house. Looking through the window in the front door I could see the phone sitting on a table next to a La-Z-Boy in the living room.

I broke the window.

"Lord have mercy." Ray Hall stood with his hands on his hips in the open barn door. A breeze moved through the barn and Calvin's body moved back and forth, the rope creaking against the wood beam.

"He was sad, Ray, but I had no idea. . . ." I still held the smelling salts in my hand but my head was clear, the crisis past. "Who would have thought a man could kill himself over a dog?"

Ray didn't answer. He walked around the open space down the middle of the barn. There were empty stalls on either side of the wide aisle and lofts on each side above the stalls. Ray looked up at Calvin Haines's body and breathed through his mouth. The smell of death mixed with hay and dust was wrenching.

"You touch anything?" Ray finally asked.

"No. My first reaction was to try to get him down, but he was obviously dead. I thought you'd want to see him the way I found him."

Ray nodded and continued to look. Finally he began his cigarette ritual and walked outside, sliding the barn door closed behind us. "Shew! Stinks, don't it?" He inhaled deeply on his unfiltered Camel.

I lit my pipe and we just stood there outside the barn, smoking and watching the road. Gilbert and Gaylord Carmack would be along shortly to remove the body. The homely twin brothers were the co-captains of the volunteer fire department and manned the life squad ambulance. Ray had called them just before he left Baird.

A year earlier I would have felt compelled to say something in such a situation. I am a preacher, after all, and talking is how we earn our living. Appalachia places no such demand on the clergy, however. People don't feel compelled to talk about every feeling and experience that comes their way, and they don't expect their ministers to do so, either. They expect us to be there, to stand firm and resolute, as they do, in the face of hardship and pain, but they know that some things go too deep for words. So we just stood there and smoked and sighed. If either of us felt the need to speak he could, but it wasn't expected.

Finally Ray took a breath and straightened up. "Wasn't your fault," he said.

"Oh, I guess I know that, Ray. A man decides to kill himself he's going to find a way. I just wonder if he gave me some signals that I missed. I keep going over it in my mind and, for the life of me, I can't think of anything." I picked up a stick and used it to clean out the bowl of my pipe.

"He didn't kill himself," Ray said.

We were talking so slowly, so conversationally, I didn't catch what he said at first. Then it sank in. "What? Someone killed him. How—"

"They tried to make it look like suicide but they must have been in a hurry."

"They?"

"Whoever. Had to be more than one. Calvin was big. Too heavy to be pulled up that high by one man." He lit another cigarette. "Here come the boys."

I looked out to the road but I didn't see any traffic. Then I heard an engine laboring up the mountain and in a few seconds the old red Cadillac ambulance swung around the corner. The Carmacks saw us and drove through the yard to where we were standing in front of the barn.

They coasted to a stop and climbed out—two identical Ichabod Cranes with soup-bowl haircuts, big ears, long hooked noses, and no chins whatsoever. They were wearing bib overalls and new white T-shirts. As always, Gilbert's right cheek was bulging with a wad of tobacco. Gaylord (pronounced GAY-lurd) held his chew on the left side. It was one of the few ways to tell them apart.

Ray walked up to greet them. "Hey, boys."

"Ray."

"Ray."

Ray flipped his cigarette into the grass. "Cal Haines is in there hangin' dead from a rafter. We need to get him down and I need to take a look at him. Then you can run him in to Perry to Doc's for the autopsy."

The Carmack twins both nodded solemnly and walked into the barn. I thought briefly of warning them about the smell, but then I remembered that they were also the local "honey dippers." They picked up extra money by cleaning out septic tanks, cesspools, and outhouses. No smell on earth could bother the Carmack twins.

The rope which held Calvin Haines was wound around an upright post on the right side of the barn and tied about chest high. Ray, Gilbert, and I reached up and took hold of the heavy braided cord and pulled down, raising Calvin's body and giving Gaylord the slack he needed to untie the knot.

But Calvin's weight had pulled the rope so tight the knot

wouldn't come undone. Gaylord picked and pulled at it until our hands and arms began to fatigue and we had to rest.

"Maybe if I had some pliers," Gay said in his slow, deliberate drawl.

"Ain't we got none in the unit?" Gil answered as slowly.

"What the hell we need pliers for in the unit?"

"Well, I just thought we might have a couple o' tools in there's all," Gil said. He clearly didn't like being questioned in front of people outside the family.

"Well, we ain't," Gay said. That seemed to put an end to the discussion and they both went silent. Gilbert looked like he was sulking. Or maybe the strain of lifting Calvin Haines had caused him to swallow some of his tobacco juice.

"Just cut the damned thing," Ray said, shaking his head. "You got a knife, doncha?"

Both of the brothers smiled as they pulled Barlow pocketknives from their overalls. What with the tobacco juice, big false teeth, and their natural homeliness, Carmack smiles were not to be enjoyed so much as tolerated. They were the only two people I have ever known whom I preferred to be with when they were morose and taciturn.

We hoisted Calvin up again and Gaylord went to work with his knife. "I got 'er now," he said after a couple of minutes. And sure enough, the end of the rope was brushing the ground at my feet.

It occurred to Ray and me at the same time that we didn't have enough rope left to let Calvin down easily. As high as he was hanging, we would run out of rope before his feet were on the ground.

"Well, hell," Ray said, shaking his head. "Gil, you and Gay get over and kinda catch him as we let him down. Try not to let him fall."

But, of course, they did let him fall. It wasn't entirely their fault. As soon as Gilbert let go of the rope, the weight seemed to double and our tired arms had trouble holding Calvin up. The rope began to bite into our hands, then it began to slide and burn our palms so we had to let it out fast, hand over hand. But we got tangled up in each other's arms and let it out too fast so the Carmacks weren't quite in place yet and Calvin Haines came crashing down on top of Gaylord, who subsequently crashed into Gilbert, who wound up on the bottom of the pile with Calvin on top of him and Gaylord on top of Calvin.

Ray looked down at the mess on the floor of the barn. "I'm sure glad we waited for you boys to get here and help us," he said.

CHAPTER 4

"LOOK AT THE ROPE BURNS ON HIS THROAT," Ray said, squatting next to Calvin Haines's body. Gil and Gay Carmack were standing behind him looking over his shoulder. Every time he pointed something out they elbowed each other and nodded knowingly. "Those didn't come from him jumpin' outta the loft with the rope 'round his neck. He was hauled up, slow. Probably several times before they finally left him to hang. His neck ain't broke. He strangled, slow."

"Why several times?" I asked. I was squatting on the other side of the body, fumbling with the smelling salts in my pocket.

Ray shrugged. "You gonna be okay?"

I swallowed and nodded.

"I don't want you passin' out on me."

"I'm okay, Ray. Why did they hang him more than once? You mean he was hanged somewhere else, then moved here?"

He looked around at the floor of the barn. "Nawp. They pro'ly done it all right here. Torture maybe."

"Lord."

"Yeah. An' looky here." He lifted Calvin's wrist. "His hands were tied. Balin' wire, most likely." He looked around again, as though he expected the wire to be tossed aside in a ball on the floor. It wasn't.

Ray stood up, dusted his hands on his thighs, and looked up at the loft. "Also, if you measure the rope from where it was tied, you'll see that there wasn't enough length for Cal to stand in the loft, put it around his neck, and then jump off."

So Calvin Haines hadn't committed suicide; someone had killed him. Tortured him to death. Why? Good lord, it was hard enough to imagine a man hanging himself over a dog. The thought of murdering someone over a dog was just about more than I could fathom. And why torture him? What could he have done to make someone hate him that much?

Ray walked over to the dead dog lying on the dirt floor of the barn. The weather was cool enough that the flies weren't out in force yet, but a few brave souls had found her blood. He knelt down and laid his hand on her head, stroking it gently. "Marietta Trueblood," he said softly. "Damn it."

Gaylord Carmack whistled softly through his teeth. "No stuff?

That-there's really Mary-T?"

"I ain't never seen her this close," Gilbert said.

Gaylord turned his head and spit a brown stream halfway across the barn. "What's she doin' here?"

Ray pointed to the dog's nose. "See that white spot shaped like a heart?" He wiped some blood away with his thumb. "All the True-blood beagles have that mark. It's her, all right. I heard Calvin bought her last winter after his bitch took sick and died."

Gilbert shook his head. "Lord, Ray. She's . . . famous!" He spit.

Ray looked up to where Calvin's body had been hanging and then back to the dog. "Sons o' bitches made him watch. They killed her in front of him before they killed him."

"Consider how many are my enemies," I said. "How they hate me with cruel hatred."

Ray looked at me with a question in his eyes.

"Just quoting scripture," I said. "Something Calvin said."

"Looks like he had it right." He stood again, slower this time, as though the sight of the dog had aged him. "Gil! Gay! Take Calvin on in to town. Tell Doc I need a time of death, close as he can guess. I'll call the sheriff and make my report, for all the good it'll do." He grabbed a burlap bag that was hanging over one of the empty stalls. "Me and the preacher'll bury the dogs."

It was after noon when we finally sat down on the porch of Calvin Haines's house. The dogs were buried and the Carmacks had left for Perry. I hadn't done the whole funeral, but I had said a prayer over their broken bodies. And I had said the words of com-mittal as we shoveled the dirt over them. I don't know; it just seemed like the right thing to do. Ray had found a stash of Coors long necks in a refrigerator on the back porch and neither of us felt like leaving yet. Ray sat in Calvin's rocking chair and I sat on the steps, leaning back against a porch post. Ray lit a Camel and I fiddled with my pipe.

"I never would have known this place was here if you hadn't shown me on the map," I said. "It's hard to believe a little valley like this could be hidden down in these mountains. It's so pretty."

Ray blew some smoke and sipped his beer. "Quiet, too. You can see why Cal liked it."

I'm a city boy, out of my element in the Appalachians. I usually like quietude for about fifteen minutes, and then I find it spooky. I like noise. I turn on the radio or television almost by habit the minute I enter my house. But there was something pleasant and peaceful about the quiet in Cut-Through Valley. A constant breeze seemed to blow through the trees, and the soft shushing noise it made as it passed through the new leaves was just enough to notice but not enough to bother you or keep you awake at night. I could still hear birds singing. The squirrel in the tree around the side of the house had driven away his adversary and was no longer chattering, but I could hear him bounding through the branches. Just enough noise to remind you that life goes on.

"Tell me about Calvin," I said between puffs on my pipe. The breeze was making it hard to keep it lit.

Ray sighed. "Calvin was born right here in Cut-Through. Lived here all his life as far as I know. Went to school with me and May June when we walked to the one-room in Baird. It's gone now. Used to sit where the high school sits now." He took a swig from his beer and tossed the empty under the porch. It clinked against a dead soldier from another time. "You want another one?" he asked.

I shook mine and, seeing there was only an inch or so left in the bottom, nodded yes.

He was back in a few minutes with two cold ones. He took up where he had left off. "Cal married his school sweetheart, Martha Benning, right after school and they had three kids. Treasure, the oldest, is a librarian up in Cincinnati. Blessing owns the Box Car Diner in Perry—"

"Bless Keifer? She's his daughter?" I asked, surprised.

Ray nodded. "You know her?"

"I've met her. Naomi and I eat at the Box Car sometimes when we're in town. Good burgers."

Ray nodded again. "She's a pistol."

Bless Keifer was a voluptuous redhead in her late thirties. She had the body of a woman ten years younger, a friendly smile, and a slap on the back for everyone who came in her place. I thought she bore a striking resemblance to Sarah "Fergie" Ferguson, formerly of the royal family, only taller.

She prided herself on remembering the names of everyone who ate in her place more than once, but she never used those names. She had a nickname for everyone. I was "Rev" and Naomi was "Honeydew." Bless's sense of humor ran to the bawdy and outrageous. I think her name for Naomi had something to do with her insistence on comparing breast size with every well-developed woman who came into her restaurant. Naomi had "won" the contest one day and her nickname was etched in Box Car history.

"She's something," I agreed with Ray.

"Her husband, Bert, died in the mines about two, maybe three years ago. She worked as a waitress at the Box Car, and when Bert's pension and life insurance came through, she bought the place."

I just nodded. The mines had left widows all over Durel County. It was nice to hear about one who had gone on to make something of her life. Most I had met were sitting on their porches, surrounded by dirty children, trying to live on their dead husbands' pensions and getting old before their time.

"Cal and Marty had a son, Victory. Died in a car accident when he was in high school," Ray said. "Cancer took Marty about ten years ago."

"What about the dogs?" I asked.

Ray took another long pull from his beer and looked off into space. "Cal retired from farmin' about nine, ten years ago. Sold off most of his big equipment 'cept the tractor and rototiller and bush hog, I guess. He'd been a beagler for some years but decided to take it up serious. His dogs were always good hunters but nothin' to shout about, you know." He started his cigarette ritual and talked as he prepared his smoke.

"Well, after he retired from farmin' he took some of the money he got from his sale and went shoppin' for a champion dog. Couldn't afford a trophy dog, you understand, one that had already won somethin' big. So he bought three or four pups with good bloodlines and commenced to trainin' 'em. Well, ol' Ras was just a natural. Like what they call a phenom in sports. Took to huntin' like he'd been doin' it from the womb. Usually you gotta run a pup with an older dog so they learn, but Ras just naturally knew what to do, Cal said.

"When it come to showin' him, he seemed to know what that was all about, too. Stood up pretty as you please. Hold his tail up and, well, you wouldn't believe it if you didn't see it yourself, but I swear that dog would sorta smile at the judges when they come to look him over.

"Maybe one dog in ten thousand has what Ras had," Ray said. "After a couple o' years and Erasmus was winnin' ever'thing in sight, Cal sold off them other dogs and bought himself a bitch with the idea of breedin' Ras and sellin' his pups. He wouldn't put Ras out to stud 'cause he said that dog's semen was like gold and he didn't have no intention of just spreadin' it all around the state.

"Well, the bitch died with her first litter and they lost all but one of the pups, which Cal gave to Blessing. It was kinda scrawny and no account, probably woulda been the runt. It shook Cal up so, losin' the bitch and the pups and all, that he said he'd never breed dogs again. Damn near broke his heart, seein' her sufferin' like that and nothin' he could do to help her."

Ray tossed his empty under the porch with its predecessors and I followed suit. We both stood and started toward our cars, me to my VW and Ray to his old Willys Jeep. When we got to the Jeep, he stopped and lit another cigarette. He wasn't done talking.

"Then last winter he surprised everyone by plunkin' down a big pile o' money to buy Mary-T. She was one of the top three beagle bitches in the state, maybe in the top ten in the whole country. Never said how much he spent on her, but the word is it was over $3,000."

My chin must have dropped to my knees. "Three thousand—"

"Costs money to breed champions," Ray said. "Probably took every cent Ras won that year to buy her." He smiled, sadly. "Now you think a dog ain't worth killin' over?"

"But they killed the dog, Ray. Why would they kill a $3,000 dog? Isn't that like killing the goose that laid the golden egg?"

He nodded again. "Yep, but maybe they figure that if they got the onliest eggs and the goose is dead, maybe that'll drive the price up. Like when one of those artist fellers dies and the price of his paintings doubles the next day."

He had lost me. "Ray, I don't get it. What are we talking about here?"

He dropped his cigarette in the grass and ground it out with his heel. "Pups," he said, quietly.

"Pups?"

"Mary-T was nursin'. Someone's got them pups and is probably tryin' to sell 'em right this minute. If our illustrious sheriff gets off his ass, he can most likely wrap this thing up by noon tomorrow."

I followed Ray back to Baird. That is, I tried to follow him. Ray drives like he's the Mario Andretti of the mountains. My little VW just couldn't keep up. By the time I pulled up in front of the diner he was already sitting down to his lunch. I joined him at the counter.

Since I don't pay for my meals at the diner, May June doesn't ask me what I want and I usually don't order. She just serves up about twice as much of whatever she's cooking than I really need. Today it was thick slices of rare roast beef on slices of griddle-toasted day-old sourdough bread with mayonnaise and mustard. Two sandwiches. She also slid a soup bowl full of potato salad next to my sandwiches. A can of icy cold Budweiser and a bowl of cherry cobbler completed the feast. And that was lunch.

I sagged in defeat before the mountain of food. "May June, this is supposed to be lunch. I can't eat all of this."

She swatted me with her dish towel. "Nonsense. You didn't come in for breakfast, which means all you had was coffee and tobacco. It's near two o'clock. You gotta be starvin'."

Ray gave me his you-don't-argue-with-May-June-about-food

look and I surrendered. His lunch was identical to mine and he'd obviously just had this same conversation with his wife. The beef was delicious. I noticed on the blackboard above the range that it was also on the menu for dinner. Roast beef and mashed potatoes with gravy. I'd be back later.

"You call the sheriff?" I asked Ray.

He nodded and took a double bite out of his sandwich.

"And?"

He shook his head. His mouth was too full to talk.

"No? No, what?"

Ray swallowed, took a drink of Bud, and sighed. "He says it sounds like suicide to him. He don't have time to fart around with a suicide investigation when there's real crime going on all over the county. Those are his words." He shook his head and took another bite.

I was amazed but not surprised. Sheriff William B. Fine was Ray's second cousin and a consummate Southern politician. A little spidery man with an Alfalfa haircut, the only crime that interested him was the kind that was going to get him reelected. People outside of the county seat in Perry, especially hill people, rarely voted. Even if they did, there weren't enough of them to affect an election. There were only about forty persons living in Baird, the biggest town in Three Mountain Township. No one knew how many lived back in the hollers, and those who lived there liked it that way.

"Did he see the body?" I asked.

Ray nodded. "Doc says it was probably murder but he can't say for sure. He don't expect the autopsy to tell him much more. Billy says that without proof he has to treat it as suicide. . . ."

"But what about the length of the rope? The marks on his wrist?"

"Rope was cut. Wrist marks could have been self inflicted."

"That's ridiculous."

"Well, hell, yes, it's ridiculous!" Ray said, pushing his plate aside and drawing the cobbler to his chest. "But what do you expect of that little peckerwood?"

"Did he tell Blessing, at least?" I asked.

"Nope. Says I got the call, I'm the peace officer of record. I'm the one to tell her. How you like them apples?"

"What are you going to tell her?" I had finished one sandwich. I pushed the other away and grabbed my cobbler. May June swooped down on the beef, wrapped it in plastic, and plopped it down on the counter next to me.

"For your midnight nosh," she said.

"Nosh?"

"Snack. It's Yiddish."

"I know what it means, May June. I guess I'm just surprised to hear it . . . here." I indicated the diner.

"Oh, you'd be surprised, preacher. We hillbillies get television and some of us even know how to read." She put on a deep hillbilly accent: "Wha ah cayun even saafur up t'mah twelve tams tables." I saw her slip a wink at Ray and I knew I had been had. Again.

"You know what I mean," I said.

"She's just funnin' ya," Ray said. "She likes to do that. Pull out new words and flash 'em around like silver dollars. Show off her worldly wisdom." Now Ray winked at me.

"What were we talking about," I asked. I really had forgotten.

"You were about to agree to come with me into Perry to tell Bless Keifer that someone killed her daddy over a couple o' dogs."

I nodded to him as May June took my empty beer can and put a mug of steaming coffee laced with Sweet'n Low and milk in front of me. Of course I would go with him. It was one of the things I did as pastor of Baird Methodist and unofficial deputy constable of the township.

In the eight months since I had come to Appalachia, I had learned that ministry in the mountains is the chaplain style of ministry. I preached on Sunday, and I visited the sick if and when I knew they were sick, and the elderly when they asked for me. During the winter I led a ladies' Bible study and prayer group on Wednesday mornings, which shortly became a gossip circle that allowed the ladies to keep each other up to speed on who was sick and from what. Mostly, though, the people of my vast parish wanted to be left alone. They'd call me when they needed me.

So I spent most of the cold rainy winter playing checkers with Ray and drinking coffee at the diner. Evenings, Naomi and I played euchre with the Halls, watched television, and, once a week, went into Perry to see a movie. From time to time I accompanied Ray in his capacity as constable. I went with him to inform loved ones when someone died on the roads or in the mines. I went with him to the hospital when someone shot a husband or wife or lover. I went with him when he had to arrest someone he didn't want to arrest. I was the unofficial chaplain to the township police force of one.

So, of course, I would go with him to talk to Blessing Haines Keifer about her dead daddy. I went home to change clothes. Our escapades at Cut-Through Valley had just about ruined my suit.

* * *

It was about 3:00 p.m. when I met Ray outside the diner. He was in the Jeep with the motor running. A big manila envelope lay on the passenger seat and I held it in my lap.

"My report to the sheriff," he said, nodding at the envelope. "He ain't gonna like it."

I raised an eyebrow. "Oh, really?"

Ray smiled as he shifted the Jeep into first gear. "Screw him," he said, and sprayed the front porch of the diner with gravel as we hit the road.

Perry isn't far from Baird, if you go in a straight line. But you can't go in a straight line, of course, this being Eastern Kentucky. So it took us nearly an hour to make the thirty-mile drive.

At four o'clock in the afternoon the Box Car Diner was mercifully empty of customers. Lunch hour was well over and the dinner crowd hadn't started to arrive yet. Ray told me on the way to Perry that the Box Car had originally been a real dining car from a train. The first owner had had the thing towed on a trailer to its present location on a corner near the edge of downtown, where it did a booming business in hamburgers, hot dogs, and fries for nearly twenty years. Finally the state board of health had demanded some changes, and the owner had remodeled the place around the old dining car. Subsequent changes over the years had seen the dining car disappear and the diner itself expand without ever giving up its friendly, coffee-shop atmosphere. We found Bless Keifer in the kitchen, laughing at her own jokes.

". . . ain't much to look at but she sure is fun to dance with!" She laughed loud and long at the old punch line. Two cooks were leaning against the big range and four waitresses in pink uniforms were sitting at a table, smoking cigarettes and drinking coffee. They laughed enough to keep their jobs.

Blessing Haines Keifer was a big woman. Probably five-ten or -eleven, with wide shoulders and high, round breasts. She was wearing a man's white shirt and tight blue jeans. Her waist was small—or at least seemed that way. Naomi always said it was just Bless's bust size that made her look that way. No slouch in the chest department herself, Naomi would know about that kind of thing, I guess.

"Well, look who's here," Bless said, noticing us as we stood in the kitchen door. "The Rev and Grey Ray. You boys want a cup o' joe? Piece o' pie?"

Ray took in the kitchen scene and shook his head. "We need to talk, Bless, honey. Is there someplace we can sit down with you for a few minutes?"

I was still struck with how much she resembled the Duchess of

York. Red hair, freckles, round, healthy figure. A little older and bigger but not bad, all in all. She must have read the serious intent of our visit in Ray's voice and face.

"Why, sure they is, Ray, darlin'." She walked between us and out into the dining room. Near the kitchen door, one booth table was strewn with coffee cups, ashtrays, ledgers and other papers. "Step into my office," she said, indicating the booth. We slid in.

"A constable and a preacher both come callin'," she said. "It can't be good news. Is it Daddy?"

Ray sighed and nodded. There was no easy way to say what he had to say. No way to soften it or take the hurt out of it. Ray did it as well as anyone could. He reached across the table and took her soft, pink hand in his big rough one and he looked her right in the eye. "Bless, honey, I'm sorry. Your daddy's dead. Someone killed him in his barn last night."

CHAPTER 5

LIFE PREPARES US FOR LOSS.

The act of being born is an experience of loss. Warm and comfortable, we are yanked into a cold, frightening, bright world for which we are not prepared and into a life for which we did not ask.

From then on it's just one loss after another. Our parents do less and less for us and we, eventually, have to do for ourselves. We get too old or too big to do the fun and comforting things of childhood. Maturity and responsibility are thrust upon us whether we want them or not.

Our pets die. Our movie idols and sports heroes die. Our grandparents die. Eventually our parents and friends die. We aren't ready for it, exactly, but we are prepared.

It's one of God's severe mercies that the little losses we suffer throughout our lives prepare us for the bigger ones yet to come. By the time the big losses arrive we have developed ways of handling them, of grieving. And each person's way of grieving is uniquely his or her own.

Blessing Haines Keifer wasn't ready for her father's death, but she was prepared. She had buried a brother, a mother, and a husband, so she was better prepared than most. Upon hearing Ray's sad news, she took one short breath, like a gasp, then a long one. She closed her eyes and breathed deeply and evenly for a few moments, her breasts pressing against her man's white shirt as she tried to stay in control.

"How'd it happen?" she asked, when she could talk steadily.

"Well, we don't know, exactly," Ray said. He went on to tell her what he did know and he told it all, just as it had happened.

"They tortured him?" she asked. Ray nodded. "And they took the pups," she said. This was for confirmation, not a question. Ray nodded again.

Bless took another deep breath, then she turned her head and yelled to the kitchen, "Roy Don! Can I get a pot o' coffee out here?"

"Right away, Miz Blessing," came the prompt response from the kitchen. We sat in silence until a black cook—a thin, bald man in his fifties—came from the kitchen with a pot of coffee and three mugs. He placed them on the table, looked at Blessing, shook his head, patted her shoulder, and shot us a disapproving look before going back through the swinging doors. The kitchen staff was listening. Bless poured coffee for all of us without asking.

"I guess I better call Treasure," she said. "She'll want to come down for the funeral. When you suppose I ought to have it?"

Ray looked at me. This was my territory and I picked up the ball. "Your dad's body is at the coroner's office right now. You'll want to call a funeral home and have them pick up the body, then you can make the arrangements with—"

"Whiteker," she said. "LeRoy buried my husband and Momma, and his daddy buried my brother."

"LeRoy's a good man," I said. "I can call him if you like. Then you can meet with him after your sister gets here and set up the arrangements."

She shook her head. "I'll call him." She took a long hit on her coffee and looked back to Ray. "Ray, why are you and the Reverend here? Why isn't the sheriff or one of his deputies telling me this? This ain't even in your jurisdiction."

Ray fingered his coffee mug for a moment. It was cracked, and the crack was stained dark from gallons of coffee that had been poured in and out of the mug. "I'm the one found him."

He paused and started over. "No, that ain't exactly true. The Reverend here found him. But I was the peace officer what caught the call. It's my responsibility to tell the next of kin."

She nodded. "What else?"

"Well, I guess the sheriff and me don't exactly see eye to eye on this thing."

"He thinks my daddy killed himself?" she asked.

Ray nodded.

Bless slammed her hand down flat on the table so hard that coffee sloshed from my mug. "That's bullshit, Ray. You know that."

"Yes'm."

"My daddy would never have killed himself over a dog. He was gonna do that he woulda done it when Momma got the cancer and died or when Vic drove his car off that ridge. Both of them things nearly killed him. And when my Bert died, Daddy cried like a baby. Bert was like a son to him. But Daddy weren't no fool. He never woulda done it over no damn dog."

"That's why I'm here, darlin'," Ray said. "The sheriff's given me my head on this. I'm gonna look into it myself."

Blessing was crying now. Finally, the dam had broken, or at least cracked. She didn't bawl or wail. Her chin quivered, and tears leaked steadily from the corners of her eyes and flowed, one after another, down her cheeks. She wasn't wearing makeup, so she didn't try to dab at them with a tissue or a handkerchief. She just let them flow down over her pretty freckled face.

Ray sipped his coffee and took out a little dime-store notebook from his shirt pocket. He licked the lead of a stubby pencil and prepared to write. "What I need to know, hon, is who might want to do such a thing to your daddy. Who were his enemies. Who hated him enough to make him suffer like he done."

She wiped her eyes and thought for a moment, then she shook her head. "Daddy didn't have no enemies. He was a lovable, likable, old hillbilly. I never knew a soul wasn't glad to see him comin'."

"What about jealousies?" Ray pushed on. "Whoever killed your daddy probably killed the two dogs and took the pups. Could it be someone who was jealous of Erasmus Wishbone winnin' all them prizes?"

That hit a nerve. Blessing's face hardened just a fraction and she let a tear fall without brushing it away. No tear followed in its track. "Conrad Foley," was all she said.

Ray stopped writing and looked up in surprise. "Your daddy done business with the Foleys?" It wasn't *just* a question. I mean, it was but it wasn't. It was phrased in the interrogative, but the intensity with which he asked it made it something more.

Blessing shook her head. "Naw. Conrad tried to buy Ras a couple o' times last year. Daddy wouldn't even talk to him about it. Word was he was powerful disappointed. Finally found something his money couldn't buy, I reckon."

Ray put his pencil and paper away, took a sip of his coffee. "Luther and Conrad Foley," he said, shaking his head. "Who'da thunk it?"

Blessing nodded. "I know."

I had no idea what they were talking about.

Thirty minutes later we were on our way to the sheriff's office in Ray's Jeep. There were no seat belts, and the Swiss-cheese muffler and the wind rattling through the canvas top made talk nearly impossible, but we managed by screaming at each other on those rare occasions when Ray slowed down.

"Foleys are bad people," Ray said, shifting gears, stopping and starting in the town traffic.

"Bad how?" I shouted.

"They're the closest thing to the mob you can get in these-here hills." He shook his head in disgust. "Gambling, prostitution, usury, extortion, pornography, you name it. It's been a family business for over a hundred years."

"Why haven't they been busted?"

"Ray shifted gears again and squinted in thought. "Smart. Richer'n God. Big-city lawyers. They're pure white trash, hillbilly criminals. But they got street smarts like a New York drug dealer."

"Dope?" I had begun to learn the strange code of sentence fragments, single words, and expressions that passed for communication when you rode with Ray in his Jeep.

Ray shook his head. "Nawp. It's the one thing they stay clear of. Ain't sure why. I think one of Luther's grandchildren got into some trouble with it and now he won't go near it." We stopped at a red light in the center of town and could return our voices to something like normal volume.

"Why would this Foley—"

"Luther."

"Why would Luther Foley be interested in Calvin's beagles?" I asked.

"Money," Ray said, popping the clutch and throwing the Jeep around the corner into the parking lot of the county courthouse. The sheriff's office was in the basement, around back. "Luther Foley does everything for money. It's his god and his only true love. His wife, Annabelle, is just like him, and his son, Conrad, is a chip off the old block with one exception."

I took the bait. "What's that?"

"C and W," he said, smiling at a private joke.

"C and W? Country and western music?"

Ray nodded. "Yep. He's a fanatic. He's got a house in the hills down by the county line at Beresford. They say it's a shrine to country and western music. All his life ol' Conrad has wanted to be a singer and songwriter. Built a studio and everything."

"Really? He ever do anything big?"

"Sold a song once, I think to Waylon or Willie or one of them. But I don't think they ever recorded it. He's got six kids and he named them all after C and W stars." Ray cut the motor and we got out of the Jeep. He lit a Camel and I started loading my pipe. "I thought we'd stop by and see what ol' Luther's been up to lately before we go back home. You don't mind, do you?"

I shook my head and shrugged. "Maybe I'll go see Naomi. Meet you back here in an hour?"

The courthouse was a big, brick building with pillars on the front, cannons, park benches, and concrete picnic tables on the yard under ancient sycamore trees just starting to bud. Eventually the leaves would be as big as dinner plates, but now they were about the size of a half-dollar.

The liar's bench was full, as it always was when the sun was out, and the four old men on and around it were smoking and laughing. They waved to me as I circled around the side of the courthouse and across the yard to Percy Mills's office across the street. I didn't feel particularly favored by the greeting. They waved at everyone.

Percy Mills held court a couple of hours every day on a bench on the courthouse lawn, directly across the street from his office, dispensing free legal advice and making appointments with people whose problems were too complex to work out on a park bench. The office to which he directed those folks was above a yard-goods store owned by his wife. Percy's bench was empty, so he was either at his office or gone home for the day. Court was no longer in session at that hour.

I crossed the street in the middle of the block and took the stairs up the side of the Mills building to the legal offices above the store. A light was burning in the window, so either Percy or Naomi was still working.

I went in without knocking. The front office was empty. Percy's son, David, served as his father's investigator, secretary, paralegal, and partner. Originally slated to inherit the practice, David had decided, upon graduating from law school and passing the Kentucky bar exam, that he didn't like litigation and courtrooms. He was content to let his father argue the cases while he provided support from behind the scenes. Had Mills and Son practiced their profession in England, they would have called David the solicitor and Percy the barrister. In Kentucky they called Percy a lawyer and they called David, David.

David was gone for the day, his desk clean and empty. The office smelled of coffee, pipe tobacco, leather, and furniture polish. A smoked-glass partition divided the front office from the back. The left half of the partition had a door with PERCY MILLS stenciled on the glass. It was dark within. The right half had a door with MEET-ING ROOM stenciled on it. A light burned on the other side, and the sound of an adding machine clicked and ratcheted from within. I heard Naomi laugh from the other side of the glass and I knocked, rapping my college class ring on the door.

Naomi opened the door, still laughing. She stopped laughing when she saw me, and a look of surprise washed over her face. "Dan. Dan! Hi! What are you doing here?"

I shrugged. "I had to come into town on business. Thought I'd stop by and see if you wanted to have dinner or something."

She frowned. "Oh, how sweet. I'd love to, but. . . ." She lowered her voice and came out into the outer office, shutting the door behind her. "I'm with a client right now."

I was disappointed. "Oh, okay."

"We're still on, aren't we? For tomorrow? Why don't you stop and pick up some hamburgers and we can have a quick lunch right here?"

"Well, I—"

The door behind Naomi opened and a handsome young man stood there, backlighted in gold and brown from the meeting room. His hair was razor cut and long, just over his collar. His beard was trimmed like King Arthur's. His shirt was pin-striped and rolled up at the French cuffs, and his silk tie was pulled loose at his neck, below his unbuttoned shirt collar. His suit coat was hanging over his arm. He was, maybe, twenty-six or -seven. Naomi's age.

His voice was a deep, rich baritone. "Naomi, why don't we call it a day? I can come back in tomorrow morning and we'll finish it up then." He flashed me a quick smile and focused back on her. He had a soft, aristocratic, southern accent.

Naomi looked back at the guy and then at me and then at the guy again. "Oh, no! I don't think that would work, Andy. I've still got time tonight and I've got other clients coming in the morning. A couple of hours here and we—"

I interrupted by extending my hand to the handsome young man before me. "Dan Thompson," I said. "The fiancé."

Naomi was flustered. "Oh, excuse me." She introduced us: "Dan Thompson. Andrew Perlstein." We shook hands. His grip was firm but not crushing.

"Don't let me interrupt your work," I said. "I just wanted to say hello and let you know I'm still alive." I turned to Perlstein. "Nice to meet you, Andrew. How's your dad? Meyer, isn't it?"

"Call me Andy," he said. "You know Dad?"

"Just by reputation."

"Well, he's fine. Enjoying retirement. I wish he didn't enjoy it quite so much. I could use his experience and expertise at the store."

I nodded sagely and managed to not stroke my chin. "Well, good luck with Uncle Sam."

He nodded his thanks and, in spite of myself, I liked him.

I kissed Naomi on the cheek. "See you tomorrow," I said.

She buzzed me on the cheek and said, "Tomorrow, noon."

I turned to leave as they went back into the meeting room. I noticed as the door closed that the remnants of a Chinese take-out meal were scattered over the table with the IRS forms and stacks of papers and receipts.

If a therapist had asked me at that moment what I was feeling, I would have had a very difficult time pinning it down. Disappointment, certainly. Anger, probably. Jealousy, yes. And maybe a little anxiety and fear. Hey, the guy looked like a young Al Pacino, was rich, and was within a year or two of her age.

Yes, anxiety. And maybe a little fear.

Ray was talkative so I didn't have to be. We were at the Road House, which was just what its name implied. It was on the east side of Perry, about two miles out of town on Route 80 where it forked with the Old Misner Road. It had a long scarred bar, a pool table, a television that played sports all day every day, a foosball table, and peanut shells on the floor. Patrons of the Road House were throwing peanut shells on the floor long before it was the popular thing to do in yuppie restaurants and bars. The only food on the menu was a pork tenderloin sandwich as big as a porterhouse steak. It hung over the edges of the bun a good three inches all the way around. The beer was ice cold and served in long-neck bottles with little six-ounce glasses turned upside down over the top. You could get fries if you wanted them. We did, golden brown and salty. We were sitting at the bar and Ray was going through a thick file, trying to keep it out of the spilled beer.

"Okay," he said, pushing his tenderloin plate aside and draining the last of his second beer. "Prostitution. He runs a whorehouse in a double-wide trailer out by the truck stop near the freeway. Calls it a dorm for the drivers who want a clean bed to sleep in overnight." He scanned a couple of pages, tilting them to the light from the pool table. "Says the state police busted a couple of his girls for propositioning in the parking lot. Musta got overanxious. The girls implicated Conrad, but the sheriff doesn't want to move on their testimony alone. Can't say I blame him."

Ray paper-clipped the pages together and moved on to the next stack. "Usury. Hard to prove. The victim has to testify that he borrowed money from Luther at illegal rates. Problem is that these people are usually trying to pull a fast one themselves with the money, so they're understandably reluctant to help. Couple of folks seem to be into old Luther for a tidy sum, but that's only speculation."

Again, he clipped the papers together and moved on. I nibbled at my fries. They were cold.

"Gambling. Says he's got a poker barn over the county line and a floating poker game over here."

"What's a poker barn?" I asked, not really caring. I was still trying not to think about young Andrew Perlstein. You ever try not to think about something?

"Usually a run-down barn or shack where someone runs a poker game, maybe some slot machines. Illegal booze and maybe a couple of girls to entertain the customers and keep them around the tables. He used to have one on this side of the line until a Perry city council member got shot in an argument a couple of years ago. Sheriff made him move it across the county line. Says here that they think he's got slot machines and payoff pinball in half the roadhouses in the county. Usually hides them in a back room." He managed to catch the bartender's eye in a split second, something I'd been trying to do for ten minutes. "Couple cups o' joe here, Benny?"

The bartender brought us two big, steaming mugs, sugar, and cream. No Sweet'n Low. I added sugar to mine and lit my pipe. Ray lit a Camel.

"You ask me," Ray said, clipping the pages together, "he's probably running punch boards, numbers, and book. Nothing here about any of it, though."

He picked up the last packet and unclipped it. "Ah, the miscellaneous file," he said, rubbing his hands together, then licking his thumb. He paged through the stack one sheet at a time. "Moonshining, of course. Let the Feds worry about that. As long as it's good quality and no one gets hurt and he doesn't make too much of the stuff.

"Suspected of growing marijuana. No way, sheriff. Maybe his grandchildren got a little stash out in the woods but not old Luther."

He flipped through several more pages.

"Looks like they got Luther and his family pegged for every unsolved crime in the last ten years." He stopped at the last two pages. "Hm-m-m. This is interesting. Looks like Luther may be branching out." He handed the pages to me one at a time. They were standard sheriff's department reports of officers responding to calls. Speculations and guesses were written on the back of each report.

"Arson," he said, with the first page. "Old bra factory burned down last year right before you got here. Says the insurance company paid off on it but they didn't like it. A pickup truck tied to the Foley family was seen in the area a couple of hours before the fire."

He handed me the second sheet. "Doggin'."

The report was that of a raid on a dog fight in a barn in the southern part of the county. Over a hundred people had been in attendance, and nearly $30,000 had been confiscated. The bodies of four dogs were found in an open pit behind the barn. On the back of the page it was noted that the forty-nine people arrested on cruelty to animals and gambling charges all pled guilty and were fined. The maximum fine was $50. Conrad Foley was the first person to pay his fine. The second and third people were Hank Williams Foley and Johnny Cash Foley.

"Don't tell me," I said, handing the page back to Ray. "Hank and Johnny are Conrad's sons."

Ray smiled and nodded.

"They're some family," I said.

"Oh, they're pistols, all right. Wait till you meet 'em."

"I'm going to meet them?"

"Why sure," he said, standing. He dug into his pocket and pulled out some bills, which he tossed on the bar. "We're gonna go see 'em tomorrow."

"Why me?"

Ray chuckled. "Well, you're my deputy constable, aren't you?" He slapped me on the shoulder. "Come on, let's go home."

I slid off the barstool and followed him out. Two men called his name and waved as we left. I didn't really want to go with Ray the next day. I wanted to have lunch with Naomi and try to convince myself that I had nothing to worry about from handsome young furniture store magnates named Perlstein. On the other hand, I had seen Calvin Haines hanging from the rafters of his barn. I had seen the marks on his neck and his bloated purple face. And I had seen his daughter's tears.

If for some reason Ray wanted me to go with him to talk to the Foley family, and if that trip would somehow lead to finding the people who caused all this pain, well, okay. Sure I'd go with him.

Naomi would understand.

CHAPTER 6

RAY DROPPED ME OFF at about eight o'clock that night, and the loneliness hit me the instant I walked into the parsonage. It felt like a lead blanket had been draped over my shoulders.

What was wrong with me?

It was so damned quiet in Baird. Too early for crickets or cicada to be singing at night. Too cold for birds. No wind rattling the screens. Just quiet darkness out of every window. No children talking and laughing and arguing.

I turned on the television, but the reception was lousy for some reason and I could only pull in an independent station from down around London or Corbin. They were running an old "Maverick" rerun, and much as I enjoy watching James Garner I couldn't help notice how much he'd aged since he was a young Bret Maverick. It made me feel old, too. I turned it off and tried the radio. A sports talk show from Cincinnati, talking about football in April. None of the compact disks my kids had brought me sounded good, and my old cassette tapes seemed old and boring . . . like me.

There was, as usual, nothing to eat in the fridge except lunch leftovers—a sandwich and some vegetable soup in a thick, fatty clump, which was just as well because I wasn't really hungry anyway. I was just empty. Food wouldn't fill the void I felt when my kids left to go back to their mom. I took a Bud out of the crisper drawer, changed my mind, and decided on Diet Pepsi, instead.

I washed some dishes that were stacked in the sink and dried them and put them away. I straightened the living room and came within a millimeter of running the vacuum—I was that restless.

After finally using all my excuses for not working on my Sunday sermon, I went back into the office to face the lectionary and the blank piece of paper in my old Underwood typewriter. The lectionary readings still weren't firing any sparks so I decided to free associate and see what came into my mind.

Calvin Haines hanging in his barn. Blessing Haines sitting in her diner, crying and angry. Treasure Haines, whom I had never met, on her way down from Cincinnati for the funeral. The librarian. I wondered what she looked like. Some stereotypical images of librarians flashed through my mind: big, severe women in half glasses and sensible shoes. Or young women with thick glasses and blonde hair done up in a bun, trying hard to be an iceberg but seething with passion under the façade of propriety. I wondered which one Treasure Haines would be. Or maybe neither. Maybe she'd be more like her sister. Another Duchess of York.

And what kind of name was that, anyway? Treasure. Blessing. Victory. Old Calvin surely knew how to name his kids, didn't he? It would be interesting to hear what Treasure thought of her father. Blessing seemed to be . . . well . . . fond of him. I wouldn't call it smothering love and affection, exactly, but she was fond of him and her grief seemed genuine. I wondered how Treasure would react to the news of how he died. Who could hate a man enough to kill his dog in front of him and then torture him to death?

"Consider how many are my enemies; how they hate me with cruel hatred." The twenty-fifth Psalm. I looked it up in several different translations, but I liked the King James the best. I went to a couple of commentaries to see what the scholars thought and I made my decision.

It would preach.

Starting from the beginning of the Psalm, a young King David sings of his faithfulness and how sure he is that being good will eventually pay off. Eventually. At present, however, he's having a rough time of it and he reminds God that this righteousness stuff isn't as easy as it sounds. He presumes to suggest that the deity should be more attentive to the heavenly part of the bargain. David longs for the time when God will punish the wicked, reward the righteous, and put everything right.

That night, missing my kids and Naomi, and feeling sorry for myself and for Calvin Haines, I got bogged down in the sixteenth through the eighteenth verses: "Turn to me and be gracious to me, for I am lonely and afflicted. Relieve the troubles of my heart and bring me out of my distress. Consider my affliction and my trouble and forgive all my sins."

It never occurred to me that God wouldn't forgive my sins. I believe in and accept God's forgiveness. My stumble comes at the point where I have to forgive myself.

I went to bed and listened to the quiet in the house. Three nights before, I had lain in the same bed and listened as my kids talked to each other in the dark of the living room—Danny on the couch and Suzanne on a cot. I couldn't hear what they were saying, but I could hear their voices. Suzanne's giggles. Danny's gruff reproofs as he tried not to giggle.

Now it was just dark and quiet. They were gone again.

And my loneliness was my own fault.

"Turn to me and be gracious to me, O God, for I am lonely and afflicted." It seemed a fitting prayer to end a miserable day. Tired as I was, it took me a long time to finally go to sleep.

I had agreed to meet Ray at the diner at nine in the morning for breakfast and then our trip to see the Foley family. He was already at the counter, drinking coffee and eating a big plate of biscuits and sausage gravy when I walked in.

The temperature had gone down to the low forties in the night, but the sun was out, there were no clouds, and it would be warm by noon. I blew on my hands and May June slid a plate of biscuits and gravy in front of me. She dumped some scrambled eggs on top of the gravy and then sprinkled some shredded cheddar cheese over the top of it all. A Kentucky omelet. The cheese melted immediately and I dug in. It was wonderful.

A tumbler of orange juice over ice and a mug of steaming coffee topped everything off, and then Ray and I were out the door on our way back to Perry and south to the Foley place.

Technically, Ray's jurisdiction as a constable extends only to the borders of Three Mountain Township, the area around Baird—Mt. Devoux, Clark Mountain, and Pine Tree Mountain, and all the valleys and hollers that run through them. He is an appointed law enforcement officer who gets paid $200 a month and has to supply his own gun, if he wants one. Mainly, he keeps the hard drugs out (a passion with him), makes sure the moonshine is safe, and keeps the marijuana crops small enough for personal consumption of the grower only. Marijuana is the new moonshine in modern Appalachia.

People in the bluegrass state, I have found, are rarely technical. If something works, they don't ask too many questions of a technical nature. Ray Hall worked.

Ray usually enforced the law with his considerable personal presence, charisma, and reputation. That is, he could beat the crap out of just about anyone in the county and everyone knew it. No one messed with Ray Hall for long. He didn't make many arrests, usually preferring to mete out justice with a word to the wise and a thump on the head of the foolish. On those rare occasions when he did make official arrests they were always perfect, undeniable, by the book, and usually accompanied by a confession.

As a cop, Ray was a hand-hewn, mountain-crafted piece of work.

"Preacher, they's two kinds o' people in this world," he shouted as we careened through the mountains. "Cat people and dog people. Even if they never owned a dog or a cat, they're one or the other. The Foleys is dog people."

I was holding the files from the sheriff's office on my lap, trying to keep them from blowing out of the Jeep as I held on for dear life. He took my lack of response for assent and continued his lecture.

"Dog people like dogs and are like dogs. They love attention and affection. They're loyal and protective. They're up front with their feelin's and they'll do anything for a reward."

He looked to see if I was following him. I was. Sort of.

"That's the way the Foleys are. They love bein' big dogs o' the county. They like the attention they get whether it comes from folks they rip off, folks they sell hot TVs to, or the law. They see themselves as maintainin' the balance between freedom and marshal law. They're loyal only to their family and would die for each other in a thoroughbred second. Their reward is money and respect. They'll do anything for either one of those, but they prefer to get both."

"You make them sound like decent people," I said, wedging the files under my thigh and blowing on my hands. It was getting warmer but the windchill factor in the Jeep had to be fifty below zero.

"Oh, hell, no," he said, smiling. "They're crooks. Scum of the earth. It's just . . . well . . . they're predictable, that's all." He downshifted into a big cutback and shifted up again on the way out, using the speed to slingshot us out of the turn. "That family is like a big old ornery, arthritic dog. As long as you know what you're dealin' with you can handle 'im. Socio—what's its."

"Sociopaths?" I ventured.

"There you go. They know the difference between right and wrong. They just don't give a damn. Got their own code.

"Now, what you gotta watch out for is them cat people. Never know what them bastards are gonna do. They don't function like most people. Turn up their nose at normal rewards and hold a grudge for no apparent reason. Hate for the sake of hatin', just 'cause it's in their blood. They're the other one." He cocked the eye at me again.

"Psychopaths?" I tried.

"Hey, that college really works, don't it? I bet your momma's proud." He laughed and slapped my knee hard enough to leave a bruise in the shape of his big hand.

"So the Foleys are all sociopaths?" I asked.

He nodded. "Yep." His hand slammed the gearshift through another series of turns and we were on the edge of Perry. "Just like big old dogs. 'Cept maybe for Hank, Conrad's oldest boy."

"He's not like a dog?"

"Oh, yeah. He's a dog all right. A big rabid St. Bernard."

"Cujo," I said to myself.

"Bless you," Ray said. Then he winked at me and pointed his thumb over his shoulder. His .410, single-shot shotgun was lying on the floor in the back of the Jeep. A box of shells sat beside it. Somehow it didn't make me feel any better.

We stopped in Perry at the Donut Hole to get a cup of coffee and a donut and use the rest room. We weren't really hungry after May June's lumberjack breakfast, but the Hole's donuts are always fresh and hot and melt-in-your-mouth light. They lie in your stomach like a ball of lead, but they sure are fun going down. The coffee is fresh ground and comes in only one size: Jumbo. And when they put cream in it, it's real cream.

I thought briefly about calling Naomi, but it was nearly ten in the morning and she'd be in that conference room working with someone and I didn't want to interrupt. I also didn't want to know whom she was working with. If it was someone young and good looking and rich it would ruin my whole day with jealousy and doubt. If it was someone old and ugly I would feel relieved and then I'd feel guilty about feeling relieved and that would ruin my whole day, too. Ignorance, I decided, was bliss.

Then I felt guilty about that, so I split the difference and called Percy Mills's office and left a message with David.

"Ms. Taylor's with a client right now. May I take a message, Reverend Thompson? Have her return your call if she gets a chance?"

"No. Just tell her I'm with Ray and may not make it to lunch." She would understand the meaning of my being "with Ray" and would know my time was not my own.

"She will be very disappointed, I'm sure," David said, with an inflection that I didn't like but didn't know how to define. Something about the way he said, "Ahm sho-uh."

"Yeah, well, just give her the message, will you?"

"Certainly." Sut-un-lay. The jerk.

It took about an hour to wind through Perry and then south of town through the rolling hills and forests that make up the southwest quarter of Durel County. We arrived at the Foley place at ten minutes to eleven.

If you thought I was going to talk about backwoods hillbilly criminals with rotten teeth, bib overalls, and muskets, forget it. The Foley place was a small plantation much like those in Paris, Kentucky, the rich suburb of Lexington.

A long, winding driveway made of crushed brick began at Route 42 and wound over a half mile through peach and apple orchards. White rail fences divided the other land into two- and three-acre portions, some with pasture, some tilled, waiting to be planted with tobacco or corn. Field hands, black and white, worked the small plots with small tractors and hand tools, getting ready to plant within a few days.

The house itself was a Williamsburg colonial of red brick with white and blue trim. I figured it for maybe thirty rooms, it was that big. There was a six-car garage off to the left and behind the house. It, the barn, the stable, and all the outbuildings were near replicas of the house—red brick with trim. The sweet, pungent smell of hay and horse manure drifted, not unpleasantly, on the spring air.

"Still uses tenant farmers," Ray said, waving a hand at the small parcels. Some of the workers had stopped to lean on their tools and watch us drive up the lane. "Poor folks, mostly. Rent a portion and tend it. Usually make just enough to get them to next year. Bigger the family, the more area you can farm. Course, if you got a big family, you gotta farm a bigger portion. Then you gotta pay the Foleys rent on the land, and the cost of seed and fertilizer, and rent on the tools, and security fees and a hundred other bullshit fees until you got just enough left to eat rice and beans all winter and buy more seed in the spring. It's a trap." He shook his head and took a breath, let it out as the Jeep slid to a stop in front of the house. "Son of a bitch," he said.

"Looks like crime pays," I said, nodding to the house and buildings.

"That it does," Ray said, following my gaze. "Ain't an honest dollar in the place, I bet. Some say he's the richest man in the county. Some say it's Percy Mills."

"I thought Hebrew Taylor was the richest," I said, surprised. Everyone, it seemed, just accepted that as fact back in Baird. Naomi's father was not only the meanest man in the county, he was the richest.

"Oh, Hebe owns more. But there's a lot of it he can't get to. All his wealth is tied up in land and mineral rights. And it's all family land. Been in his family for years and years. I guess legally he could liquidate it if'n he were a mind, but he wouldn't." Ray took off his cap and ran his hand through his hair, wiped his forehead on his arm. We were sitting in the sun and it was getting warm.

"Luther Foley, though, all his is in cash money. He could buy most o' the county before Hebe Taylor found a buyer for his mountain. Only thing keeps him from doin' it is Percy Mills. Percy's the richest man in Perry, probably. What he don't own, he controls as legal council or controller. He's a rascal, ol' Perce. Power behind nine out of every ten thrones in Eastern Kentucky." Ray smiled in admiration and took a deep breath. "Well, we better get goin'."

When he got out of the Jeep, he left the shotgun in the back with an old army blanket tossed over it. I was glad for that. Despite everything I had read and heard about the Foley family, this house just didn't look like the kind of place where violence was possible.

I was wrong, of course.

The doorbell played the first few bars of "Release Me." We could hear it through the door. Ray thought that was funny. After a few seconds a young man in his late twenties, wearing jeans, cowboy boots, an unbuttoned western shirt, and a bad case of bed hair opened the door. He was unshaven; he didn't say anything—just stood there looking at us.

"You'd be who?" Ray asked. "Waylon?"

"John," said the young man. He tried to make his voice deep.

Ray snapped his fingers. "Course you are." Then to me: "Reverend, meet Johnny Cash Foley."

I stuck out my hand and John ignored it. Just nodded at me. I nodded back.

Ray went right on as though we had shaken hands and smiled at each other. "Reverend Doctor Daniel Thompson," he said, smiling. "Pastor of the Baird Methodist Church."

Johnny Cash Foley was not impressed. He looked at Ray. "Who are you?"

"Me? Oh, I'm Constable Raymond Hall." He pulled a badge out of his shirt pocket and showed it to Foley. I had never seen the badge before.

"You're a long way from Three Mountain territory. What you want?" This kid was hard to impress.

"Well, we'd like to speak to your grandfather, you don't mind," Ray said, still smiling. He brushed past Foley and started into the house. I followed.

"Hey!" Foley pushed the door shut behind us and followed. "You can't just push your way in here. You got a warrant?"

Ray and I were standing in the foyer, looking around. All pretense of grandeur vanished once you walked through the door of the house. The place was a wreck. To the right was what was supposed to be a formal living/sitting room. Cardboard U-Haul boxes were stacked to the ceiling. The ceramic tiles in the hall hadn't been swept or mopped in a month. Big clots of dried mud, straw, grass, and other outdoor stuff lay scattered all over the floor. The walls were grimed and smeared with hand prints, all too high to have been left by children.

"What we need a warrant for?" Ray asked as he walked down the hall. The restaurant-size kitchen was full of unwashed dishes, empty beer bottles, full ashtrays, and the smell of mold. Cobwebs ran from the corner of the counter to the oven door. "Pastor comes to pay his respects to one of the leaders of the community. He has to have a warrant? Where's that written?"

Foley hurried along, trying to keep up with us. He mumbled something as he pushed past me. "Grandpa ain't takin' visitors," he told Ray as he stepped around him and tried to block his path.

Ray stopped with his chin about a half inch from Foley's forehead. He didn't smile when he said, quietly, "The hell he ain't."

"He ain't, damn it. He's sick." He was almost pleading.

Ray examined Foley's face for what seemed like a long time. Then, finally, he said, "Okay. Where's your daddy, John? We'll talk to him."

Foley seemed to deflate with his sigh. "Come on," he said.

He led us through the house and it didn't improve much with depth. Every room was a mess, even the ones where people had been living. Dirty dishes, ashtrays, clothing, tools, car parts, animals, magazines—in piles everywhere. In every room we passed. Even the bedrooms.

Somewhere in what seemed like the northeast corner of the building, on a second floor I caught Ray's sleeve and gave it a tug. When he looked at me, I nodded toward one of the bedrooms we were passing. The bed was just a mattress on the floor and on that was a pit bull. The dog was sleeping with its head on a pillow next to that of a man who looked to be about six-and-a-half feet tall. He was wearing jockey shorts—the man, not the dog—and snoring peacefully. His body was layered with muscle—man or dog, take your pick. Long-neck beer bottles were scattered around the floor with open bags of pork rinds, piles of clothing, stacks of girlie magazines, and at least two handguns. A pile of dog poop lay prominently in the middle of the floor.

"Ain't that cute," Ray said in a stage whisper. "Hank's gettin' his beauty sleep."

"Hank?"

"Hank Williams Foley," Ray said, nodding toward the big man. "He's the one I told you about. Pure mean and evil."

John Foley appeared at our side, looking over Ray's shoulder. "Come on, you wanna see Daddy, don't ya?"

Ray put his finger to his lips and tiptoed into the room. With the stiff cover of a girlie magazine he scooped up the dog mess and placed it neatly on the pillow next to Hank Foley's left ear. Then he tiptoed back to the door.

John groaned and whispered. "Now why you wanna do that for? Don't you like livin'? Damn! He's liable to think one of us done it. You ever think o' that?"

Ray just grinned and started down the hallway. John rushed

ahead to take the lead again. Ray leaned over to whisper to me, "They all live here together. The whole family in this one house. Luther and Annabelle, their son Conrad, and his wife and their six young 'uns."

"What happened?" I asked. "The maid die?"

Ray shook his head. "I don't know, but it sure is a mess, ain't it."

And then, suddenly, the mess disappeared. John Foley opened a door and we walked into another room and another world.

It was an office as lavish and beautifully appointed as any I had ever seen. Plush sand-colored carpet. Big antique mahogany desk. Signed, tasteful prints of modern watercolors framed and hung on delicate, lovely wallpaper. Two handmade leather wing chairs faced the desk with a beautiful, antique end table between them.

But the biggest surprise was the man behind the mahogany desk. He was about my age or a couple of years older. Say forty-five. His hair was prematurely white and his complexion was bright red and healthy. His boots, which were propped on top of the desk, were snakeskin or alligator, or some other rare and expensive reptile. He wore a black western shirt with embroidered roses on the breast pockets, string tie held in place with a piece of turquoise as big as a golf ball, and a sport jacket made of glove leather. He was smoking a cigar as big as my arm, taking it out of his mouth and admiring it lovingly between puffs. The smoke disappeared so quickly that I couldn't smell it—and I couldn't have been more than ten feet away.

He looked up and smiled as we entered the office. John panted up to the desk and said, "Daddy—"

But the man stopped him with an upraised hand and slowly stood. He smiled with perfectly even teeth and extended his hand to Ray Hall. "How ya doin', Ray?" he said.

Ray took the hand and shook it. "Fine, Connie," he said. "Just fine. Your family?"

Conrad Foley shrugged and indicated the wing chairs. "Oh, you know how family is."

Ray nodded. Yeah, he knew. What are ya gonna do, right?

We just sat there for a few moments, the two of them grinning at each other. Young John took his leave and Conrad sat down behind the desk. The big leather chair let out a little woof of air but it didn't squeak.

Finally I realized why no one was speaking. There was music in the air, coming out of some hidden speakers concealed in the bookcases. Country and western music. A nasal baritone voice was singing a sad song about coming home from work and finding his wife was gone with his kids. And his dog. Run off with the guy he thought was his best friend. Directly, mercifully, it ended.

"Whataya think?" Conrad asked Ray.

"Not bad," Ray said. "Not bad at all."

"Hank Junior said he may give it a place on his next album. Says it needs work but it sounds like one his daddy might have liked." Conrad looked at his cigar. "He don't want it, Travis's agent says he's sure Randy'll like it. I call it sold."

Ray nodded again. "Sounds sold to me."

They both sat there in easy silence, and I eventually figured out what they were talking about while they listened to another awful song. Hank Junior was Hank Williams, Junior, country music recording artist and son of the late, great Hank Williams. Randy Travis was, well, Randy Travis. I'm not a huge fan of country and western music, but I knew enough to know that those guys wouldn't come within a hundred miles of the noise in that room.

When the second song finally died, Conrad Foley sat up straight in his chair and laid the cigar in a platter-size ashtray. "I reckon you're here to talk about Calvin Haines and them damn dogs o' his'n," he said.

All Ray said was, "Yup."

CHAPTER 7

PEOPLE FROM OHIO are called Buckeyes.

People from Indiana are Hoosiers.

People from Kentucky are, well, Kentuckians. You may remember the movie. Jimmy Stewart, I think. Or was it John Wayne?

Anyway, Kentuckians are pioneers, frontiersmen. They are explorers, Indian fighters, trailblazers, and what-have-you. Hillbillies, they will tell you, are from West Virginia.

West Virginians insist that they are Mountaineers. Hillbillies, they say, live in Kentucky, where the so-called mountains are really just great big hills.

In business, Kentuckians don't hesitate to call themselves hillbillies. As in, "I'm just a Kentucky hillbilly." If someone says that to you, hold on to your wallet, your truck, your dog, and your wife—and run the other way as fast as you can go. If you hear a lawyer say it, just go ahead and settle the case, you're beaten.

Whatever they call themselves, they have their own way of doing things, and a slow way it is. These are the people who invented bourbon whiskey and bluegrass. The Kentucky Derby—the actual race, itself—lasts about two minutes. Then they talk about it for a week and spend fifty-one weeks getting ready for the next one.

This slow, deliberate way of doing things is nowhere more evident than in their modes of communication. You never just come right out and say what's on your mind with Kentucky hill people. You circle slowly around the subject for a while in a seemingly simple, but deceptively intricate folk dance. You talk about family and music and cars and the weather and Wildcat basketball. Asking the time of day can sometimes be more time-consuming than buying a camel from a Bedouin tribesman. One day, maybe I'll learn how to do it.

The point of this discursive dillydallying is to get the other guy to bring up the topic you want to talk about. I don't know why this is important, but it is. I've seen it hundreds of times.

Conrad Foley probably thought that being in his own house, in his surprisingly clean office, listening to his own whiny voice singing his own whiny country and western music on the hidden speakers on the bookshelves put him at an advantage. He probably thought that popping the reference to Calvin Haines and the dogs would be a surprise maneuver that would hit Ray like a left jab when he was expecting a right cross. Not a knockout punch, exactly, but a painful blow, nonetheless.

Ray wasn't even stunned. Conrad's left jab had failed. He had brought up the subject first, and now Ray was ahead on points—a subtle but important advantage in the art of Kentucky discourse.

I, however, not so adept at Kentucky-speak, was caught by surprise, and Conrad saw it in my face. He looked at me, then back at Ray, and said, "Your partner here looks like he just seen a ghost."

Ray just smiled. "Oh, excuse me, Connie. This-here's Reverend Dan Thompson from over to Baird Methodist. He's the one found ol' Cal." He didn't try to explain why I was with him. Conrad didn't seem to care.

"How ya doin', Reverend?" he said without even a hint of sincerity. He turned back to Ray. "Shame about ol' Calvin."

"Yeah," Ray said. "I guess now you and your daddy'll never get them dogs."

Conrad lifted his hands, palms up, at his sides and shrugged.

"I heard you was tryin' to buy into beagle competition," Ray said.

Conrad nodded. "I did give it some thought, but Cal wasn't sellin'."

Ray reached into a large wooden box on Conrad's desk and extracted a cigar for himself and one for me. He lit his with his cigarette lighter. I put mine in my inside windbreaker pocket and pulled out my pipe. When Ray's cigar was smoking like a forest fire, he said, "Why you interested in beagles, Connie? I thought you was a pit bull man."

Conrad chuckled. "Gettin' too old for that happy horse hockey. Sorry, Reverend. You watch enough dogs tear each other apart it starts to look all the same. Thought I might try my hand at beaglin'. Get outside more. Breathe some clean air for a change."

"What made you change your mind?" Ray asked.

Conrad shrugged again. "You know me, Ray. I can't have the best, I don't want nothin' at all." His eyes popped wide open. "Hey! That's good. There's a song in that, don't ya think?"

"Maybe."

"Why, hell, yes, there is." He hummed a few notes, then grabbed a pencil and wrote furiously on a yellow legal pad, singing slowly as he wrote. "If I can't have the best, honey, I don't want nothin' at all."

"Connie," Ray said evenly.

"M-m-m?"

"When was the last time you seen Cal Haines?"

Conrad looked up from his legal pad. "I don't know. Maybe three, four months ago." He leaned back over his legal pad.

"What about your young 'uns?"

"Ray," Conrad said, laying down his pencil. "They ain't so young anymore. It's just that you and me are such old farts, everyone seems young to us." He ticked them off on his fingers. "Hank's twenty-nine, Johnny's twenty-eight, Waylon's twenty-six, Willie's twenty-five, Loretta's twenty-four, and George is eighteen." I pushed my estimate of Conrad Foley's age up by a couple of years. They started early with their families in the hills, though. I figured him to be forty-seven, maybe forty-eight.

"That's quite a memory you got there, Connie," Ray said.

Conrad shrugged again. He was a good shrugger. Full of expression and easy Kentucky charm. Kentuckians can say paragraphs with a well-executed shrug. "They're my kids, Ray."

"What about them? They been talkin' to Cal lately?"

"Conrad shook his head. "Nah. No reason to."

"What about your daddy?"

Conrad's face changed completely. No more smiling hillbilly now. He was dead serious. "Daddy don't talk much to no one anymore."

"That right?"

Conrad looked at Ray for a few minutes and his eyes said he was right on the edge of anger, balancing there, trying to get it under control. "How long since you seen my daddy, Ray?"

Now it was Ray's turn to shrug. "Couple o' year. Five, maybe."

Conrad stood. "Come on," he said.

And again we were following a Foley through the big mansion. This time, however, we went farther into the other world—the clean, neat part of the house. Conrad opened a door on the back wall of his office and we followed him through a control room that looked out, through a glass wall, into a state-of-the-art recording studio. At least it looked like state-of-the-art to me. Not knowing what state-of-the-art was, exactly, I was guessing, but I felt confident that my guess was pretty close. If he couldn't have the best he didn't want anything at all, right?

There were dials and lights and slide switches and microphones and speakers and monitors and stringed musical instruments of every kind and size. And there were computer screens and oscilloscopes, or things that looked like oscilloscopes, and about a thousand other things the meaning and use of which I could only hazard a wild guess.

Through the studio and another door into a small waiting-room-type place with comfortable, upholstered chairs and a table where, presumably, food was sometimes laid out. Speakers on the walls probably fed music from the adjoining studio into this room.

Through yet another door and we were in a bedroom. Big hospital bed, nineteen-inch color television, medicines, magazines, books, checkerboard, and checkers. It was a very nice version of a hospital room.

Sitting in the middle of it all, in a wheelchair, was an old man. He looked like he was over a hundred. His pajamas were sky blue with little white sailboats all over them. His bald head was covered with a wisp of thin, white hair. He was wearing a pair of BVD briefs on the outside of his pajamas, and he was asleep, his chin on his chest.

Conrad Foley walked up to the old man and gently shook his shoulder. "Daddy?" Shake. "Daddy, there's someone here to see you."

The old man stirred, smacked his lips, blinked, and looked up. Conrad said, "Ray Hall, you remember him? Constable over to Baird? He brung a preacher to see you."

The old man looked at Ray. Looked at me. Looked at Conrad the same way he looked at us—without a hint of recognition. "Go to hell!" he said, and turned the wheelchair abruptly toward the television and began to watch the blank screen.

Conrad shrugged, a little embarrassed. "Oh, Daddy, fer cryin' out loud."

"Go to hell!" He wheeled closer to the television set and leaned forward until his face was only about three inches from the screen. Conrad leaned across the old man and turned on the television. "The Price Is Right" sprang to life in living color.

Conrad looked at Ray and shook his head. "Ain't that a pity?" he seemed to say without speaking a word.

"Alzheimer's?" Ray asked.

"Who knows?" Conrad sighed. "Probably. You know, they can't really diagnose Alzheimer's till the autopsy. But that's what the doctors figure. His arteries are fine. The only other possibility is that he's just gone crazy or senile—or both."

"Go to hell!" Now the old man was yelling at Bob Barker.

We returned through the recording studio to the office and stood around for a few minutes while Ray and Conrad refired their cigars and filled the room with smoke. I left my pipe in my jacket pocket and just enjoyed their cigars vicariously.

Finally Conrad Foley spoke again. "I figured you'd be down here to talk to me as soon as I heard about Cal dyin'," he said. "It's still Daddy's county, Ray. Daddy may be crazy as a dodo bird, but people still respect him."

"They don't know?" Ray asked.

"Oh, there's probably some rumors goin' around. I reckon folks'll know sooner or later, but for now we keep it right here in this house."

"How's your momma takin' it?"

Conrad executed his perfect shrug again. "It's killin' her, I think. But you know Momma. She just wipes his chin and talks to him like they used to. All he does is cuss her. I tell ya, Ray, I could smack him when he does that."

"It ain't really your daddy talkin'," Ray said.

"I know. Still. . . ." He looked at his cigar, rotated it to keep the burn even. "I don't know nothin' about Cal Haines and his dogs, Ray. That's the truth. I offered to buy and I offered him good money and he laughed in my face. I don't take well to that kinda thing, but I got more important things to worry about." He nodded toward the door we had just come through.

"You runnin' the show, now?" Ray asked.

"Best I can. Daddy was right, though. I ain't really got the head for it. I guess I'll turn the whole shootin' works over to Loretta one day. She just got outta college and she's the onliest one's got the brains. Hank sure as hell ain't."

Ray stubbed his cigar out in the big ashtray. The stogy was still six inches long. He nodded his head about ten times like he was thinking. "You don't mind if we have a look around, just the same, do you?"

Conrad Foley smiled without showing his teeth and shook his head. "My word's not good enough for you, huh?"

"Oh, Connie, it ain't that. It's just that I gotta do my job, you know? I don't look around I wouldn't be doin' my job and I wouldn't be earnin' my pay. It won't take long."

Conrad collapsed into his chair behind the desk. "I said no, you'd be back in an hour with a search warrant, wouldn't you?"

Ray shrugged. Conrad knew that, with his reputation in the county, denying Ray permission to search would be probable cause enough for some judges—the few he didn't have in his pocket—to grant a search warrant, especially if it was being applied for by Ray Hall.

Conrad picked up a pencil and started writing on the yellow legal pad as though he had already dismissed us. "Go on, then." He hollered at the door to our backs. "Johnny!" Johnny Cash Foley had buttoned up his shirt and tucked it into his jeans. His hair was wet and combed. "Show these two around the place," Conrad said.

Johnny shrugged his whatever-you-say shrug and we followed him out.

"Take care, now, Connie," Ray said.

"You, too," Conrad said without looking up.

Johnny Cash Foley walked silently back through the house and we followed as silently. A housekeeping staff had not arrived in our absence, and everything was pretty much as it had been on our first trip through. Confusion, mess, dirt, and trash dominated.

Finally, we made it through the maze and out the back door into the backyard of the house. The lawn spread out before us toward the barn and the stable, and it was to the stable that we followed the young Foley.

The bluegrass in the yard was long in some places and dead in others. Some daffodils were trying to survive a weed attack and almost winning, but other than that, the backyard was as much a mess as the house. Beer bottles, food wrappers, and trash seemed to be thrown there from the doors and windows of the house.

Johnny Foley opened the single, walk-through door into the stable and we entered a warm, beautiful tack room that smelled of leather, horse sweat, coffee, and tobacco. Johnny stopped and turned around. He was smiling. "You ever had a real good ass whippin'?" he asked. He pronounced it "ice whuppin."

I didn't know who he was talking to, and I wanted to do one of those things where you point to yourself and silently mouth *me?* Instead, I looked at Ray. "I hope he's talking to you," I said.

Ray didn't look at me. "He is."

Johnny's smile was cocky now. "Well?"

Ray wasn't ruffled. "Boy," he said, to Johnny. "You ain't fool enough to call me out, are you?"

"Might be."

"But you ain't."

Johnny reached behind him and opened the door into the stable. "Hank, he's here." Over Johnny's shoulder, back in the shadows of the stable, Hank Williams Foley walked into view and struck a Mr. Clean pose, with his arms folded against his chest, his fists making his biceps bulge. He was not smiling.

He looked even more huge and forbidding than when he was sleeping with his pit bull on the floor mattress in the bedroom of the house. He was bigger than I originally thought. Six-feet-seven or -eight, probably. His hair was short and curly and wet. His jeans were tight and his boots had high heels and silver caps on the toes. He wasn't wearing a shirt, and I noticed that the muscles on his chest and torso seemed to be layered in great slabs. He had a tattoo over each pectoral muscle. On the right was a heart with the name *Dedra* written in it. On the left was an American eagle like the one in the seal of the United States.

Johnny stepped backward into the stable and out of sight, leaving us in the tack room.

"Where's your girlfriend?" Ray asked.

Puzzlement passed across Hank's eyes and his left pec jumped about a foot. Then the right answered.

"The dog," Ray said. "The one you were sleepin' with."

Hank smiled and it wasn't a pretty thing to behold. Most of his teeth were either rotten or broken off. "That jus' shows how much you know, buddy. That-there weren't no bitch. That were a male dog name o' Breaker."

Ray thought for a moment. "You're sleepin' with a male dog?"

The smile vanished immediately. Hank shook his head and looked at the ground. "See, now that's gonna cost ya. That dog dirt on the pillow thing, I was just gonna bloody you a mite. Now you insulted me, personal, to my facc. So now I gotta break sumpin'."

"Yeah?"

Hank nodded. "Uh-huh. Come on out here an' take it like a man."

Ray shrugged and started for the door, then stopped. "You gonna whup the preacher's ice, too?"

Hank tilted his head to look through the door into the tack room, saw me, and waved. I waved back. It felt silly. "Nah," he said. "Preacher can just watch. I got nothin' agin' him."

Ray nodded. He leaned over to me and whispered. "Watch Johnny. He comes up on my back, coldcock him with one of those bottles." He nodded to an old Coke machine in the corner. A rack beside it held empty six-ounce Coke bottles. I nodded.

"Well," Ray said, taking off his jacket. "Let's get to it." He walked toward the door into the stable, and just as he got to it, he hesitated long enough to reach out to a saddle that was hanging on a rack sticking out from the wall. He lifted a riding crop from the saddle horn and, holding it behind his back in both hands, entered the stable like Napoleon viewing a battle from a mountaintop. I followed, Coke bottle in my jacket pocket.

I had seen Ray fight before and he was good. Really good. For his age and size, he was surprisingly fast and he operated from one deadly rule, which he had shared with me one night last winter over bourbon and coffee. "Walk away," he had said. "Walk away from a fight just as fast and far as you can and keep on walkin' until your back is to a wall. If he follows you to that wall and still wants to fight, then you can figure your life is in danger. When your life's in danger there ain't no rules. Pick up the nearest weapon you can find and hit him fast an' hard. Put him down and don't let him get up again." To tell you the truth, I felt a little sorry for Hank.

Hank took a sort of boxer's stance, like the old-fashioned English thing where the guys stand straight up and hit each other until one falls down. Marquis of Queensbury by way of Nashville and Memphis. He was smiling from one side of his mouth.

Ray walked up to him and started to talk. I couldn't believe my ears. Surely Hank had watched television or movies or something. Surely he wasn't dumb enough to fall for that. Yes, he was.

Ray opened with the Butch Cassidy gambit. "Before we start," he said. "What are the rules?"

Hank dropped his fists to his side and faced Ray full on. He looked back at Johnny then back at Ray with a quizzical look on his face. "Rules? There ain't—"

Ray hit him.

A riding crop is a short little whip about two feet long. It is made of leather, wound around a plastic core, thick at one end for a handle. A leather thong wraps around the wrist to keep you from dropping it. The business end is often a wide piece of leather folded over so when you hit the horse with it, it makes a loud pop to let the horse know he's been hit. Other crops have little strips of leather dangling from the end. This kind of crop is called a quirt. Sound is not important with a quirt. It's designed to deliver a stinging pain to a horse's tough muscled flank.

Now considering who Ray was up against, the "horse's ass" pun is not totally lost on me here, but any more than a brief mention of it would draw our attention from the painful fact that Ray was applying the quirt to a man's face. And even Hank Foley's face, with its big jaw and proud nose and hooded eyes and perpetual five o'clock shadow, was more tender than a horse's flank.

Ray hit him six times, back and forth, full arm swings, and he did it so fast that his arm was a blur. Whack! Whack! Whack! Whack! Whack! Whack! The first three whacks came so fast that Hank didn't react. By the fourth he was raising his hands to his face, the fifth caught one hand and one cheek, and the sixth hit the backs of his hands. Blood was seeping out between his fingers as he staggered back.

He jerked his hands away from his face and saw the blood and let out a roar like some great wounded grizzly bear. His arms spread wide and he charged. Ray ducked under Hank's right arm and kicked out to the right, sweeping his leg under Hank's. The big man went down, face-first into the sawdust, and a little cloud puffed up around him.

Remember Ray's rules? He did. He had no intention of letting Hank get up again. He kicked him in the groin just as hard as he could. His black size-fourteen work oxfords had steel toes. Hank's butt came up into the air, he grunted, rolled over clutching his groin, and coiled himself into a ball like a snail.

Johnny was standing, dumb, his mouth open. He looked up at Ray like he was going to cry. "You bastard!" My hand went to the coke bottle in my jacket pocket, but Ray was there first. His hand shot out from his side with the quirt hanging from his wrist, and he backhanded Johnny so hard against the jaw that the young Foley fell down on top of his brother. Hank groaned again.

Ray walked back into the tack room and hung the quirt back on the saddle horn. He went to the Coke machine and bought two Cokes (one diet) and came back out into the stable. He handed me the Diet Coke.

"Hank," he said, squatting down next to the pile of humanity on the stable floor. "I think some of that dog poop slipped in your ear and right into your brain. Soon as you can manage it, I think we oughta talk."

Then he sat down in the sawdust and dirt, took a swig of his Coke, and lit a cigarette.

CHAPTER 8

"WE DON'T KNOW NOTHIN' ABOUT NO DAMN BEAGLES," Johnny Cash Foley whimpered.

Hank wiped the blood from his face with Ray's bandanna. There was only one cut, across his cheek, but it was bleeding profusely. His face looked like he had stuck it in a hornet's nest.

"Hank?" Ray said. He was standing behind them, looking at me. Hank nodded his agreement with his brother.

"Neither of you know anything about Calvin Haines and his dogs?" They both shook their heads. Johnny rubbed his jaw.

"Then what were you doin' up to his house. We got a witness puts you up there." I caught myself just in time to not look at him in surprise.

"That's impossible," Hank said.

"Why's that?"

Hank frowned in concentration. Then his eyes opened wide, but Johnny spoke first.

"Because we never been up there, that's why!" He looked at Hank.

Ray looked at me and shook his head. "Preacher, are these two peckerwoods about the dumbest couple o' clod kickers you ever saw or what?"

Hank growled. "There ain't no need to insult us to our faces."

Ray smiled. "Why's that, Hank? You gonna *whup* my *ice* again? Didn't you hear me? I got a witness puts you two boys up there." Ray walked around to face them and sat down Indian style. "Now here's the way I figure it. If you was up there and talked to ol' Cal and left, fine. No law against payin' a friendly visit to a man with a common interest. On the other hand, if you're lyin', I got to wonder why. Maybe you killed him?"

Ray just watched this fabrication sink in as he began his cigarette ritual. "So, which was it?"

They looked at each other. They both frowned in concentration. Then Hank spoke. "Wasn't me—"

"Shut up, Hank!" Johnny backhanded Hank on the arm.

"You shut up!" Then to Ray: "Was Johnny and Waylon up to

Mr. Haines's."

"When was that?" Ray asked.

Hank thought again. "Musta been about—"

"Whataya mean, when was that?" Johnny shouted. "You got a witness, you oughta know when it was!"

"Shut your food hole, John. Me and Hank's talkin' here. Show some respect."

I could hardly believe it. Instead of coming to his brother's defense, Hank Williams Foley sat up just a little straighter and the corner of his mouth turned up in a smirk.

Ray turned his full attention to Hank. "You were sayin', Hank?"

"Well, uh, it was Johnny an' Waylon went on up there . . . let's see . . . that musta been Friday last." He looked to his brother. "Is that right, Johnny? It was Friday, wasn't it?"

Johnny crossed his arms over his chest and sat there staring.

"What'd they go up there for, Hank?" Ray asked.

"Dogs."

"What about dogs?"

"They went up to give him some money on one o' them pups. Fer Daddy." He looked at his brother, then back at Ray. "It were supposed to be a surprise. That's why Johnny's mad I'm tellin' ya. You won't tell Daddy, will ya?"

Ray looked at Johnny. "That's it? You were buyin' a pup for your daddy?"

No answer.

"So what's the big secret?" Ray asked.

Hank reached out and Ray almost flinched. The big man's hand touched the constable's badge showing through Ray's shirt pocket. He smiled. "You're the law."

Ray got up and dusted the sawdust off his butt. "Me and the preacher are gonna look around a mite. You two give us about thirty minutes, then you can go back to the house. Hank, you put some peroxide on that cut, you hear?"

Hank nodded earnestly. "Yes, sir."

We walked across the yard from the stable to the barn and I saw why there were no horses in the stable. They were out in the fields, grazing and romping around. I counted five: two brown, one gray, and two tan. That's about all I know about horses. Ray flipped his cigarette into the grass and shook his head.

"What's the story with those two?" I asked. "Is Hank retarded?"

"No more'n you ner me," he said. "He's just dumb. Ignorant. Big ol' hoss like him, the family just figured he could be put to better use, so they never sent him to school."

"Better use?"

"Bustin' legs. Collectin' debts. Scarin' people. Whatever."

"And he's never been to school?" I asked, incredulous.

"Never. Can't write his own name."

"Ray opened the big red doors and we walked into a barn like none I'd ever been in before. There were a few bales of straw in the loft and a little scattered on the dirt floor. There were no chickens or hogs or cows or mules. There were no plows or scythes.

What there was, was dogs.

Kennels lined the walls and in each kennel was a pit bull. Most of the dogs looked docile enough, sleeping and lying in little piles of straw. A couple of the dogs got up when we entered, and barked happily as though they were glad to see us. A couple of others acted a little more threatening, baring their teeth and slobbering as they barked and growled. I counted eleven dogs and twelve cages. The empty cage, presumably, was for the dog in Hank Foley's bed. Breaker.

In the center of the barn were several contraptions. A treadmill was obvious. Some other things I couldn't identify. Near the back door, two poles about three inches in diameter were sunk into the floor about six feet apart with another pole running between them, across their tops, about five feet above the ground. A rope hung from the horizontal pole, and there was fresh sawdust on the ground beneath it.

Ray scuffed the sawdust with the toe of his shoe. "Blood training," he said.

"I don't think I want to know what that is," I said.

He lit a cigarette without his ritual. "They put a cat or a pup or some other live animal in a gunnysack hung from that rope. Then they let the dog kill it if he wants to eat. Dog has to work at it to jump up, grab it, and pull it down. They use it to start the dogs from pups, train 'em to like the taste of blood. Get used to killin'. Feed 'em nothin' but raw meat."

"Lord."

"Ain't pretty, that's for sure. That-there's a trainin' pit." He pointed to a small area in the center of the barn. It was about ten feet in diameter, made of three-quarter-inch plywood sheets about four feet tall. "When the dog gets bigger, they put 'im in the pit. They use another dog that ain't a fighter. It's what you might call a rigged fight."

"They train them to fight?" I asked.

"No. Pit bulls want to fight. They love to fight. It's in their blood. All dog fighters do is weed out the weak ones and encourage the strong ones." He leaned on the plywood and smoked. I lit my pipe. The barn smelled like wet dog. "You keep puttin' your strong one in here, in this pit with weaker dogs, but you keep gettin' bigger and stronger ones to put him up against. After a while, when you think he's ready, you take him to a fight and bet on him."

He straightened and flipped his cigarette butt onto the clay floor of the pit. He walked to a small room in the corner of the barn and opened the door. I looked into a miniature surgical theater.

"If a dog's valuable enough, you bring him home and patch him up and get him strong for the next fight. Ol' Luther was a better surgeon than most o' the vets in the county," Ray said.

We walked out of the barn and into the sun. It was getting warmer, and by the time we left the barn all of the dogs were barking. "Well, have we seen everything we need to see here?" I asked Ray.

"Nawp."

"No?"

"We ain't seen any beagle pups."

It was after two when we got back to Perry. I'd missed my lunch date with Naomi. Oh, well. I'd left a message with David Mills and he would have made sure she got it. He may have been a supercilious twerp but he was reliable. I called Percy Mills's office and got David again. He said that Naomi was with a client. He said he'd given her my message and asked if I wanted to leave another one. I told him I'd try again later. Ray suggested we go over to the Box Car Diner for some late lunch.

Blessing Haines was still on the job. I don't know why I expected otherwise. What was she going to do, sit at home and mope until she buried her father? The diner, I figured, was her life. She was most comfortable there. She was wearing a man's white dress shirt with the sleeves turned up, tight blue jeans, and gym shoes. Her hair was parted in the middle and flipped up at her shoulders. She waved as we came in.

There were a couple of old guys sitting at the counter drinking coffee and power smoking Marlboros. They were taking turns reading USA Today out loud to each other. One had the sports and the other read the celebrity gossip. Four men dressed in painter's whites were sitting at a table eating pie and drinking coffee, talking and laughing. Probably either just finished a job or taking a coffee break. We took a booth by the window.

Bless waved off a waitress and came to take our order. "Whata you boys have?" she asked, hip cocked, pencil poised. She had started out as a waitress and she still had the knack.

Ray closed his menu and slid it behind the napkin dispenser. "Couple o' cheeseburgers and coffee, hon. How you doin'?"

She shrugged. "I talked to LeRoy Whiteker. We're gonna bury Daddy on Friday if that's all right with you, Reverend. Probably around noon."

I nodded. "That's fine."

"LeRoy said he'd call you."

"I've been out of the office," I said. "I'll call him and arrange everything. Is there anything special you want to have said or sung at the funeral?"

"I don't know," she said, shrugging again. "Treasure's coming in tonight. Why don't we come over to the church tomorrow after we've had a chance to talk?"

I said that would be fine. "Or I could meet you somewhere," I offered. I didn't relish the idea of waiting around the church all day for them to show up.

"Could you?" she seemed relieved. Churches affect some people that way. "How about you come up to Daddy's farm about noon tomorrow?" She turned to Ray. "You find out anything?"

Ray sipped his ice water. "Yeah. I found out that two of the Foley boys was up to your daddy's place Friday last. They wanted to buy one of his pups. They put a down payment on it to hold it for them."

Bless looked pensive. "Really?"

"Yeah. Buyin' it for their daddy was a surprise I believe. Since he took a liking to beagles, they decided to buy one for him. Nothin' much there, Bless," he said.

"Mmm," was all she said. Then she seemed to realize she was still holding our order in her hand. She turned and walked to the kitchen without another word.

Ray and I lit up our smokes when the waitress brought our coffee. I looked out the window. Ray watched the people in the diner. We were both lost in our own thoughts.

"Where was everyone else?" I asked, finally.

"What?"

"Where was the rest of the family? Today, when you and Hank were fighting in the stable, where was everyone else?"

Ray looked out the window. "Oh, that. Gone. Probably out plannin' or doin' crimes somewhere. If they was there they woulda been in the stable, you can count on that."

"That might have been a little dicey," I said, wondering if the rest of the Foley brothers were built like Hank or Johnny.

He nodded. "Might. But probably not. That fight was between me and Hank. They probably woulda just let it run its course unless it got outta hand and I threatened to do him serious harm."

"That bunch is a strange family, Ray," I said as the cheeseburgers were delivered. They were a half pound each.

Ray dumped about a cup of catsup on his. "That they are. Place didn't always look like that, you know. It's always been bad, but never as bad as we saw it today. Conrad's momma and wife used to always keep it cleaned up."

"What happened?" I asked around a mouthful of cheeseburger.

"Oh, bunch o' things, I guess." Ray bit into his, leaning over the plate so the catsup wouldn't get on his pants when it dripped out. It didn't drip; it ran. "Luther's got the Alzheimer's or whatever. Connie never did want to be a criminal. Oh, he don't mind the little stuff, it's the business end that drives him nuts. All the bookkeeping and paperwork. He's just always wanted to be a singer/songwriter. Since Luther took sick it looks like Connie's been lettin' things go to hell."

"I wonder if that applies to the business as well," I said.

Ray shook his head and wiped his chin with a napkin. "Naw. It's like a machine now. Just keep it oiled and the money rolls in. He'll turn over the books to Loretta soon and things'll be back to normal."

"Too bad," I said. "Probably the best thing for the county would be for the whole family to go bankrupt."

I was surprised to see Ray shake his head as he laid down his burger. He wiped his fingers and sipped his coffee. "Let me tell you somethin' about crime, preacher," he said. He started his cigarette ritual. Ray was the only person I have ever known who could smoke and eat at the same time.

"When me and Luther Foley was boys growin' up in this county, there weren't no organized crime. None local, that is. A man wanted to gamble, he went to a roadhouse clear to hell and gone across the county line. It weren't even gamblin', to tell the truth. People from this county got cleaned out and sent home. Crooked tables, crooked dealers, crooked dice, everything. You complained, you got your head handed to ya. Games moved around a lot and the law either couldn't catch up with 'em or didn't try because they was paid not to.

"Same was true with women. Man wanted to get his ashes hauled, he had to drive clear to Corbin or London. Didn't know the women or the men who pimped 'em. You could get a dose o' the clap or any damn thing as easy as not. Half the time you lost your wallet while your pants was hangin' over the chair, and you didn't say anything 'cause you was too embarrassed and afraid to say where you lost it.

"Moonshine, same story. No regulation, no control. Back in about 1951 or so, someone served some doctored 'shine at a barn dance down to Clairborn. It was doctored with rubbing alcohol, Dan. Four people died and six lost their sight, some completely."

Ray sipped his coffee and signaled for a refill. He continued as the waitress filled our mugs. "So, then along comes Luther Foley. Him and his brothers and his son, Conrad, decide it's time to clean things up a mite. So they start buyin' up all the 'shine in the southern half of the county. They test it, make sure it's good, and then they sell it at a huge profit. Yeah, it's expensive but you know it ain't gonna kill ya or make you go blind.

"They go to the cities and they recruit some girls and they open their own house with a madam from Cincinnati—Big Jesse her name was. Standard rates, girls checked out by doctors ever' three weeks. Then they open a massage parlor in a mobile home out by the truck stop on I-65. Same controls.

"They buy out a couple o' bars and roadhouses that're dyin' and they put slot machines in 'em and these slots actually pay off sometimes. And they start some floating crap and card games and they use clean cards and they don't let you bet more'n you're carryin'."

He raised his eyebrows at me. "You make them sound like saints," I said.

He laughed. "Oh, hell, no. But I think you see what I'm gettin' at. Fact is, there's always gonna be a market for what they sell. The choice we got is, do we send people outta the county for it and pray they come back in one piece or do we turn a blind eye to Luther Foley and his family and know our folks ain't gonna get too bruised up by it?"

"What about right and wrong?" I asked, feeling every bit the Methodist minister. "What about Hank not getting an education so they can use him to collect debts, and what about the extortion and loan sharking?"

"Extortion started out as protection, and the people they protected needed it. You gotta remember, preacher, that the people who patronize the Foleys ain't saints neither. Some of the good ol' boys in these hills would just as soon rip you off or shoot you as look at you. The loan sharking ain't nice, but it ain't brutal, either."

The waitress arrived with two pieces of butterscotch pie and placed them in front of us. "On the house," she said, and nodded her head toward her boss's table. Bless waived and we waved back.

Ray pushed his empty plate aside and took his fork in hand. "Look," he said, pointing to his pie. "This is your family farm, see. It's been in the family for ten generations. Maybe more. But the land's wore out or bad or you lost your job at the mine or you been laid off or whatever. You need money to get by till you get another job or something breaks open. You go to the bank and what're they gonna say?"

"No way," I said. "No job, no money."

"Right," Ray said. "Or they're gonna give you a second mortgage and if you miss a payment they take your farm. But probably they aren't gonna loan you any money at all on accounta they don't think you can pay it back and what the hell they want with a farm, anyway? They want cash. But let's say they take the farm." He made a sweeping motion above his pie. "But not ol' Luther Foley. He just loans you some money on a couple o' acres. The interest is high, yeah. Say thirty, even fifty percent. But it don't come due for a couple months. You got that money interest free for sixty, ninety days, sometimes. You pay the vigorish when you pay off the loan. If you don't pay off the loan you lose the acres." He cut into his pie and put a big morsel in his mouth. "But you don't lose the whole farm," he said around the pie. "That's how the Foleys work their loans."

"What about Hank breaking legs and twisting arms?" I asked.

"Used to be that's the way they did it, yeah," he said, taking another bite. "But not anymore. Hank's more for show and tradition than anything else. Besides, there's always someone tryin' to horn in on the action. Hank handles most of that. Him and Johnny."

"You still didn't answer the part about right and wrong," I said. The pie was delicious.

Ray smiled. "And I ain't gonna. The Foleys wouldn't be in business if there weren't a market for what they sell. The right and wrong part is for you preachers to figure out."

Blessing came up to us when we took our checks to the register. While she rang us up she asked Ray, "What you gonna do now?"

Ray took a toothpick out of the holder and stuck it in the corner of his mouth. "Keep my eyes and ears open," he said. "Keep lookin' and hope somethin' pops up. That's about all we can do, hon. We got no leads, no suspects, nothin'."

"Then what you gonna keep your eyes and ears open for?" she asked. "What you hopin' to find?"

Ray looked at her, then me, then her again. He took the toothpick out of his mouth and examined it. Finally, he spoke. "Beagles," he said. "Somebody's got them pups."

We drove back to Baird in silence. I know it sounds dull, but it wasn't. Silence is a difficult thing to achieve with another person. Usually we feel like we have to fill the air with words or something's wrong with our relationship. But occasionally, we meet someone with whom we are so in sync, so in tune, that we can just be quietly together, let our minds work, without feeling uncomfortable.

Somehow Ray and I had managed to achieve that with each other. It was nice.

On the way I thought about our conversation in the diner. Was vice really inevitable? Should we really roll over and let it happen? Just as long as it didn't hurt decent people very much? Was there really such a thing as a victimless crime?

As a minister I had always scoffed at the notion. There was, after all, right and wrong. The Bible said so. The Ten Commandments weren't just the ten suggestions—as the bumper sticker says. God had certain behavioral expectations for human beings, and we ignored those expectations at our peril. Life has a way of dealing severely with people when they consistently defy God's moral laws. But that was the problem. I was talking about the moral law. Perhaps Ray was right. Maybe the moral law and the civil and the criminal law were three separate things and should be kept separate. Maybe we had to make room in the world for those among us who were merely immoral but were only hurting themselves. And their families? And their communities?

By the time we got to Baird I had a headache.

It was too early for supper and too late to start anything, so I picked up the mail and went back to the parsonage and tried to think of something to do. I was too restless to work on my sermon and I didn't know enough to work on Calvin Haines's funeral service.

The mail consisted of a gas and electric bill for the church and another one for the parsonage. I tossed them on my desk. John Hazzard, the Chairman of the Administrative Council of the church, would pick them up Sunday. There was also a newsletter from the church of an old seminary buddy of mine (depressingly successful and very religious) and an invitation to have lunch the following Wednesday with the Perry Chamber of Commerce at the Pine Room of the Perry Inn. All of the clergy in the county, it seemed, were now honorary members of the Chamber of Commerce, thanks to the machinations of their president, and my friend, funeral director LeRoy Whiteker.

LeRoy included a personal note in my invitation. He was ready to start teaching me the game of golf again. We had started last autumn and I thought I was hopeless. LeRoy loved the game and insisted that I would, too, under his tutelage. He also included an off-color joke. Lunch, he said, would be on him. What the heck; I marked the RSVP card that I would be there and put it in the mailbox.

The rest of the mail was advertisements, requests for donations, and memos from the district and conference offices. I threw them all away.

Having satisfied my conscience with some actual preacher work, I turned on the stereo and found a classics station in Lexington, put on a pot of coffee, dug my big briar pipe out of a desk drawer, found my Civil War book, took off my shoes, and settled down on the couch for some serious relaxation.

CHAPTER 9

IT WAS THE TELEPHONE that woke me up.

I jumped off the couch, disoriented, trying to remember where I was and what day it was. I looked at my watch and it was after six. A two-hour power nap. Now I'd never be able to get to sleep at bedtime. Damn.

The phone continued to ring, insistently, accusingly. I didn't have an answering machine. No one did outside of Perry. I put off getting one because I was afraid the rural folks would think it uppity and citified.

On about the seventh or eighth ring I cleared the sleep out of my throat and answered. "Hello."

Nothing.

"Hello?"

Silence. I was just about to hang up when a voice finally spoke up. It was male and it had a very slight Kentucky accent. Other than that, all I can tell you is what he said: "Leave it alone, preacher." That's it. Then he hung up.

I didn't think much of it at the time, though later I would wish I had. Preachers are often targets of crank callers. We're listed in the phone book as "Reverend," and our phone numbers at home and at work are in the public domain. Some people seem to get their jollies saying anonymous dirty things to ministers, supposing we'll be shocked and scandalized. This wasn't dirty but I put it out of my mind as just another crank.

Then the phone rang again. I jerked it up, ready to give the caller a chewing out. "Hello!"

"Where the hell you been? I been callin' you all day." It was LeRoy Whiteker.

"I've been with Ray," I said, a little relieved to hear his voice.

"You get the invitation to the Chamber luncheon?"

"Yeah, I'll be there. Nothing I love more than spending the afternoon with a bunch of small-town Southern Republicans." I tried not to let my smile show in my voice, but I probably failed.

"Oh, it's an experience, all right. Don't worry though, it ain't contagious," he laughed. "You talk to Bless Haines?"

"Yeah. She says they want to have the funeral on Friday. That's fine with me. About noon?"

"Yep. Service here, then the interment at Holy Hill. Darlin', I don't know. Ask your mother. You want to ride with me in the hearse or you gonna drive?"

That confused me for a moment, then I realized he was trying to talk to me while his kids climbed all over him. His kids always climbed all over him. He had three, all under twelve years old, and they worshiped him. They also lived upstairs in the big house that served as his home and business. They didn't seem warped, though.

I always got the distinct feeling that LeRoy wanted me to ride with him at funerals. Preachers and funeral directors are more alike than you might realize. Most people tend to respect us and the jobs we do, but neither of us gets invited to many parties. "I'll ride with you," I said.

"All right. Wanna get something to eat after?" he asked.

I shrugged, then realized he couldn't see me. "Sure."

"Okay, then." He paused, then said, "Sweetheart, I'll help you with that in a minute, okay?" He paused again, then said, "I gotta go, Dan."

After I hung up I sat there looking at the phone, thinking about my own kids and how they used to crawl over me and how it used to irritate me because I was so tired from working too many hours helping other people solve their problems.

And for just a brief, fleeting moment I hated LeRoy Whiteker for his big, warm, cozy house, and his success, and his beautiful Miss Eastern Kentucky wife, and his three loving children, and his ruddy good looks. Then I felt ashamed of myself. And I felt sorry for myself. And ashamed of myself for feeling sorry for myself. And. . . .

I decided to go down to the diner and get some of May June's chicken-fried steak and home-fried potatoes—that night's special. Maybe I'd even have a piece of her sugar and cream pie. Food like that might not cure depression, but it would distract me from it for a while.

I stayed to play checkers with Ray and got home in time to catch the news and Letterman's "Top Ten List" before I hit the sack with my Civil War book. I managed to get through the entire Chattanooga campaign before my eyes were heavy enough to sleep at about 2:00 a.m.

I walked down to the diner at about 9:30 Thursday morning, the first day it really felt like spring, and had oatmeal with honey and raisins and cinnamon toast. Three cups of coffee, the Perry newspaper, and my pipe brought me into the land of the living by 10:30

or so when Ray came in from the constabulary office just a few feet from the diner and next to the post office.

"Anything?" I asked him as he sat down at the counter.

He shook his head. "Nah. Didn't expect there to be anything this early. I been on the phone puttin' word out, though. I want them pups found and I want the name of whoever's got 'em."

"You offering a reward?" I asked.

He gave me one of his looks. "Yeah. The reward is I don't kick someone's butt, which I *will* do if I find out someone bought one o' them pups and didn't let me know."

May June picked up my oatmeal bowl, which was big enough to require both hands. "Dad, how's folks supposed to know if they bought the pups you're lookin' for? They's folks sellin' pups all over the county most o' the time."

Ray sighed and gulped the coffee she gave him. "If they buy a beagle pup, they call me. *Any* beagle pup. That's the deal."

May June nodded. "Well, that can't be too good for the beagle business. But with the whole litter to unload, I reckon you got a chance of one or two of 'em getting called in."

There didn't seem to be anything else to say, so Ray and I talked about baseball and what little hope the Cincinnati Reds had of making it to the playoffs. But then you never knew about the Reds. Ray follows the Cincinnati professional sports teams because they're the closest ones to where he lives. I follow them because Ray does.

About 11:00 I made my way back to the parsonage to change clothes for my meeting with the Haines sisters. I was supposed to meet them at their father's farm at noon and it was a good forty-five-minute drive up the mountain.

My old Volkswagen was running rough in spite of the warm weather, and a few times I wondered if it would make it over the mountain. I was about fifteen minutes late getting to Calvin's farm, but I didn't think it would matter. In the mountains and hills of eastern Kentucky they call it AST—Appalachian Standard Time— and it means you get there when you get there, as close as you can to the time you intended.

There was a black Toyota with Ohio license plates parked in the yard of the house when I rolled to a stop and the Veedub wheezed and coughed itself into silence. The Toyota was one of those souped-up, sporty models. I've never been into cars, so that's about all I can tell you. All it needed was numbers on the sides and STP stickers on the windows and it would have been at home on the speedway in Daytona.

I knocked on the door of the house and got no response, so I wandered around back, thinking they might be in the yard or out at the barn, looking at where their father had died.

A woman was standing beside the place where we had buried the dogs, looking at the ground. When I came around the house she must have sensed my presence, because she turned and started toward me, walking carefully, trying to balance on high heels that were sinking into the soft earth.

When she got close enough, she extended her hand and put on a small smile. "I'm Treasure Haines," she said. "You must be the Reverend."

Hers was not a face meant for smiling. Not that her smile was in any way unpleasant or unattractive, you understand. It's just that smiling creates a curved line in the middle of the face, and her face was all straight lines and angles.

I'm not doing this very well, so let me start again.

Everything that her sister was physically, Treasure Haines was not. Where Blessing was round and plump, Treasure was angular and thin. Where Blessing was red-haired and freckled, Treasure's hair was raven black and her skin was milky white. Blessing's face was open and humorous and pleasant, her eyes sparkling even in grief. Treasure's face was serious and clouded, and her black eyes were impenetrable. She looked like a model—one of those who's famous not because she's beautiful, but because you just can't stop looking at her.

Striking. I guess that's the word.

Five-feet-nine or -ten inches. Weight, I wouldn't know. I'm not good at weights, but she was thin. Hardly any chest to speak of. Her hair was cut in a China-doll style, high in the back and flipped up around her face on each side. She wore a black business suit with no blouse.

I did some quick mental arithmetic and figured she had to be nearly my age or a couple of years younger. Put her age at forty. But her alabaster skin showed not a single wrinkle.

"Everyone around here just calls me Dan," I said, trying not to trip over my jaw.

"Everyone around here calls me Treasure," she said, one corner of her mouth turning up in a reluctant smile. "It's a horrible name, isn't it?" Not really a question, she was just seeking affirmation.

"Well, it's unusual," I said.

"I go by T. R. in the city, but that wouldn't do here. Here, I'm Treasure." She sighed.

"What's the R for?" I asked, inanely. Was I flirting with her? This woman I'd just met, whose father I was going to bury tomorrow? Was she flirting with me?

"Nothing," she said, shaking her head. "There's no middle name. I just made it up."

"Like Harry Truman?" I said.

"That's right," she said, as if she had only just now remembered that the late president didn't have a middle name either, only an initial. "Harry S Truman, no period after the S. My father used to call him Harry-ass Truman."

I laughed, but she didn't. She was aware of her looks and how smiling seemed to detract from her striking appearance. It occurred to me that she had said "my father" instead of "daddy" like most of the folks around Durel County, and she had no accent.

"You don't sound like a Kentuckian," I said.

She started to walk toward the house. "How's that? You mean because I don't say *ain't*, and *y'all*, and *y'hear*?"

I walked beside her to the porch, shaking my head. "You don't have an accent."

She nodded emphatically. "Thank you for noticing. I worked for a long time to lose my accent. Is it really gone? All of it?"

"I would say northern Ohio or Wisconsin. Maybe Illinois."

That seemed to please her. "Good. Who says you can't take the country out of the girl?" She sat in one of the rockers on the porch. "Blessing's going to be late. She had to go talk to Mr. Whiteker. A problem with the casket or something."

"Ah," was the only thing I could think of to say.

After a few seconds of silence she asked me, "Did you know my father, Dan?"

"I met him the day before he died," I told her. "He came to see me about doing a funeral for one of his dogs."

She shook her head slowly, the little points of her hair flipping from side to side. "Erasmus Wishbone," she said. "My, how he loved that dog. You know he sent me a picture of Ras one time? What was I supposed to do with a wallet-size picture of a beagle puppy? He did have a sweet face, though. Ras, I mean."

I just nodded. Another silence stretched out. I realized at just about the same time she did that I was looking at her.

"Is something wrong?" she asked. "I mean, other than the obvious?"

I looked away, embarrassed. "I'm sorry. I guess I was just thinking about Mrs. Causey."

"Causey. Causey? I don't think I know her."

Now it was my turn to smile. "You wouldn't. She was the librarian of my elementary school."

She understood at once. "Let me guess," she said. "Big, broad-shouldered woman with half glasses and gray hair in a bun? Could say 'Sh-sh-sh' loud enough to knock down a wall?"

"That's her," I said. "Librarians have changed a lot, haven't they?"

She leaned back in her rocking chair and stretched her long legs out in front of her, toeing off her high heels. "Librarians used to be bibliophiles. Bookworms. At the college where I work we don't even call it a library anymore. It's called the 'Info-center.' Audio, video, computers, CD-ROMs, DVDs, computer networks, the Internet . . . and a few books. Libraries are just one of the stops on the information superhighway." She sighed again.

"You work at a college?"

"The College of Mount Saint Michael," she said, as though it bored her. "Started by some nuns about fifty years ago as a school for girls. They went coed in the early eighties for financial reasons. Real small. I think our total student enrollment is about eight hundred."

She stood, suddenly, leaving her shoes on the porch. She wasn't wearing hose. "Would you like something to drink? I made some coffee and I think there's some beer and pop in the fridge."

"A diet pop would be nice if you have it," I said. "If not, just some ice water."

"Come on," she said. "We can talk while I fix it."

I followed her into the house through a cluttered old living room with a hook rug, couch, easy chair, nineteen-inch television, and an old spinet piano. The dining room, to the left, held a table and eight chairs, but the table was filled with old and new mail, newspapers, magazines, brochures, and junk. At one end, a small area was cleared away to make a work space. A legal pad and a coffee mug full of pencils lay where Calvin Haines had left them.

The kitchen was like the rest of the house: appliances thirty years old but still functional because they saw little use, linoleum floor, and a bare light bulb hanging from a wire in the middle of the room. The room was big enough to hold a kitchen table and four chairs and still leave plenty of walking around space. The table was Formica, scratched and scarred. It probably dated back to when the girls were little. Cal Haines could have afforded better, he just chose not to.

Treasure noticed my examination of the clutter that lay everywhere. Every flat surface looked like the dining room table. "I've been trying to go through some of my father's clutter, to see what kind of shape things are in," she said. "So far, as you can see, it's been hopeless. He had his own way, and it's a far cry from the Dewey decimal system. I think it'll take days to get to the bottom of all his stacks. He was kind of a pack rat."

I leaned against the counter and admired the efficient, athletic way she moved as she talked, rummaging through the cabinets, looking for glasses. She opened the refrigerator, started to reach in, and then stopped, her back still to me. "The only diet drink he has is . . . is . . . Barq's grape . . . grape . . . soda." And then the dam broke. She coughed out a huge sob, turned, and leaned on the back of the chair as she cried. I stood up and moved to her, took her in my arms, and hugged her while the tears flowed. She pressed her face to my chest and laid her hands on my shoulders. Her hair smelled of flowers and her back was firm and well-muscled.

After a couple of minutes, she stopped crying, sniffed, and sat in the chair she had been leaning against. She took a paper napkin from a plastic holder on the table and wiped her nose and eyes, not looking at me. Finally, when she thought she was under control again, she said, "I'm sorry. That's the second time I've done that. I thought I could handle it better."

Second time? She had cried only twice and she was embarrassed about it? The man was her father for heaven's sake. But then she was a control person, you could see it in her demeanor and her appearance. Crying meant being out of control and she didn't like that one bit.

"It's okay," I said. "You have a right. He was your father."

She nodded. "It's just that when I looked in the refrigerator and saw the way he lived and ate. He always had that Barq's diet grape soda in there for my mother. After she died he just kept it around." She hiccuped and sniffed. "I think he started drinking it just because it reminded him of her. I don't know. It was just so . . . him."

She stared at the tabletop for a few moments and then looked up at me and took my hand. "Thanks for being here."

I squeezed her hand and felt a little guilty for enjoying the feel of her skin so much.

"Well," she said, slapping her thighs. "I guess it's just going to go to waste now. We might as well drink it." She stood and took a deep breath, opened the fridge again, and brought out two tall sixteen-ounce bottles of the grape soda. They were capped with the old-fashioned pry-off caps, but an opener was on the string attached to the door handle and she used it to pop the tops.

She handed me mine and sat hers on the table. "Will you excuse me for a minute? I'm going to get out of this suit and into something more appropriate for the farm. I feel like I've slept in this thing." She fanned the jacket in and out from her chest.

I smiled at her and winked.

"Just make yourself at home," she said and left the kitchen. I heard her go up the stairs.

For a couple of minutes I just sat there looking at all the crap stacked around the kitchen. No dirty dishes, but papers, books, ledgers, fliers, mailers, and periodicals seemed to have sprouted from the cracks in the walls.

I took my grape soda into the dining room and sat in the chair that had been Calvin Haines's work seat at the big table. Nothing jumped out at me. Just junk.

A statement from a stockbroker in Louisville.

A stack of bills. The one on top from a veterinarian in Perry.

Some farm magazines and a big checkbook in a binder with the stubs left in the book. I looked at the stubs but found nothing of interest. Calvin paid his bills and deposited his social security checks. There were some deposits that looked like they were bigger than Social Security would account for, but not big enough to jump off the page and scream at me. Maybe he sold a dog or won a prize at a dog show or something.

The yellow legal pad was the short kind, about eleven inches long instead of fourteen, and half the paper had been used. There were impressions on the page from things that had been written on other pages, now gone. I looked in a wastebasket by the leg of the table but it was nearly empty, just a few scraps of plastic wrap and what looked like a cigar ash, still intact.

I eyed the pencils in the coffee cup and considered doing what they always do in the movies—rubbing the pencil over the page to see what pops up. I wondered if it would work. Well, nothing ventured. . . .

It worked too well. Words, numbers, phrases, doodles—all cropped up on the page. I was excited at first and then disappointed. What did all that stuff mean? Did it come from the last page or several previous pages?

I tore my page off, folded it in quarters. I was going to put it into the inside jacket of my windbreaker which was hanging over the back of a chair in the kitchen, when Treasure came down the stairs.

She was wearing baggy faded blue jeans and a tan T-shirt with her college's name on the front: MT. SAINT MICHAEL ARCHANGELS. It was obvious that she wasn't wearing a bra. She had taken the time to fix her makeup and run a brush through her hair, which was now held in place by a dark blue bandanna tied as a band across the top of her head. She looked very, very nice.

"You find something?" she said, seeing the paper in my hand.

"Maybe," I said, shrugging. I took the paper to her and opened it. "These things were written on your father's legal pad before he died. I was going to give them to Ray Hall, the constable in charge of the investigation, and see what he thought."

She nodded. "I know Ray. Bless told me he was investigating our father's murder. She looked at the paper, shrugged, and handed it back to me. "Dad was a doodler."

I went with her into the kitchen and put the paper in my jacket pocket. Put the jacket on. Took a swig of the grape soda. She took a swig of hers and I watched the muscles in her throat move. It was a nice throat.

"You want to see the rest of the farm?" she asked.

I didn't know what else there was to see that I hadn't seen already, but I nodded. "Sure, why not?"

She took my hand and we went back through the house to the front porch. "I love this place," she said. "I grew up here. Lots of nice memories."

We were standing on the porch and she was looking out over Cut-Through Valley, her head tilted slightly to the side, as though she were looking at a photograph of a child.

That was when Blessing's car came shooting up the lane and roared to a stop in the front yard. Treasure let go of my hand and her shoulders sagged a little. "Oh," she said. "Blessing's here."

CHAPTER 10

BLESSING HAINES KEIFER CLIMBED UP THE STEPS to the porch and embraced Treasure with a quick kiss on the cheek. "How's sis?" she asked, holding Treasure at arm's length and looking at her. "Skinny as ever, I see."

Treasure wiped a tear from her cheek and tilted her head. "I work hard to stay this way. You look good, Bless. How are you?"

Bless shrugged one of those expressive Appalachian shrugs that said more than a two-hour monologue. They stood there looking each other over, affection and something else in their eyes. Maybe a little competition? I tried to imagine them in high school, going after the same boys. Blessing was probably the cheerleader, robust, healthy, vigorous, and sexy. Treasure would have been the president of the student council, beautiful and aloof. Blessing was homecoming queen; Treasure was queen of the prom.

Blessing favored her father, his open, good-natured expression and vibrant, home-fed appearance. Treasure must have taken after her mother. There had been a brother, Victory. I wondered what he had looked like. I hadn't seen any pictures in the house.

Bless broke off the inspection of her sister and spoke to me. "How ya doin', Rev?"

I nodded and winked.

She nodded at her sister. "This 'un here didn't get in until early this morning and then she come straight here. This is the first time we seen each other in . . . what?"

Treasure pondered for a moment. "Two years, maybe?" Then to me: "I got held up at work yesterday. A glitch in the computer at the library. I didn't get in until about four this morning."

"Well, since you all already introduced yourselves we can go on and talk about the funeral," Blessing said, sitting down on the porch. "You got any more o' that soda pop?"

Treasure went back into the house for another bottle of soda and Bless breathed a long sigh. "I had to get away from the diner. Word's gotten around and folks is comin' in payin' their respects. It's nice of 'em but after a while it gets to be too much."

"It's quiet here," I offered. *Empathetic response* they call it in the psychology texts.

"Yeah, it is. I always loved it. Treasure couldn't wait to get away. I think the quiet drove her crazy. She needed action, you know?"

"She was just telling me how much she liked it here," I said.

Bless nodded. "Yeah, for a day or two. It's like a retreat for her. But then she'll get restless again. Have to get back to the city. Me, I never would have left here if Bert hadn't died. After that, though, I just couldn't stand livin' here and seein' all this stuff every day."

"Bert was your husband?"

"M-m-m." She nodded again. Leaned her head back against the post.

"You lived here after you were married?" I asked.

"Yeah. Me and Bert and Daddy. It was nice. Then Bert didn't come back from the mine one night and we started to worry. Daddy had always told him not to go up there by hisself, but Bert was just headstrong enough to do it anyway. 'Sides, winter was comin' and we needed to put up some coal.

"'Bout midnight me and Daddy went up to the mine and found him. A widow-maker had fallen in. Daddy said he probably never knew what killed him."

I let a few seconds pass before I said, "I'm a city boy, Bless. What's a widow-maker?"

She looked at me and smiled. "I keep forgettin'. You're a stranger in these parts." She leaned on her accent, teasing me. Then: "A widow-maker is what the miners call a petrified tree trunk. A million years ago, when this was all flat, it was covered with forest just like it is now. When the mountains were pushed up, trees were buried. Some rotted to make the coal, but others were just petrified. The miners bore shafts into the mountains and sometimes they cut a petrified tree trunk right in half. The top half stays in the ceiling of the mine until one day it just drops out. Maybe a thousand pounds of petrified tree trunk slidin' out of the ceiling and crashin' to the floor, leavin' a big hole where it was. The most dangerous part is that it don't make no noise until it hits the floor . . . or some miner." She sighed again. "These Kentucky mines is full of 'em."

She paused and looked out into the mountains that spread out beyond the barn. "I sat right here that night, waitin' for him. If you go up into the loft of the barn you can see the entrance to the shaft, yonder." She nodded her head in the direction of the barn.

When Ray first told me that Bert Keifer had died in a mining accident, I had assumed it was in a company mine, perhaps in an explosion or a cave-in. In fact, he had died in one of the hundreds of little family coal mines that dotted the county, gathering coal for his family. It was like a story from a historical novel, yet it had happened just a few years ago.

"He didn't work the mines regular on accounta he was afraid of the black lung," she said at length. "Hell, we both was. I was content to be poor as long as he and Daddy were healthy. Damn mine got him anyhow.

"At least it was fast. I don't think I coulda stood to watch the black lung take him, slow and painful-like. He was a strong man and he liked livin' too much to die slow."

She looked at me and bowed her head. "I'm sorry. I guess you know all about black lung, what with your girlfriend's daddy and all."

"You didn't tell me you had a girlfriend," Treasure said, coming out of the door with a diet grape soda in each hand. She handed the full one to Blessing.

Bless took the soda and drank from it, wiped her mouth on her sleeve. "He's datin' that Taylor girl, Naomi."

Treasure looked directly at me, the corner of her mouth turning up just a little—the closest she could let herself come to a smile. "Is she pretty?"

Blessing nearly choked on her grape soda. "Pretty! Damn, girl. She puts the likes o' you and me to shame, I can tell ya. An' she's young, too. Don't that just put a stitch in your side?"

"She's not *that* young," I said.

Treasure leaned up next to me and let her breast brush my arm. She looked up into my face under hooded eyes and took a long, long drink from her soda. "How young is she?"

I sneaked a look at Blessing, who was shaking her head and smiling. "Well," I said, "She's about—"

"Damn, you don't change, do you, Sis?" Bless stood. "You just can't stand to see a single man go off with another woman till you've dumped him, can you?" She started into the house. "Naomi Taylor's in her mid-twenties, she's college educated, she's pretty as all-get-out, and she's got boobs bigger'n mine." She held the screen door open for us. "Besides, he's a preacher."

Treasure continued to look at me. "What's that got to do with anything?" she said. I wondered the same thing.

"It means he's here on business," Blessing said, still holding the door open. "Anything else'll have to wait till after Daddy's buried."

Treasure gave a little shrug and turned to follow her sister into the house. I followed after taking a second to breathe a huge sigh. She had freshened her perfume since I hugged her by the refrigerator. Chanel No. 5 hung in the air on the porch.

I got back to Baird in the middle of the afternoon, just in time to find four guys putting up scaffolding around the church's steeple. They were big-gutted, hairy men, working in their shirt-sleeves and sweating in the spring sun. One of them was smoking a cigarette and doing a lot of pointing from the back of a big truck, so I took him to be the boss.

"Are you Walter Rudepohler?" I asked him.

He took off his Beech-Nut gimme cap and wiped his brow, looked at me. "Yeah." He flipped his cigarette into the road and tugged his Rolling Rock T-shirt down over his belly.

I yelled over the noise of a coal truck roaring down the road, just a few feet from the apron where Rudepohler had parked his truck. "I'm Dan Thompson, the minister here." I hooked my thumb over my shoulder.

His face brightened and he crouched down and jumped heavily from the back of the truck. "Oh, sorry. I'm Walt Rudepohler. We're supposed to fix your steeple." He extended his hand and we shook. His hands were callused and heavy. "Took us long enough, I guess. But we're on 'im now."

Actually the contract had been signed the previous fall, using the money left to the church by an elderly couple who had died in a house fire the summer before. Rudepohler was supposed to start construction as soon as he finished another job he was doing in Perry. But then the cold, rainy, gray Appalachian winter had set in and all outdoor work had stopped until spring. We had hoped to ring the bell for the first time in half a decade on Easter Sunday, but the delay had made that impossible.

"Well, it's good to see you," I said. I pointed to the steeple. "What do you think?"

"No problem," he said, following my gaze. He consulted a clipboard in his hand. "If the winter hasn't made it any worse, I figure it'll take us about five days. Probably come in right around what we bid."

I nodded. "Great." Now the other men had gathered around us. When the boss didn't work, the crew didn't work, I supposed. Walt introduced the rest of his crew.

"This-here's John, my brother." To John: "This is the Reverend, this-here church."

John nodded. He was the same size and shape as Walter, but he had a big woolly beard that came down to the middle of his chest. His shirt was plaid, buttoned up the front, and had the sleeves cut off at the shoulder.

"These-here two no-accounts are Orville and Howard Cartrite." They were carbon copies of the Rudepohler brothers, only younger and not as hairy. They both nodded to me, embarrassed. Said "Reverend," simultaneously.

"Well, you been introduced now. No need to stand here playin' pocket pool." They all nodded again and went back to work. Walt turned back to me. "We'll take 'im down in pieces, save what we can, redo the underworks and put 'im all back together in workin' order. We'll check the bell post and reinforce it, too, if you want."

It sounded good to me so I said, "Great," again, since he seemed to be waiting for some kind of affirmation.

He said, "Okay, then," and we stood there looking at each other and the steeple. Finally, I realized that he was waiting for me to say something or leave, so I left.

I still had to figure out what I was going to say at Calvin Haines's funeral. And I still hadn't written the first word of my Sunday sermon.

My big old study Bible was open on my desk when I sat down, that verse from the twenty-fifth Psalm staring up at me, still: "Consider how many are my enemies, and how they hate me with cruel hatred."

It's attributed to King David. Whether he wrote it or collected it, no one is sure, but we always assume he wrote it. Besides being a warrior and a king, old David was quite the singer/songwriter. An early Renaissance man, I guess you could say. I wondered what he was talking about, specifically, when he had written those lines. I studied the rest of the psalm and found nothing to nail it down. Certainly David knew about trouble and pain and enemies. His first child died in infancy. His son raped his daughter. His favorite son hated him and tried to murder him. His best friend died under torture, and his king falsely accused him of treason.

How was it that such a great, great man could be so beset with misery? Are the great people among us always destined for misery? Do they bring it on themselves, or is that just how it works out? Is it some sort of natural balancing thing? Greatness has its price?

If you put King David and Calvin Haines down across the table from each other, they could probably match each other misery for misery. David's might have been of a greater and larger scale, but Calvin's were no less painful.

Calvin had watched his wife die of cancer. He had seen his only son buried after dying in a car wreck. Then the substitute son had died in a coal mine, the place he feared most. Finally, when Calvin's life had begun to have some balance, some meaning, some satisfaction in it, he had found his beloved Erasmus Wishbone kicked to death, and watched his pretty little Marietta Trueblood kicked to death, as well. And then he had been tortured to death and hanged in his own barn.

"Consider how many are my enemies, and how they hate me with cruel hatred." Did he really have a lot of enemies? Did they really hate him with cruel hatred? Or was his miserable death just a case of nature exacting her revenge on him for being a truly good and decent man? I didn't really believe that to be the case, but how could I explain that to his daughters?

I sat there at my desk looking at my Bible and letting my mind free associate until the racket of Walter Rudepohler's crew began to drown out any attempt at concentration. Exhausted and depressed, I decided to go get some supper. May June's Thursday night special was chicken and noodles with homemade bread and string beans. If the crowd wasn't too bad I'd run my theological musings by her. May June's no theologian but she's smart and kind. When you're preparing a funeral sermon, those two are worth more than all the theological insight in the world.

I exited the building through the main door of the church so I could see how Rudepohler and Co. were getting along with the steeple. Plaster dust and sawdust coated everything in the back of the sanctuary and hung in the air. Walter Rudepohler was directing the action from the little entrance room of the church, what we call the narthex, his hand on the bell rope, as the men packed their tools onto the truck. We exchanged greetings as I stepped past him and onto the concrete steps outside.

"How long's it been since this thing was rung?" Walter asked.

I stopped and turned back, took my pipe out of my pocket. "Ray says about five years," I told him, coming back up the stairs into the little cubicle. "It flipped all the way over and got stuck when some kids were ringing it on New Year's Eve."

"That Ray Hall you're talkin' about?" he asked.

I said that it was and he nodded. Ray was a man to be believed. If he said it was five years then it was five years and not a day more or less.

Walter rubbed his mouth and chin as he looked speculatively up the rope to where it disappeared through a small hole in the ceiling of the narthex. He gave the rope a tentative tug and I heard metal creak against wood up in the tower, about thirty feet above my head. "Hm-m-m," was all he said.

"I tried it a couple of times," I told him. "But it sticks after one clunk."

He gave it another tug, putting more muscle into it. It clunked and the rope stuck. "If all they did was flip it over, you ought to be able to flip it back with a couple o' good hard pulls," he said, tugging on the rope, lightly at first, then with more effort, putting his considerable weight into it.

The bell clunked, creaked, and groaned. Then, on about the fourth or fifth tug, there was a loud splitting sound from above. The rope went slack in Walter's hand, and I realized that it was wood that was splitting over our heads and now the splitting had turned into breaking. Walter looked at me and I think it dawned on both of us at nearly the same instant what had happened.

The big carpenter grabbed me by the arm and nearly threw me out of the door as the bell came through the plaster ceiling like a rock through onion skin, bringing boards, lath, nails, and plaster with it.

I stumbled going across the threshold and felt myself falling, trying to grab something and only catching air. The ground fell away from my feet and I was going down the concrete steps, my legs flailing like my arms. I started to fall as I reached the bottom when the side of my face slammed into something big and soft. As I tried to look up at what had stopped my egress from the church, a different something big and soft and heavy slammed into my back and I was falling again, this time on top of whatever it was that stopped me the first time.

The first thing I heard was coughing. Then swearing.

"Damn, I can't breathe. Get off me, you two." This came from under me and above my head. It was John Rudepohler, Walter's brother.

I was having trouble breathing myself, and suddenly a great weight was lifted off my back and I rolled off of John and onto the gravel beside the road. I looked up to see the Cartrite brothers pulling Walter up by his arms and dusting him off. He pushed them off and grabbed his cap from the older one, Howard, I think it was.

"You okay, Reverend?" he asked, checking himself for damage. Finding nothing serious, he advanced on me and offered me his hand.

I took it and he pulled me to my feet. "I'm okay," I said. "I think."

"Well, I ain't," John Rudepohler said. He was rolling onto his hands and knees. He groaned as he stood, rubbing his big butt. He pulled the back of his pants down a couple of inches and tried to look over his shoulder, turning around like a dog chasing its own tail. "Damn! I think I'm bleedin'."

Walter walked over and checked John's butt. "You're okay. Have Jean Ann put some peroxide on it." He looked his brother over. "Put some on your elbows, too."

Walter sighed and lit a cigarette while he looked up at the door of the church. We both went up the steps and looked at the wreckage. The bell was bigger than I had imagined it would be, maybe three feet from top to bottom. The ball on the clapper was nearly as big as a softball. As we stood there looking at it, I couldn't help wondering if we didn't look like big-game hunters standing over a particularly vicious man-eating lion that had been terrorizing the village—one that had nearly gotten us with its cunning and ferocious blood lust.

"Thanks for the push," I told Walter. "You move pretty good for a—" What was I going to say? A fat man? A man your size? Which amounted to the same thing.

He just harrumphed. "She woulda put a right smart lump on your head, that's for sure." He looked up through where the ceiling used to be. I could see the early evening sky through the clear plastic his men had stretched across the missing pieces of the steeple high above. "I'm sorry, Reverend, but I'm gonna have to charge extra for this part. We weren't expecting her to come all the way down and through like this when we wrote up the estimate."

I shrugged. After eight months in Appalachia I was beginning to pick up the language.

"See ya tomorrow," he said.

I just nodded as he went down the steps to the truck, slammed the door, and gunned the engine. He had referred to the steeple as "him" and the bell as "her." Was there any significance to that, I wondered. I must have still been in shock, thinking, as I looked up through the hole in the ceiling, about widow-makers.

I decided to change my clothes before I went to the diner. I'd torn the knees of my jeans and the skin underneath as well. I followed Walter Rudepohler's advice and poured some peroxide on my cuts and rubbed some witch hazel into my bruises, not knowing what it did exactly, but comforted in the knowledge that May June, our local granny woman, swore by the stuff.

I got to the diner at about 7:30 and Ray hadn't come in yet. May June slid a big bowl of chicken and noodles with carrots and celery chunks in front of me. The broth was thick as gravy, the noodles were as big as my thumb, and the chicken was lean and tender in nice long strips. The bread was whole wheat with real butter, sweet and cold. Ice water in a Mason jar and coffee in a big mug were placed on either side of the place mat. She promised coconut cream pie for dessert. Lord!

"He called about an hour ago," she said, when I asked after Ray. "Said he had some trouble with the Jeep and he'd be late. I asked how late and he said that would depend on how soon I hung up and told the Carmack twins to go get him." She wiped away an invisible spot on the counter and shook her head. "He gets testy when the Jeep breaks down."

"I could have gone to get him," I said. She just made a popping sound with her lips and flipped her towel at me. "Phut!" I had no idea what that meant.

Darnell Kody came in carrying a bowling ball bag. Darnell's a big pear-shaped man whose face is constantly smiling. He has Down's syndrome and he's the town fix-it man. Give a broken mechanical something to Darnell and he can fix it. That's all. Don't even ask. Ray says it's a gift from God to balance out Darnell's other deficiencies. He can't read or write. I'm not sure it's a fair trade for Darnell but I didn't argue the point too enthusiastically. Darnell was keeping my Veedub running with spit, chewing gum, and baling wire.

"How's the Bug, Reverent Dan?" Darnell asked me. May June slid a piece of pie in front of him. He apparently didn't pay for *his* meals either.

"It's a little weak going uphill," I said. "But other than that it's fine, Darnell. How about you?"

His smile almost slipped a fraction. "You better bring 'im over and let me take a look," he said. "May be the timin'."

"May be the fact he's got about a million miles on that thing," May June said. "When you gonna let Ray help you get somethin' better?"

Ray had been pestering me to trade the Veedub on something more mountain-worthy all winter, but I hate buying a car like I hate going to the dentist. It is such a hassle. All that dickering and lying and horse-trading. And no matter how it came out, I always felt like I was getting cheated. A former parishioner of mine was a car dealer and he asked me, one time, if I knew how to tell that a car dealer was making a lot of money from the car he sold me. I said that I didn't. He said, "He sells you the car!" Then he laughed. Then he said: "If he does that, he's making a whole lot of money, no matter what he says."

I looked at Darnell and tried to change the subject. His bowling ball bag was sitting on the floor next to his stool. "You going bowling, Darnell? Or are you just getting back?"

His smile turned up a couple of notches and he gave his oh-shucks shrug. "I don't bowl, Reverent Dan. You know that."

I didn't, but I let it pass. "Well, I saw your bag there. You tryin' to sell your bowling ball?"

Now his transparent face said: *I've got a secret!* "Ain't no ball in that bag," he said.

"Well, don't keep us guessin' all night," May June said, trying to lean over the counter. It was no use. All she managed to do was mash her breasts nearly into my pie. "What you got in there's such a big secret?"

Darnell smiled and looked at both of us, then shrugged. "Dog."

"Get on down the hill!" May June said. "You got a dog? I never knew you had a dog." She winked at me.

"Just got 'im," Darnell said, reaching down to pick up the bag.

May June gave me a quizzical look. Could Darnell really have a dog in that bag? "Well, let's see him," she said to Darnell. "What kind you get?"

Darnell reached into the bag and, hearing the little yelp and squeal come out as his hand went in, I knew what he was going to say even before he opened his mouth. I just knew and I couldn't believe it would be this easy. Ray was driving around all over the county looking for the Wishbone/Trueblood beagles and—

"Beagle," Darnell said, lifting the puppy from the bag. "His name's Little Ray." He looked up, deadly serious. "You don't think Ray will mind if I name my dog after him, do you, May June?"

May June looked at me and our eyes locked. I felt my pulse quicken and a chill running up my back. May June could feel the same thing, I could tell. On Little Ray's snout there was a heart-shaped white spot.

"Oh, I don't think he'll mind at all," she said to Darnell, "I don't think he'll mind one little bit."

CHAPTER 11

I NEARLY JUMPED OUT OF MY SEAT. I would have, in fact, if May June hadn't put a painful, viselike grip on my wrist. The pain shot up through my elbow to my neck and sizzled there. I sat back down, and she let go.

Her face was flushed but other than that, you wouldn't know that she was excited. She put her hands together in front of her bosom and said, "Well, ain't he the one! Why, Darnell, he's just purdy as a picture. Lemme hold 'im."

Darnell proudly handed the pup to May June, who took it and cradled it in her arms. "Oh, he's a fine one, he is." May June continued to coo and baby-talk to the dog, examining every inch of him as she did. "And healthy as a hog on corn, I'd say. Gonna be a fine hunter, this one."

Little Ray was following May June's hand as she moved it around him, trying to bite it, snapping at it. Finally, exasperated, he barked at her. "Oh, and listen to that voice. He's gonna be a singer, for sure."

She handed the pup back to Darnell, who cuddled and petted him and scratched his ears. Little Ray settled down onto Darnell's lap.

May June leaned on the counter again. "Okay, Darnell," she said. "Where'd you get him? What did you pay? Tell us the whole story." She leaned in close.

"Can't," Darnell said. He clearly wanted to.

"Can't? Whataya mean, ya can't?" May June asked. "You mean you don't even know how much you paid for a dog? Come on, Darnell, you ain't that slow."

"It's a secret," Darnell said, looking over his shoulder and leaning down toward May June.

I leaned in with them. "I've been wanting to get a dog for Naomi, Darnell," I said, playing on his innocent good nature. He had a tremendous crush on Naomi, would do anything for her. "If I knew a secret way to get her a really special dog, wouldn't that just make her happy?"

Darnell frowned, looked around for a moment, then back to May June and me. "They're kinda expensive," he said.

I pulled out my wallet, opened it, looked in. "How much?" I asked, frowning.

"I paid a hunert dollar fer this 'un," he said, awed by his own extravagance.

The dog he was holding, according to Ray, was probably worth ten times that. The last litter. The last Wishbone/Trueblood beagles. I frowned, shook my head, riffled the bills in my wallet, and finally said, "Well, I guess Naomi's worth it, don't you?"

He nodded vigorously.

"Well, who do we talk to?" May June said.

"You can't tell no one else," Darnell said.

"Not a soul," I added.

"You know the junkyard?" We both nodded. The only Durel County junkyard sat on the west side of Perry about eight miles out of town, eighteen or twenty miles east of the expressway. Everyone called it the junkyard except Trent and Floyd Feuchs, the owners, whose billboard sign read FEUCHS AUTO PARTS. "I was down there gettin' a part for Ms. Musgrove's Dodge." He scrunched up his face. "I don't remember what it's called but I drew a pi'ture of it an' they helped me find one from another old Dodge in the yard. Her Dodge ain't run so good since she got that tune-up down to Melrose. . . . "

"Darnell," May June said, gently, patting his hand. "The dogs."

"Oh, yeah," he smiled. "Well, they got this feller workin' there in the yard. I come up on him whil'st I was lookin' around and he had these-here pups in the back of this big ol' Caddy. In the trunk? I come up and looked at them pups and I say as how they sure are purdy. And he asks me how I'd like to buy one right now for a hunert dollar."

"You had a hundred dollars with you?" I asked.

He looked at me like this was the silliest thing he had ever heard. "Naw, Reverent Dan. Daddy always tol' me never carry more money than I can afford to lose, an' I don't."

"Well. . . . "

"I went to the bank and drew it outta my savings account and then I went back." He smiled proudly.

"You done that all by yourself?" May June asked, the pride flowing out of her voice. "You done that?"

Darnell nodded. "Them ladies at the bank helped me. I can sign my own name."

"Well, I guess we know that, Darnell. Since you got your license you can darned near do anything you set your mind to. We know that. Don't we know that, Reverend?"

I nodded. "This fellow you bought Little Ray from, Darnell. Did he tell you his name?"

"Yeah."

"Do you remember what it was?"

"Yeah."

"Well. . . ."

"George."

"His name was George?" May June asked. "George what?"

Darnell shrugged.

"So," I said. "If I want to buy Naomi a beagle, all I have to do is go to the yard and ask for George?"

"Or you can just walk back through there and find him like I did," Darnell said. He crooked his finger and beckoned me forward. I leaned in and he whispered, "He ain't too smart."

"He isn't?"

"He's not as smart as me."

"Why's that, Darnell? What makes you say that?"

"He couldn't remember my name, but I remembered his," Darnell said, his chest expanding with pride.

"He couldn't remember your name?"

He whispered again. "He kept callin' me Lenny."

I could see the heartbreak in May June's face. "You called him George, and he called you Lenny?" she asked.

Darnell nodded. "Just like in that movie about them two guys. He was real nice, though."

"I bet he was," May June said.

May June and I sat on the porch waiting for Ray until it got too cold to be outside, then we sat a while longer. May June seemed impervious to the damp spring air. Once, she got up to refill our coffee mugs, and when she came back out she had one of Ray's old fishing jackets for me and a ratty old quilt for herself. While we waited we talked about the dogs.

"It don't make sense," she said. "Those pups are like gold and this George fella is sellin' 'em for less than a pet store."

"Maybe word has gotten out," I said. "Maybe he's afraid of Ray."

She shook her head. "I don't think so. If he was afraid of Ray he woulda taken 'em outta the county, which I figured was what had been done all along. I allowed as how them pups was long gone by now."

We sat and stared across the road at the Mountain Baptist Children's Home. Only eleven kids were in residence at the big facility that, at one time, had held close to a hundred. A few lights were on in the dorms, but it was quiet. At the main building, a light was on in the administrator's office. The Reverend Doctor Jerome Bretz had been brought in just after the first of the year to run the place.

He was a stooped, balding, bespectacled little man who wore rumpled three-piece suits. Terminally serious, he had not reciprocated my two attempts at ecumenical hospitality. He was also a fanatic about paperwork, as the light in his office proved.

Paperwork.

"What about the kennel club?" I asked May June. "Wouldn't those pups need to be registered to prove their worth?"

She rocked back and forth in her rocker for a minute, thinking. "It depends," she said, at last. "If you're gonna show them dogs for their looks and their breeding, then they got to be registered with the kennel club. But if you're gonna run 'em in hunting and tracking competition then no one gives a hoot about no papers. They're bein' judged for their ability and their performance. If you know that they're the Wishbone/Trueblood beagles, well, so much the better. If they're all marked like Little Ray, any dogger in the county could pick 'em out. Any dogger in the state for that matter."

"Maybe whoever took them doesn't know that," I said. "Maybe he thinks that since they're not registered and he doesn't have the papers to do it, maybe he thinks they're not as valuable. . . ." I let it trail off because I didn't know exactly where it was going.

"Or!" May June said, as the Carmack twins pulled up in front of the diner in their big pickup truck. "Or maybe he don't know what he's got. Maybe he thinks they're just some cute beagle pups. But then, why steal 'em? And certainly no one killed Calvin Haines for a bunch of cute pups."

Ray climbed out of the truck and thanked the twins, walked wearily up onto the porch, and sat down on one of the old chrome-and-vinyl kitchen chairs. "Mother, have you got any more of that coffee?"

May June puttered into the diner and came back with a steaming mug for her husband. "Well, what happened?" she asked him, wrapping her quilt back around her shoulders.

"Oh, the damn thing. Brakes aren't workin' right and I didn't want to chance drivin' back over the mountain. I left it in town. I'll call tomorrow and tell 'em what to do." He sighed and took a long gulp of his coffee.

"Any luck with them pups?" May June asked, winking at me.

"Nah! I'm beginnin' to think them pups is gone. I woulda heard by now. Either that or they're dead. If someone took 'em and they wasn't weaned yet and he didn't know how to care for 'em, he mighta killed 'em."

"Oh, I don't think so," May June said, trying hard not to smile. "I think them pups is still right here in the county somewheres."

Ray looked into his coffee mug. "Well, I don't know what would make you think that. I been all over the county leavin' word at every gas station and tavern. . . ." He leaned forward and looked at her. "Did someone call?"

May June shook her head. "Not on the phone, they didn't." She smiled at me and I smiled back.

"Okay, you two. Just what the hell's goin' on here?"

May June sighed and spoke as though she might be recounting the weather, offhandedly, matter-of-fact. "We found 'em."

"You found 'em?"

She told him the whole story about Darnell Kody and his bowling ball bag and the guy who called himself George.

And when she was done all he said was, "Well, I'll be damned." Then he went through his cigarette-lighting ritual, and when he had taken another gulp of coffee and a big, satisfying drag on his Camel he said, "George and Lenny, huh?"

May June nodded. "That's the names of those two fellas in that book, *Of Mice and Men*. Lenny's the retarded one and—"

"I know, Mother. I read it in high school and we rented the movie last winter." Ray leaned forward, elbows on his knees, smoking. "Well, I guess we got us a call to make tomorrow, preacher."

"We do?" I asked. I was thinking about the work on the steeple and how I wanted to be there when Rudepohler started again in the morning. And I was thinking about Calvin Haines's funeral at noon. I said as much to Ray.

"Walter Rudepohler don't need you lookin' over his shoulder," Ray said. "And we'll get you over to Whiteker's in plenty o' time for you to send Calvin on to glory. Besides, my Jeep's in town. You gotta drive me in to get it. While we're at it we'll stop by Feuchs Auto Parts and meet this George fella."

"What time?" I asked, resigned to the trip.

"Oh, about seven, I guess."

"Are you going to call the sheriff and let him know what's going on?" I asked. "Maybe get some backup?"

Ray stood and stretched, flipped his cigarette butt into the road. The Mountain Baptist Children's Home was completely dark now, as was the rest of the village. The only lights still on were the streetlight above the volunteer fire department near the road just south of the children's home and on the porch where we sat.

"Nope," Ray said. "This is more of a personal thing now."

"Personal?" I asked.

"Preacher," he said, "Darnell Kody is as kind and sweet a man as ever walked the face of this cursed earth. He never has, in his whole life, intentionally hurt a living soul—man, ner beast—with word or deed." Ray stuck his hands in his pockets and stared straight ahead. "That George feller, whatever his real name is, thinks he's better'n Darnell 'cause he's read a book or seen a movie. Do you understand what I'm saying?"

I nodded, not realizing that he couldn't see me.

"He messed with Darnell Kody 'cause Darnell's big and retarded and kind and gentle. Made fun of him. Mocked him." Now he took a deep breath and let it out. "Well, sir, I won't have that. I just won't have it."

"Preacher, we gotta get you somethin' else to drive," Ray said. His knees were crushed against the dash of my VW. May June, believe it or not, was in the backseat behind Ray, her legs angled sideways along the seat and her feet behind me. I was wearing my gray funeral suit, white shirt, and blue-and-maroon-striped tie. Ray was in his usual uniform, his funeral suit in a garment bag in the front trunk of the Volkswagen. May June was wearing one of her multi-hued floral church dresses, hose, hat, and tan gloves. She had been generous with the honeysuckle perfume. Ray lit a cigarette and started to crank down the window.

"Dad, my hair!" May June shouted from the backseat.

Ray shook his head and tossed the cigarette out the window and rolled it back up. He looked very uncomfortable.

You know those snakes they put in the fake cans of peanuts, so when you open the lid the snake comes flying out? Whatever they must look like when they are scrunched inside the can, that's what Ray looked like in my VW.

"Damn thing ain't big enough to fart in," he grumbled. "How come you keep shiftin' gears ever' time you go up a hill?"

"I think it's the load we're carrying," I said.

"Thanks a lot!" May June said from the backseat.

I shook my head. "I meant—"

"She knows what you mean, preacher. She's just givin' you a hard time. Ain't that right, Mother?"

May June giggled. "Darnell says maybe it's the timin'."

Ray harrumphed. "It ain't the timin'. It's the whole damn car. It's twenty-five years old, for cryin' out loud. Preacher, we gotta get you somethin' better'n this. Next week you and me are goin' to see Barret Smith about a trade. He probably won't give you doodly for this pile o' crap, but he won't skin ya either. Barret, he's been in the car business for twenty-five years and his daddy before him and *his* daddy before him. You don't stay in the car business that long by screwin' people over. Not in a town the size of Perry, you don't. Besides . . ."

"Okay," I said.

". . . he just runs the place with his daughter. Just the two of 'em there, and no salesmen or anyone to try to pressure you just to meet their whatchacallit."

"Quota," I said.

"So how much money you got to spend on your new unit?"

I thought for a moment. "I've got just over four hundred dollars in my savings account, and two hundred in my checking. I'll owe my ex-wife four hundred dollars in child support at the first of the month, but I'll be getting another paycheck by then."

I thought a big dose of reality might put an end to the conversation. Ray knew how much money I made. Everyone in the church did, or could. It was published in the church newsletter every year. But I was sure he hadn't given it the kind of scrutiny a bank would when I asked for a loan. Parishioners usually think of their pastor's salary when it comes up for review at the end of each year, and then they think of it in terms of how much it is costing them and couldn't they really get by with a less experienced minister who would cost them less?

Ray scrunched up his face so that it now matched the rest of his body, looked straight ahead through the windshield, and started his cigarette ritual. When he finally got the weed going to his satisfaction he took a deep drag and cracked his window again. May June sighed loudly from the backseat, but he either didn't care or didn't hear. Then he nodded his head a couple of times and said, "Okay. Okay. We can work with that."

Damn.

By 8:30 a.m. we had dropped May June off in Perry to do some shopping before the funeral and made our way out Route 48 to Feuchs Auto Parts. The Feuchs brothers themselves were there to greet us.

"You wanna talk to George?" asked Floyd.

"What you wanna talk to him about?" asked Trenton.

Trenton and Floyd Feuchs were stereotypical Appalachian hill-billy garage monkeys. Since I had moved to Appalachia, eight months before, I had become a little dismayed that no one ever seemed to match the Hollywood stereotypes I had brought with me. The Feuchs brothers now stepped onto the stage to prove that there was, indeed, a grain of truth to those celluloid images. My faith in the big screen was restored.

Floyd was the older of the two by about five years. I put him at maybe thirty-five or so. He was about five-feet-eight-inches tall and—I'm not good at weights, but—he wasn't fat or thin, just average. He wore a tan gas station uniform with his name stitched over a breast pocket full of tire gauges, pens, tiny screwdrivers, rulers, and eyeglasses, taped at the nose. His clothes were grease-stained and dirty, as were his hands. There was black stuff encrusted under his fingernails, and a couple of those were black from having been smashed. He held a pinch of snuff the size of a lemon in his lip, and about four of his upper front teeth were missing. The crown of his billed cap read I HAVEN'T HAD SEX IN SO LONG, I FORGET WHO GETS TIED UP.

Trent was about thirty. He was thinner than Floyd and a couple of inches taller with a little pot belly that looked like a volleyball sticking out over his belt. The belt aided and abetted a pair of clip-on suspenders in holding up a pair of old pin-striped suit pants that rode nearly up to his shoulder blades in the back and looped down under his belly in the front. His shirt was plaid and frayed and buttoned at the throat. His billed cap was pulled down so that his head filled it, and there was nothing printed on it. He hadn't shaved in a couple of days, and his breath was so bad that I could smell it every time he talked. He dipped snuff with the same enthusiasm of his brother but had managed to save one of his front teeth—though it was slightly crooked and stained mahogany.

"We need to talk to him about some dogs he's sellin'" Ray said. "You two know anything about that?"

The brothers looked at each other and shrugged. They didn't. We were in the little shed that served as their office. There was a green metal desk and a filing cabinet, neither of which saw much use, it seemed, from the pile of stuff on top of the desk and the flood of stuff coming out of the filing cabinet. There were also some girlie calendars and about a thousand car parts lying around on counters, floors, and chairs, and soaking in pans of kerosene. I figured that the kerosene pans was why the brothers chose to dip snuff rather than smoke. They may have been ignorant, but they weren't utterly stupid. They were sitting on two car seats that formed a triangle with a kerosene heater as the base, drinking coffee around their dip. Even without cigarettes the place could go off like a bomb at any moment.

"Well, where can I find him?" Ray asked. Clearly the Feuchs brothers had no intention of leaving the shed.

"Yonder," Floyd said, moving his hand in the direction of the door.

"Out in the yard," Trent said, nodding.

"What's his full name?" Ray asked.

They looked at each other and shrugged again.

"You got a guy workin' for you and you don't know his name?" Ray asked.

"Don't work for us," Floyd said.

"Used to work for ol' Bill," Trent said.

"If you can call that work," Floyd said.

Trent snorted, nodded several times, and they both kinda chuckled.

Ray looked at me and shook his head as if to ask, *Have you ever seen anything so pitiful?* What he said was: "You're sayin' he came with the place? What?"

"Good way o' puttin' it," Floyd said.

"Come with the place," Trent said.

"Kinda comes and goes as he pleases," Floyd said.

"Where's he live?" Ray asked.

"Here," Floyd said.

"Here in the office?"

"Nah. In the yard. Sleeps in the cars far as I can figure," Floyd said. "He don't do no harm and he probably keeps the kids out. They think he's a crazy man, eat 'em if'n he catches 'em in the yard."

"He don't bother us and we don't bother him," Trent said. "'Sides, I don't think he really would eat them kids."

"What he does eat, though, we don't know," Floyd offered. "Only seen him a couple o' times myself. Never have talked to him. When ol' Bill sold us the place he said George was harmless. Still, I always take my rat killer with me I go inta the yard."

"Rat killer?" Ray said.

Floyd rolled to one side, slopping coffee on the car seat. Behind his right kidney was a small holster with a semiautomatic pistol strapped into it. "This-here take care o' any rats jumpin' out o' them old cars. *Any* rats. Four legged or two," he said with a nod.

Trent reached under the car seat he was sitting on and brought out a child-size baseball bat with some nails driven into the fat end. It was about two-and-a-half feet long and very ugly. Red stains tinted the wood around the nails.

"That red stuff's just some old paint from whackin' cars but it surely throw a scare inta anyone tries to mess with you," Trent said, smiling with his solo tooth. He tested the bat for heft and balance. "Yessir. Any nigger want to give us trouble, they gone find out fast they come to the wrong place."

Again Ray gave me one of his looks. "Oh yeah," he said. "When the fifty colored folks who live in this county rise up in armed revolt, the first thing they're gonna do is get together and say, 'Hey, let's go out and rob those two sorry-ass peckerwoods got the junk-yard outside o' town. Steal some o' that incredible wealth they got hid in their shed.'" He shook his head and turned to leave. I went with him.

As we opened the door to step out into the junkyard, Floyd called to Ray and we turned to look back into the stinking shed. "It's good to know there's others in this county with a clear head." He nodded several times, dead serious. "You never know. You just never know what them coons is thinkin'."

"Good luck findin' George," Trent said. He, too, was nodding seriously.

"You ever hear such an ignorant pile of manure in your entire life?" Ray asked as we walked through the yard. "I swear. And this George fella is supposed to be the crazy one." He lit a cigarette and looked out over the acres and acres of smashed rusting cars. "Well," he said. "Let's go find us a crazy man."

CHAPTER 12

I LATER LEARNED that Feuchs Auto Parts covered about thirty acres, but at the time, it seemed to go on forever. The piles of cars, trucks, vans, panel trucks, and non-automotive junk rolled out before us in a seemingly endless series of small hills. It looked as though ol' Bill, the previous owner, had tried stacking the cars until the stacks fell over into large piles. Then he just threw more cars on the piles. Some of the car-hills were nearly thirty feet high and didn't look very stable.

I kept thinking about the rats that Floyd and Trent had talked about—the four legged kind and the two legged kind. I wasn't all that anxious to meet either. Was this George guy really crazy? He lived in a junkyard! The local kids were afraid of him. No one seemed to know anything else about the guy. How crazy was he? Ray didn't have a "rat killer" with him.

I was dressed for a funeral, hoping desperately to keep my suit clean and my shoes free of mud. Ray was in his work uniform and walking like he was leading Pickett's Charge. After a few minutes he stopped and looked around, ground out his cigarette, and listened. Birds, cars creaking in the breeze, a chain saw somewhere off in the distance. Ray cupped his hands around his mouth and said just above conversation volume. "George? George, you around here? My name's Ray Hall and I need to talk to you." He listened again. Nothing.

We walked some more and within a few minutes I was lost in the maze that was Feuchs Auto Parts. If we got separated I would never be able to find my way back out of the place. And I kept getting this feeling that I was being watched, that if I turned around quick enough I would see someone ducking behind a pile of Dodges or Fords. I knew it was just paranoia, but I couldn't shake the feeling and I shivered as I walked, trying to stay close to Ray.

He stopped again to listen and continued this pattern, listening, calling, walking for three more stops. I was utterly lost and getting more and more spooked as we listened. The chain saw was no longer buzzing and the birds seemed to be on break. The cars creaked and whined and I kept hearing skittering noises from deep within the piles of junk.

I looked at my watch, amazed to see that it was nearly 10:45. We'd been walking through the junkyard for nearly an hour and half. I needed to be heading back to Perry, getting ready for Calvin Haines's funeral, talking to Treasure and Blessing about last-minute things that always come up before funerals. I was gathering breath to say as much to Ray when he held up a hand and stopped again.

He cocked his head to listen and held his breath. I did the same and we both heard it at the same time: a yelp. That's all I can say about it. It wasn't a bark or a woof or a yap. It was the unmistakable yelp that puppies make when they first start to vocalize. Ray took a couple of steps to his right and stopped again, waiting.

Yelp!

We began to move, as quietly as we could toward the sound, and stopped beside a low, spread out pile of Cadillacs, listening again.

Yelp!

Ray pointed into the pile, then held his finger beneath his nose. The sound was coming from deep in the pile of cars. He wanted to locate it as quietly as we could. He motioned for me to go to the right around the pile and he would go to the left. I did not like this idea but I didn't say so. I moved to the right.

Now the yelping was coming more often, one pup being joined by the others. They were probably hungry, I figured, calling for their mother who was buried out at the Haines farm.

I moved on around the pile of big cars, noting the wide tail fins on the bottom and the reduced size and sleeker lines on the top. After a while it seemed that I had surely gone farther than half the way around and I was beginning to wonder what had happened to Ray when I found him leaning up against the front bumper of a pink, convertible Eldorado. When he saw me he pointed down beside the car and I saw the entrance to a tunnel that undoubtedly ran to the center of the pile.

I pointed to the knees of my neatly pressed suit pants and he just smiled and shrugged. After a couple of moments enjoying my discomfort he relented and whispered to me to stand guard at the entrance of the tunnel while he crawled through and checked out the other end.

My relief lasted only until Ray's butt disappeared into the tunnel, and then my paranoia came on in full force. The birds were off their break and refreshed, singing in full throat. The breeze had picked up and the cars were creaking and groaning worse than ever. I kept imagining a rat running around inside the tunnel as Ray tried to crawl through, only to be confronted by a club-wielding lunatic with bugs in his hair and blood in his beard, waiting at the other end to bash his brains out.

The wait went on and on. I looked at my watch again and discovered that I'd been waiting about fifteen minutes. What could be taking so long? Where was Ray? How long should I wait? What if he didn't come back out of the tunnel? Go for help? How? Where? To whom? The Feuchs brothers didn't seem like a very good choice. Did they even have a phone in that shed they called their—

A scream.

My heart and stomach leaped into my throat and I nearly wet my pants. I may have even yelled in answer. It was a male voice. It was high pitched and it was . . . what? Angry? Yes, that was it. It was an angry scream. It wasn't from pain or fear or surprise or horror or any of the other things a human might scream about. It was anger, pure and simple.

Again. Louder. This time followed by some crashing and bashing around and the sound of glass breaking.

I gave the knees of my pants a moment's consideration. The image of a sleek, black rat with gleaming eyes and a long tail flitted across my mind and was gone as I dove into the tunnel and began scrambling into the darkness.

My journey didn't go quickly because the tunnel was a winding thing of varying heights and widths. At one point I had to lie down and crawl on my stomach, and at another I had to pull myself through on my side, using one hand to pull and the other to push. I grabbed something jagged and felt the skin on my right hand tear open and willed myself to ignore it.

Another scream and more crashing.

Finally, huffing and puffing and cursing the extra ten pounds I'd put on over the winter, I made it to within a few feet of the other end of the tunnel and realized, as I stopped to catch my breath, that there was no more noise coming from within the Cadillac mountain.

Now what? Go forward and investigate? Go back and call for help? What about Ray? What if he was hurt? What if the person who hurt him was waiting for me?

I looked around, using the light from the end of the tunnel, to search for a weapon. Anything I could swing or throw or use to defend myself. The best I could come up with was a broken piece of mirror about eight inches long and maybe three across, jagged at one end. I took off my tie and wrapped it around the wide end of what had probably been a rearview mirror. Thus protected from further cuts, I crawled slowly toward the light that was filtering through the end of the tunnel, controlling my breathing, trying to come up with a plan that wouldn't get me killed.

The only thing I could come up with was the element of surprise. Whoever George was, he would not be expecting an explosive attack. Would he? Of course not. If he did, he would have already started down the tunnel, or he would have at least looked down the tunnel to see if an attack was coming, or he would have. . . .

O, lord.

He would have done something to bring the tunnel crashing down on whoever was attacking him and used another route to escape. Whether or not an explosive attack was a good plan, that's what George was going to get. The thought of the tunnel crashing down on top of me was enough to propel me out of it like a rocket.

I took three deep breaths, got into a sort of crouched, cramped version of my high school football lineman's stance, rocked back and forth a couple of times, and exploded out of the tunnel ready to slash and cut anyone or anything that got in my way.

"Simmer down, preacher, the battle's won," Ray said. He was sitting on the ground, leaning back against the door of a green Coupe DeVille. He was holding a blue bandanna to the side of his head and sucking on the knuckle of his right hand. "Meet George," he said.

The pile of Cadillacs wasn't really a pile, it was a ring. The automobile doughnut encircled an open space about twenty-five feet in diameter. It reminded me of the forts I used to build out of junk and scrap lumber with my friends when I was a kid, only this was the kind we dreamed of building. George had stretched a tarp across and over some of the cars to form a shelter. The doors had been removed from the cars, as had been the seats, which were on the ground around a campfire ring with a metal grate over it. An unbroken windshield sat across two stacks of concrete blocks to form a table, and one of the empty cars was full of canned goods, dry firewood, and clothing. All in all, George's fort was homier, more comfortable, and generally nicer than the Feuchs brothers' office shed. The only thing marring the childlike charm of the fort was the owner who lay on his back in the center of it.

"George?" I asked Ray.

"I reckon," he said, looking at the bandanna. He dabbed it against his head again, looked again, frowned, and stuffed it into his pocket. "Big maniac come screamin' outta nowhere and tried to coldcock me with that tire iron yonder. Damn near took my head off—and woulda if he hadn't screamed. I just had time to duck and he caught me with a little chip shot. Hurts like a bastard, though."

I stood over George and tried to make him fit into the neat little campsite. He was big, maybe as big as Ray. Six-six or -seven. Two-forty or -fifty, probably. Long hair, matted and dirty, probably brown. Big beard that had never been trimmed from his neck or cheeks, curly with pieces of breakfast still hanging in it. No blood, though. He was wearing army camo fatigues and combat boots. His teeth were stained but straight and all present and accounted for. His age was a complete mystery.

Ray came up and stood beside me. "Glass jaw," he said. "I got a lucky punch and down he went. Crazy as a bedbug."

"What about Darnell?" I asked. "He wasn't too crazy to make fun of him."

Ray walked toward another Cadillac but I couldn't make out the model. He opened the passenger door, which creaked and groaned and drug on the ground. Inside the car was full of paperback books. Many had missing covers and most were water damaged, torn, bent, and moldy. "He read the same book I did in high school," Ray said. "Darnell must have reminded him of the Lenny character is all."

"Did you find *Of Mice and Men* in there?"

"No, but I'll bet it is, or was." He reached in and grabbed a handful of books, tossed them back in as he read the titles. "*Tale of Two Cities, Moby Dick, The Pearl, Madame Bovary, The Rise and Fall of the Third Reich.* George don't believe in pollutin' his mind with trash like mystery and romance novels."

George groaned. I jumped. Ray turned and walked to the heap of humanity in the center of the fort. He slapped George lightly on the face and jiggled his shoulder. "George? George! You hear me?"

George groaned again and his eyes came open. He blinked a couple of times, shook his head, brought his hand up, and scratched his beard. Finally, his eyes focused on Ray. "Who're you?"

"Name's Ray Hall. I'm a county constable." Ray took his badge out of his shirt pocket and showed it to him.

"Who's he?" George asked, nodding toward me.

"He's a reverend."

"Chaplain?"

"That's right. You feel like talkin'?"

"No." He started getting up and Ray stood up straight. His knees popped.

"Why not?" Ray asked.

George rolled to his hands and knees, the better to rise to his feet. Without warning he screamed again, came straight up, and took a roundhouse swing at Ray. "Incoming!"

Ray easily ducked the "incoming," stepped forward, behind the swing, and popped George on the jaw with a right jab. George dropped like a big sack of rocks, out like a light. Ray shook his head and looked at me. "Man with a jaw that fragile, you'd think he'd be more careful 'bout choosin' his fights."

He bent and grabbed a handful of George's shirt collar and

began dragging him to a place directly across from where I had entered the fort. "He's got an escape tunnel over here," he said. "Probably shorter and straighter than the one we came in." He bent, looked around for a couple of minutes, and then said: "Yeah. Here it is." He started to crawl into the backseat of a car and then turned and dragged George after him.

As George's feet disappeared into the car, Ray called out to me. "Hey, preacher. Bring the dogs."

I looked around, only now remembering the sound that had brought us here. There were no dogs. "What dogs?" I shouted toward where Ray had been.

"The pups," Ray's voice was fainter, now seeming to come from over the tops of the cars instead of from within them. "Darnell said he kept them in a car trunk."

I walked around the fort, listening for puppy yelps. I rattled a couple of cars, not ready to spring open every trunk I saw, afraid of startling a rat. Finally I heard it again. A muffled yelp from within the trunk of a black Lincoln that had somehow managed to make it into this exclusive General Motors domain. A sacrilege?

I got my fingers under the rim of the trunk and started to yank when it popped open and glided easily up. Inside the trunk space was a green army blanket, a small, chipped bowl of water, a hubcap with a few pieces of dog food still lying in the bottom, and five beagle puppies who mistook me for their mother, savior, lord and master.

"Good lord, what happened to you?" LeRoy Whiteker stood at the backdoor of his home and business looking obscenely neat and handsome. Give actor Alec Baldwin a few more years, gentler eyes, and a squarer jaw, and you have LeRoy. He made his navy blue pin-striped Brooks Brothers suit look like an Armani. His black Bostonians shone like mirrors.

I put on my best hangdog expression. "Ray Hall, five beagle puppies, and a crazy man at the junkyard happened to me." Out in the VW a puppy yipped to punctuate my reply.

LeRoy looked past me to the car, smiled, shook his head, and looked at his watch. Then he looked at me and pulled a face. "You know, you got a funeral in forty-five minutes."

"I'm not here to pass the time of day, Lee. Help?"

He smiled a handsome, blindingly white smile and stepped back from the door. "Come on in. We'll see what we can do." Then he yelled into the house: "Andrea! Break out the needle and thread, honey. We got an emergency."

Fifteen minutes later I was showered and standing on a kitchen chair while the beautiful Andrea Whiteker tacked an inside cuff to the pants of one of LeRoy's suits. She was as pretty as he was handsome, former Miss Eastern Kentucky. LeRoy was about my age and I figured Andrea to be six or eight years younger, maybe in her early thirties. Naomi and I had gone out with them several times, and LeRoy was trying to teach me golf so he'd have someone to golf with, his assumption being that most people don't like to play games with preachers or undertakers. He was right.

Most people think of preachers and funeral directors as serious, humorless, depressing people who couldn't have a good time with a hundred-dollar bill in a two-dollar whorehouse. And to give such folks their due, most of the preachers I know pretty much fit that description.

I think about partying, the last group of people to come to my mind are a bunch of Methodist preachers. Funeral directors, ministers, and cops. These are people you want to be there when you need them, but you also want them to leave you alone until that time comes, right? Come on, admit it.

Well, your loss. Some of my best friends are funeral directors and cops, and let me tell you something, those guys know how to have a good time. I could psychologize about it but I don't. LeRoy and Andrea are my friends and I don't try to analyze anything that has to do with my friends.

They had three kids, two girls and a boy, so beautiful they made your heart ache just to look at them. The kids were in the yard playing with the pups. Being raised in a funeral home didn't seem to have warped them in the slightest. They played Monopoly on the floor of the casket display room and earned spending money somberly greeting visitors at viewings and funerals. Death? Oh, yeah, well, it's the end of life. What else did you want to know?

They hadn't seen Calvin Haines hanging in his barn.

LeRoy had found one of last year's suits—he bought three new suits every year—a gray pinstripe, and it almost fit me. He was a couple of inches taller and not quite so beefy as I, so the legs of the pants were a little long and the waist was a little tight, but Andrea was making short work of those problems with some basting tape and a sharp pair of scissors. He brought in a white shirt and a maroon tie with little flecks of gray in it and they fit okay. The jacket was a little snug in the shoulders but I could button it over my gut, so I wasn't complaining. He'd also run some of that liquid shoe polish over my shoes and they shined like his. So that was his secret.

When Andrea was done I looked myself over in the mirror above their fireplace and was pleasantly surprised. LeRoy stood next to me and we could have been brothers. Me the older, fair-haired, husky, gruff one who took after his father; LeRoy, the pretty, smart, girl-chasing, charming one who took after Mom.

Andrea giggled. "Well, Butch and Sundance, you gonna stand there waiting for GQ to show up and sign you, or are you gonna bury Calvin Haines?"

LeRoy looked at his watch and dashed through the connecting door from his living room into the funeral home just as the mantle clock chimed noon.

The Methodist funeral, like the Methodist wedding, is a brief affair. We are not gathered together to wallow in sentiment, the founders of the church seemed to think. We are, rather, come together to remember our place in the universe, a place which God has given us as a gift. A very small place in a very big universe.

Like the lilies of the field and the grass of the pasture, we spring up, we live, and we are gone, all in a blink of the cosmic eye. Life, no matter how brief it seems, is a gift, and the value of the gift is not diminished by its brevity. The Lord gives and the Lord takes away. Blessed be the name of the Lord.

I know it sounds cold, but it isn't, really. It's two hundred years of tradition and theological thought packed into twenty minutes, like thirty pounds of goose down stuffed into a six-foot-square comforter. The comfort is not in the content of the ritual as much as in the doing of it.

So I did the ritual.

I read the traditional words from the Scriptures. I prayed the traditional prayers and, when we got to the cemetery, I spoke the traditional words of interment. For the homily I spoke on the text Calvin Haines had spoken to me. I talked about how enemies came in many forms and how he had, with faith and hard work, overcome many—poverty, lack of education, the deaths of his wife and son and son-in-law, the greed and envy of his adversaries.

At the request of Treasure and Blessing I did not mention the manner of Calvin's passing. Suicide or murder, it was still officially undetermined, and besides, they wanted the service to focus on his life, not his death. Pretty smart for a couple of hillbilly girls, huh?

The sisters cried quietly at the funeral home, and at the cemetery they leaned on the arms of their father's friends—doggers and farmers and old hunting and fishing buddies and their wives. When it was all over everyone milled around the grave site while the cemetery workers smoked cigarettes by the hearse, waiting to fill in the grave. I shook hands with some folks I knew and was introduced to some others. Everyone said what a wonderful job I did and how I had captured Calvin perfectly in my text and homily. They stood around for a while, talking, smoking, remembering Calvin, and then they drifted away, some to their cars, some to other sites in the cemetery to pay their respects to their own dearly departed. Some were somber, some laughed as they talked, remembering a favorite story.

Treasure and Blessing talked and laughed with them, and I drifted over to the hearse and stood by LeRoy. We took out our pipes and lit up, talked to the cemetery workers about the weather and the Cincinnati Reds and the Atlanta Braves and largemouth bass.

When LeRoy started talking about golf the workers drifted away, and as soon as they were out of earshot, he changed the subject again.

"I dated both of them," he said.

For just the briefest moment I thought he was talking about Herman and Carl, the cemetery workers, and the image that came into my brain was so funny I nearly laughed out loud, which wouldn't have done at all. It's one thing for the mourners to laugh at a story or a memory. It's quite another for the preacher and funeral director to laugh about something just between the two of them. It isn't done.

I followed his gaze toward the Haines sisters where they were talking to the last of their guests, wishing them well and thanking them for coming. They both wore suits. Bless's in a green so dark it was almost black, off the rack from a department store in Lexington and then altered to fit around her bosom. She wore a scarf with green and black swirls around her neck to hide her cleavage, and it was fastened with a black cameo pin. Treasure was in the black suit I had seen her in the day before, open at the throat with a strand of pearls around her neck. I realized as I watched them that while they looked nothing alike they shared the same skin, milky white with freckles—Bless's more prominent on her face and neck, Treasure's sprinkled delicately over her nose and cheeks.

"They must have been something," I said, with maybe a little too much lust in my voice, a little too much sigh.

"Oh, yeah," LeRoy said. "They were that. Had every boy in the high school panting after them. Treasure more than Bless but only because she was less approachable. You know how high school boys are. The harder it is to get, the more desirable it is. Bless was just this good old country girl with a big laugh and boobs to match. Saucy and sexy. Treasure always seemed more exotic, more aloof, I guess you'd say."

"Not too aloof," I kidded him. "She went out with you."

"Twice. She knew I was gonna inherit my daddy's business—"

"And she didn't want to be married to an undertaker?"

"She didn't want to be married to anyone in Durel County. Hell, anyone in Kentucky for that matter. She had her eye on bigger things. Took off for Cincinnati as soon as she got outta high school and never looked back. I guess she finally found what she was lookin' for." He knocked out his pipe in the palm of his hand and slipped it into his jacket pocket where it disappeared without making a bulge. It was one of those pencil stems like Bing Crosby used to smoke. My large bowl imperial always made my suit coat look like I was carrying a bowling ball in my pocket. And when I knocked it out on my hand I ended up with pipe ash all over my pants. LeRoy's hand was as clean as the day he was born.

"What about Bless?" I asked. "What was she like?" We were both leaning against the hearse looking out over the cemetery. I laid my pipe on the hood to cool off and go out.

"Well, I got to second base," he said, smiling to himself. "And it was a great inning, too. But she had a thing for Bert even then. He was a senior and we were juniors, and he played football and I ran cross country. She was a cheerleader for the football team and I guess it was just fated or something. Before I could get back up to bat in the next inning she'd dumped me for him."

"Broke your heart," I said.

"Mighta. Only Bert was such a good guy you couldn't be mad at him. He was just as plain as a pair o' brown shoes and twice as comfortable. Easygoin' and pleasant even then. I mighta envied him, but I sure never hated him."

"You buried him, didn't you?"

"Yeah. Him and Mrs. Haines and Vic. We've buried damn near everyone in this county for the last sixty years except the Catholics, the Jews, the Seventh Day Adventists, and the coloreds. They all got their own people. So I guess we're talkin' about the white protestants and the heathens." He sighed. "He died in the family mine. Widow-maker got 'im. Wasn't much left to bury. I told Calvin I'd do my best if he wanted me to, but he finally agreed to a closed casket. It was a shame. The death, I mean, not the closed casket."

The sun was getting hot against the black hearse so I stood up and unbuttoned my suit jacket, stretched my back. The Haines sisters were waving to the last car to pull away from the grave site. They turned and came toward us. "Those two girls have seen more than their share of tragedy," I said.

"Yeah," LeRoy agreed. "I'm glad you caught the guy that killed Calvin. It doesn't bring him back, but they at least don't have to live with the mystery of it, not knowin'."

I had told LeRoy and Andrea Whiteker about my morning at the junkyard while Andrea was adjusting the suit for me to wear. They had both laughed through most of it and I didn't realize until this moment, standing in the cemetery, that after all I had been through, I didn't really consider Crazy George a suspect.

Up until the moment I saw him I was sure he had killed Calvin Haines in some kind of insane ritual. The longer I walked through that junkyard with Ray the more sure I became. Crawling through the Cadillac tunnel, toward what I feared was my own death, my mind had seized on the truth of his guilt as though it were proven.

Then I saw him lying there in the dirt and saw the food scraps in his beard. And I saw him come up and take off after Ray again, and Ray put him down again with one pop on the jaw. Without realizing it, without really thinking about it, I had dismissed George as a suspect in the death of Calvin Haines.

Maybe if Calvin had been killed by a single blow to the head with a tire iron. Maybe if he had been strangled by hand. Maybe then I could believe George was the killer. But, as it was, I couldn't see George having the patience, much less the desire, to torture a man to death by hauling him up and down on the end of a rope.

I told as much to LeRoy and he took it all in, but he didn't have time to respond. Just as I was finishing my speech he gave me a quick warning glance and looked over my shoulder.

"You ladies look radiant, today," he said. "Was everything all right?"

Blessing shook our hands and wiped a tear from her eye with a man's handkerchief. "It was wonderful," she said. "Lee, you did a wonderful and sensitive job, as always. And Dan, you sounded like you knew Daddy all your life. Thank you, both."

"Yes, thank you," Treasure said, shaking our hands as well. "It was a very nice service. Very nice."

We both told them it was our honor to be of service, and they turned to walk back to their car. LeRoy called out that he'd have the flowers from the funeral home delivered to Bless's house. Bless nodded and waved. LeRoy got into the hearse and I went to the passenger side to get in, too, when I heard my name being called.

Treasure was making her way back toward the hearse and I met her halfway. She took my arm to keep from falling off her high heels. "I'm sorry," she said. "We told LeRoy we'd give you an honorarium and then we both forgot to bring it here. I was wondering if you were going to be at home tonight."

"Don't worry about it," I told her. "I don't do it for the money."

"I know you don't. I know you would have done it for nothing if we were poor or if we asked you to. But we aren't and we didn't. I also know what these hillbillies pay you so I'm not going to stiff you on a funeral honorarium. If you'll be home around eight or so

I'll bring it by on my way into Perry."

"You been staying out at your dad's house?" I asked.

"Yes, I'm going to give a little time to my sister before I have to go back to work. Is that all right if I bring the check by?"

I shrugged my best impression of the great Appalachian shrug. "I'll be there," I said.

"Good," she said. She then stood on her tiptoes and kissed me on the corner of my mouth. "Thanks again." Chanel No. 5 again. My mother's scent. Naomi's scent. Heaven sent.

LeRoy was watching us through the rearview mirror of the hearse. "That reminds me," he said as I got in. "I don't have an honorarium check for you. The girls said they wanted to give it to you personal."

"Okay."

"Well?"

"Well, what?"

"Well, was that what your little talk with Treasure was all about? Your honorarium?" LeRoy looked devilishly interested, a twinkle in his eye.

"Yeah, she said that she'd bring it by the house tonight," I said, strapping on my seat belt.

"Did she, now?" LeRoy grinned as he started the engine.

"Lee."

"Okay. I was just playin' with ya."

"She's bringing me a check. Hopefully a really big one."

"Okay."

"That's all."

"Okay."

"I'm nearly a married man. Naomi and I are engaged."

"Okay."

"She's not even my type," I said.

"What type is that type?" he asked.

The type who doesn't wear underwear to her father's funeral, I wanted to say. *So when she stands close to you and you sneak a peek down the front of her jacket, you can darned near see heaven. The type who kisses you on the corner of your mouth all proper-like, then presses her tongue ever so gently into that little place where your lips meet at the side of your mouth. The type who leaves a trail of Chanel No. 5 wherever she goes so that the only thing you can think of when she leaves the room is her.* But it would have been a lie to say those things because that was exactly my type. That was the type that destroyed my marriage. That type was what dreams were made of and. . . .

What I said to LeRoy was: "Too skinny."

CHAPTER 13

I CALLED NAOMI when I got back to the funeral home and, amazingly, she was free. She had worked through lunch and agreed to meet me at Grandma's Kitchen (Ho-o-o-me Cookin'!) about a block from the courthouse. Grandma's was one of those restaurants that changed hands every year or so. People seemed to eat at the place and think, "Well, hell! I could do better than this!"

Only they couldn't. Naomi said that before it was Grandma's it was the J&J, and before that it was the Courtview Diner, and before that it was Roy's Restaurant. None of them had made it for more than eighteen months. Grandma was halfway to that fatal mark, having opened in July of the previous summer, just before I arrived in Durel County.

If the midafternoon crowd was any kind of barometer, Grandma may have found the secret to success in the restaurant business in Appalachia. She had transformed the storefront into her own dining room with round tables, checkered tablecloths, blue china, unmatched silverware, and linen napkins. There were only two sandwiches on the menu: one-third-pound hamburger and grilled cheese. The rest was given to huge breakfasts (served all day) and dinners. The specialty of the house was fruit or vegetable pie—apple, cherry, blueberry, blackberry, raspberry, pumpkin, rhubarb, and sweet potato.

Grandma Simmons, herself—a little wisp of a woman with osteoporosis, gray hair, and chin whiskers—took my order for beef stew over jumbo buttermilk biscuits. I passed on the pie; LeRoy's suit pants were pinching my love handles as well as my conscience.

Naomi came in just as one of Grandma's granddaughters brought my iced tea (sweet) in a pint Mason jar and my conscience got another pinch. Naomi looked wonderful. Robust. Athletic. Healthy. Her lush figure was set off by a black mini-dress with a white collar and a small gold cross hanging just above the V of the neckline. Her black hair was down in a pageboy that caught the light and reflected in blues and greens that set off her hazel eyes. Her cheeks were flushed and her smile was fresh and innocent with the tip of her tongue peeking out between her teeth.

I fell in love all over again.

She bent over me, kissed me hard, and said, "M-m-mh." Then she sat down next to me at the round table and took a big gulp of my iced tea. Grandma's granddaughter appeared at her shoulder and she ordered the grilled cheese sandwich and coleslaw. Finally, the business of lunch taken care of, she leaned her cheek on her hand and looked at me, still smiling.

"You look good enough to eat," she said. "New suit?"

"Maybe," I said, shrugging. "It's LeRoy's. I'm hoping he doesn't remember who he loaned it to."

"LeRoy Whiteker's? You're wearin' LeRoy Whiteker's suit?" She looked at it again. "I bet this is a good story."

So I told her the whole story. Everything from Calvin Haines's death to his funeral. It took us through most of my beef stew and all of her slaw and grilled cheese. Grandma's beef stew had just enough brown sugar in the gravy to awaken my sweet tooth, so I broke down and ordered the sweet potato pie. Naomi said she'd just have a bite of mine.

"So you got the dogs?" she asked, grinning.

"They're over at LeRoy's right now, playing with the kids. I'm picking them up on the way home."

"What you gonna do with them?" she asked, slicing off a paper-thin piece of my pie and dabbing it in the whipped cream.

"Ray wants them. I guess they're evidence." She nodded, thinking, eating my pie. A whole bite this time. The race to the crust was on. "What about you?" I asked. "How's the tax business?"

My pie was now safe. She laid down her fork and rolled her eyes and her face came even more alive than it usually was. "Don't ask! My lord, Dan, these people are a mess. You should see the way they keep records."

"Worse than me?" Mine had been the first tax return she had prepared that year, digging through my shoebox full of receipts. She laughed out loud.

"Ha! These folks make you look like a C.P.A." And with that she was off, talking in a language I didn't understand and, in truth, didn't care to learn. Money was never really interesting to me. Oh, I like it well enough and it's more fun to have it than to not have it, but it's not something I give a lot of thought to. Lots of ministers are like that. If I can keep my car running, pay the rent, and still have enough leftover for comfortable shoes, books, pipe tobacco, and a bologna sandwich now and then, I'm happy. My ex-wife found my attitude infuriating. I think Naomi looked at it as a challenge.

So she talked. On and on and—I'm not proud to admit it, but—to this day I can't recall even a single word of what she said. I put on my interested and concerned face. I laughed where I should laugh and I shook my head where her tone indicated that a head shake was appropriate in affirming her own exasperation. I was attentive and empathetic, and I didn't hear a word she said until the pie was gone, the coffee was cold, the iced tea was warm, and she looked at her watch and said, "Oh, my gosh. I've got to get back. I'm supposed to meet. . . ." Someone. I don't even remember who it was.

She kissed me again as she stood up to leave. "Maybe I'll get off early tonight," she said. "See ya." And she was gone.

I ordered another cup of coffee and, finding an ashtray on my table, I lit my pipe. Ray says that once you go south of the Mason-Dixon Line they not only have smoking sections and non-smoking sections in restaurants, they have smoking-required sections as well. We aren't technically south of the MD in Durel County, but tobacco is a cash crop here, and it is accepted with a lot more tolerance than it is up north.

I sat in my blue cloud and continued to think about what I was thinking while Naomi talked about tax returns. And if you think it was Treasure Haines and her lack of underwear, you're only partly right.

Mostly I thought about George.

Who was he? How did he get the puppies? Why did he get them? And what part did he play in Calvin's death? And what about the Foley family? That whole trip had been an interesting adventure, but it hardly seemed very productive.

I pulled my funeral notes out of LeRoy's inside jacket pocket, turned them over, and tried writing a list of questions that needed to be answered. They all led to pretty much the same place: Who killed Calvin Haines and why? List making isn't my style. I'm more a stream-of-consciousness kind of guy. You put the ingredients—facts, questions, ideas, impressions—into the pot you call a brain and you let them bubble and simmer for a while and then you pour them out and see what you've got. Kind of like Grandma Simmons's stew.

Well, it works in sermon writing.

I paid the bill, left a healthy tip for Grandma and her granddaughter, and headed back to LeRoy's to get the pups and go home. Funny. Eight months in Baird and I already thought of it that way. Home.

Rudepohler and Co. were hard at work on the church steeple when I arrived late in the afternoon. I left the pups in the car and rolled down the windows, figuring I'd only be a couple of minutes, but I thought I ought to at least check in on the workers.

Walter was wearing a T-shirt that said CO-ED NAKED CONSTRUC-TION on the front with a hammer and saw crossed like a coat of arms. Under the graphics the fine print read PLUMB AND SQUARE IN THE COOL, FRESH AIR. He was wearing a different cap, too. Black & Decker, I think. He saw me pull in and motioned me over to the steps that led to the front door of the church under the steeple.

"Rot," he said, holding out a piece of wood for me to examine. I examined, not knowing what I was supposed to be seeing. He pressed his thumb into the center of the chunk which was about as big as his hairy forearm, and it flaked away like a dry sponge. "Leak in the roof let water in and rotted the wood supports." He tossed the rotted wood into a pile at the bottom of the steps.

"That why it came down?" I asked.

"Nawp."

Ah. Now things were obscure. "So what—"

"It was cut," he said. "Come on." He walked through some more trash, into the back of the sanctuary. Lying across the back of two pews was a rotted beam about eight feet long and six inches square. It was broken off at both ends. In the middle was a big metal contraption which was used to hold the bell. Walter pointed at one end of the beam and I could see where it had been cut about halfway through with a saw.

"Last crew that worked on it started the job and didn't finish it," Walter said. "See, it weren't flipped over, 'cause it was hung from a bracket on the bottom of the beam to prevent that from happenin'. Way I figure it, the bell wouldn't ring because the beam shifted and wedged it up against the side of the steeple. Last crew you hired to fix it started to and then realized what a big job it was gonna be an' said, screw it." He paused for a moment, realizing where he was, and then shrugged. "Anyway, the cut in the beam weakened it and when I put my ass into it she broke through and came down."

I was looking at the cut in the beam and thinking about a phone call I had received. *Let it be. Leave it alone.* What did that guy say? Something like that. The wood was so old I couldn't tell how old the cut was, but I knew that no one had ever been hired to fix the bell. Maybe someone didn't want us to find those pups and was willing to demonstrate that desire in more than just words.

No. That was just paranoid. Someone in the church had probably tried to be Mr. Fix-it and given up when he saw the enormity of the task. I'd check with Ray.

"You okay, Reverend? You look a little peaked."

I shook off a little chill that ran up my back. "Yeah, I'm fine. Just thinking about yesterday. I don't think I thanked you for that push."

Walter chuckled. "Thank John. He's the one what broke your fall."

I put out my hand and he took it in a strong, sandpapery grip. "I'll do that," I said.

"What you got in your bug, there?" he asked as we walked back down the steps toward the road.

The pups had been wound up from playing with the Whiteker kids and they had bounded all over the interior of the VW and the exterior of me as we drove through Perry. Once we were out on the road, however, they had huddled into a big ball of beagle fur on the backseat and fallen asleep. Now, as Walter and I approached, they were bounding again, having awakened from their nap, their energy renewed. Upon seeing us coming toward them, they went into a frenzy of yipping and yapping.

"Well, lord, look at that," Walter said. Then: "Hey, John, come look at this."

John materialized from the dust around the steeple and walked over, a smile breaking across his face. "Well, I'll be. You a dogger, preacher?"

I shrugged. "No, I'm just getting ready to deliver them to Ray Hall. They were Calvin Haines's pups. I guess they're evidence in his murder."

They were both looking at me with their mouths open. When I stopped talking they looked at the pups and then back at me.

"Them are the Wishbone/Trueblood pups?" John said.

"Erasmus and Marietta's?" Walter said.

"I'll give you a thousand dollars for one," John said.

"I'll give you twelve hundred for first pick," Walter said.

"Fifteen," John said.

I held up a hand. "Uh, guys. They're evidence. You'll have to talk to Ray Hall about it."

They looked at me again and both nodded, then they walked away arguing. "I seen 'em first."

"I made the first offer."

"Pissant offer, you cheap prick."

"Gotta start somewheres."

"Well, I'm startin' with choice female. I'll pay two thousand dollars."

"The hell you say."

Like that.

Ray and May June hadn't come back from Perry, and Darnell Kody was minding the store and post office. May June was serving turkey for dinner so she didn't have to stay around and cook all day. All Darnell had to do to the three turkeys was put them in the oven at the right time and turn up the flame. The smell of roasting turkey permeated the diner. It's one of those smells you love or hate. I love it.

Darnell was peeling potatoes when I arrived with the pups and he was only too glad to take them off my hands. He said they'd be good company for Little Ray and he'd turn them over to Ray when he and May June got back from town.

When I left the diner one pup was licking the metal leg of a table, one was chewing the cuff of Darnell's pants, one was chewing his own tail, and the other three—Little Ray, included—were sniffing the floor searching out microscopic particles of dropped food.

Darnell was peeling the potatoes and talking to them like they were a group of friends who had dropped by to keep him company. "I thought what we'd do is, I'd finish these-here potatoes and then we could go out and play some ball or maybe chase some squirrels. Whata y'all think about that? Gotta get that chasin' instinct in you while you're young. Maybe work on your barks a little."

I decided that the beef stew and jumbo biscuits were going to leave no room for turkey and dressing. I went back to the house in time to wave good-bye to Rudepohler and Co. and give a quick inspection of the work to date before I went in to put up my feet and do some serious reading about the Civil War. My inspection took about thirty seconds as I couldn't tell what the hell was going on and didn't really care as long as someone else was doing it and paying for it.

The reading became napping, and when I woke up it was dark out and I was hungry again. Well, not hungry exactly, but wanting to eat. I think it had more to do with the empty house than with my empty stomach. Turkey and dressing still didn't sound right so I made myself an egg sandwich and opened a Diet Pepsi and turned on the network news. People were still killing each other in ever more brutal and inventive ways. Three big trials were keeping the cable watchers glued to their sets. The President's approval rating was down. Teenage pregnancy was up, as were hard drug and handgun use. Reading and math scores were down. Some were blaming the President. Some were blaming Satan. And some were blaming God. No one was blaming himself, of course. It was depressing and the egg sandwich was giving me indigestion.

I thought about calling Naomi but didn't. It was too late or too early or something. To tell you the truth, I'm not sure why I didn't call her but I didn't. Who knows? I decided to take a walk instead.

I picked up my pipe, keys, and lighter, and put on my Bengals jacket and a VW gimme cap Ray had given me for Christmas as a gag, then left the house unlocked.

It was chilly for April but not cold. The sky was clear and the stars were bright like tiny chips of crystal. The air was clean and crisp and it felt good to be outside. I walked north along Route 42, away from the diner, down past Weems's big house (he owns Weems Hardware in Perry and Weems Sawmill on Pine Tree Mountain). About two hundred yards and I was then at the edge of town so I turned around and walked the other direction, south on Route 42.

When I got to the Mountain Baptist Children's Home, I crossed the road and walked up the long, semicircular driveway. The place was dark except for a couple of lights in the dorms. All the way up the driveway to the main building and back down to the road on the other side and I was at the south end of town, right next to the Baird Volunteer Fire Department, under the only streetlight in town.

I crossed the road again and thought about going into the diner to see what was going on but decided against it. I wanted to find out what Ray discovered about junkyard Crazy George, but I knew he wouldn't discuss it in front of customers and the place was still hopping and noisy. I ducked into the store, picked up a quart of cherry cordial ice cream out of the little freezer in the corner, and left the money for it on the counter. May June wouldn't have let me pay if she had seen me, but she was busy with customers in the diner on the other side of the wall and at times like that she used the honor system in the store.

Back out on the street I walked past Aunt-tiques, which was still closed. Past the small dormitories that the church had built for the city kids who come down to do mission work and home repair for the poor and elderly, and back toward the church. Not much of a walk, but better than nothing, I figured.

Treasure Haines's black Toyota was sitting empty in front of the house. She came out of the screen door as I was clomping up the steps. "Oh, there you are," she said. She closed the door behind her and shrugged. "Sorry. I knocked and when you didn't answer I thought maybe you were in the church or something, so I kinda invited myself in."

"It's okay," I said, meaning it. She was wearing a white T-shirt, blue jeans, gym shoes, and denim jacket. Her makeup was soft and nearly invisible, giving her a relaxed but sassy look that was very becoming. She looked great. "We're not much on privacy here," I continued. "I don't think Ray bothers to knock. I'm just glad I wasn't in the shower." I tried a self-deprecating smile.

"Would that have been bad?" she said, flirting playfully, laughing and taking my arm. "What you got there?"

"United Dairy Farmers Cherry Cordial. Want some? I also make coffee." I held the door open.

"Sure," she said, letting one corner of her mouth smile. "I

shouldn't, but what the heck."

So I made coffee and dipped us both huge portions of that wonderful ice cream and we talked, sitting at the kitchen table. I told her about the investigation of her father's death and the arrest of Crazy George. Then, because she was a good listener, I talked about my background—my big churches and my big education—and then the affair and the divorce and how I came to be pastor of Baird Methodist Church. I talked about my ex-wife in a few neutral sentences and I talked about my kids until I embarrassed myself.

She told me about her life. Leaving Appalachia with her high school diploma and going to the big city of Cincinnati. She spent a little time being wild and crazy, she said, and then a lot more time working and going to college and nearly starving until she finally, after seven years, got her B.A. in library science with a minor in computer technology. Then three more years of shared apartments and rowdy youth and a master's degree and a job at the county library, and finally her own gig (her words) at Mount Saint Michael College. She talked about her father and her brother and her mother and she cried. And I talked about my kids some more and almost cried. And then we just sat there in the silence for several minutes, thinking.

"You miss your kids, don't you?" she said. She laid her hand on top of mine just like May June had done, but somehow it didn't feel the same.

I nodded, afraid to talk. Afraid of what I was feeling. Afraid to think about it and afraid not to.

Someone knocked at the door. I looked at the clock on the wall above the stove and noticed that it was about quarter after eleven. Ray might knock at the time of night. May June certainly would. The only other person I knew who would come to my house that late and who would knock on the door was Naomi.

I swallowed.

I got up, feeling guilty and feeling stupid for feeling guilty. I hadn't done anything wrong. And feelings don't count, do they? Or fantasies?

I turned on the porch light and opened the door. Before it was even three inches open a handgun about the size of a howitzer swung up through the opening and stopped, pointing at my face. A gravelly voice on the other side of the door said, "Turn it off."

I turned the porch light off.

It wasn't Naomi.

CHAPTER 14

THERE WERE THREE OF THEM. The one with the gun was shorter than I, maybe five-eight or so. He hunched his shoulders under a herringbone topcoat, and his face was pinched like he had just smelled something rotten or sour. He squinted like his eyes hurt.

The second guy was about my height or maybe a little more. He was lean and angular but not the way mountain people are. His was a gray, unhealthy, city kind of lean with bones sticking out on his face like a bag of horseshoes. He wore a dirty, tan, belted trench coat hanging open and a black suit with a white shirt and thin black tie.

Number three was big, heavy, and mean looking. He was probably six-three or -four, and his brown knit sport coat had to be a size fifty, and even then I don't think it would have buttoned around his gut. His face was pocked with acne scars and his nose had been broken, probably several times. He was sweating, not wearing a topcoat, and he smelled of cooking spices.

Pinchface looked at us while the other two looked around the living room of the parsonage. After they all seemed to get their bearings, he waved the gun around at waist level like they used to do in the gangster movies.

"Over there."

I looked at Treasure and she shrugged.

"Over where?" I said. I was filled with an unnatural desire to laugh. This was too ludicrous.

"Center of the room," Pinchface said.

Treasure and I moved to the center of the living room between the television and the couch, next to the coffee table. "Here?" I asked.

"Strip."

"Excuse me?"

"Your clothes," he said, smiling. "Take 'em off."

"Why?" I no longer wanted to laugh.

He brought the gun up and sighted down the barrel at my face. "Because I got a gun, and I said to."

Treasure said, "Oh, great," and took off her denim jacket. She started unbuttoning her blouse.

"There you go, tiger lady," said Pinchface. "You, too, Reverend."

The other two men were watching Treasure. She didn't seem to notice, or if she did she wasn't about to give them the satisfaction of being embarrassed. She was now defiantly bare-chested, unbuttoning her jeans.

I started getting undressed. "You seem to have the social advantage on us," I said, trying to sound flip. It went right by them. "You know who we are but you haven't introduced yourselves."

"You couldn't leave it alone, could you?" Pinchface said. The other two kept watching Treasure. The big one was smirking.

"I'm sorry?"

"The old guy over in the valley. The one with the mine and the dogs. You just can't leave it alone, can you? You and that constable just gotta keep stickin' your noses where they don't belong." He didn't seem interested in Treasure at all. He was watching me. I hoped it was because he thought I was a threat.

"Look," I said, stumbling around over my blue jeans, trying to get them off. "I'm a minister. I buried Calvin Haines because I was his minister. I don't know who you are or what you're talking about or what it is I'm supposed to leave alone."

"I'm Lewis, this is Bobby, and that's Franklin," he said, pointing to the skinny one and the big one in order. "Franklin likes to be called Frank."

"How ya doin'?" big Frank said, smiling at me.

"I've been better."

"What we're talkin' about here is you not doin' what you're told. What we're talkin' about is me tryin' to tell you to leave it alone and you actin' like you got rocks in your head or somethin'." Pinchface was getting angry, waving the gun around. "Everything. Socks, too."

Treasure and I were in our underpants and socks. We removed the rest of our clothing. I left mine in a pile at my feet and she tossed her panties defiantly at his chest. She didn't even try to cover herself. I wanted to, but it didn't seem right if she was going to be so damned brave.

Bone-face Bobby went into the kitchen and came back out carrying two chairs. He placed them in front of the television, back to back, kicking the coffee table over so they would fit. He said, "Sit."

We sat. Frank pulled several pairs of handcuffs out of his sportcoat pockets and chained us together and to our chairs. Ankles to the chair legs, wrists together, and then around the backs of the chairs. We could wriggle but we couldn't really move.

Pinchface Lewis sat on the couch facing me and crossed his legs. I could feel Big Frank move in behind me, facing Treasure. I could also feel my breath begin to shorten and my heart double its pace. Fear. Cold, nauseating fear. Bobby started wandering around the room, knocking things over, breaking things.

Lewis lit a cigarette and considered it, examining its length, enjoying the taste of the tobacco and the rush of the nicotine.

At length, he spoke. "What are we going to do with you, Reverend?"

I decided that it was a rhetorical question. I stayed quiet. Bobby knocked over the bookshelves I had built from cinder blocks and one-by-eight-inch pine boards.

"You and that constable are like a couple o' old ladies. Bothering people. Asking questions. Making trouble. You keep that up, someone could get hurt."

Big Frank took that as his cue and hit Treasure. From the sound of it, it was an open hand slap, but Frank's hands were as big as baseball gloves. Treasure's head snapped back into mine and we both nearly went over. Treasure groaned and I strained against the handcuffs.

"What do you want? Just tell me and I'll give it to you," I said, trying not to sound as desperate and afraid as I felt.

"Oh, yeah, now you want to cooperate. I tell you, it does my heart good to see chivalry still alive. A man wanting to protect a poor defenseless woman. Sell your own soul to protect a woman, wouldn't you? Can't stand to see her hurt."

Frank hit Treasure again. This time backhanded, because she tilted the other way. She tried to stifle a scream but it slipped out, sorrowful and full of pain.

"Please!" I begged, letting the desperation out. "What do you want?"

Lewis looked at his cigarette again. "You know, for a little thing, a cigarette can cause a whole hell of a lot of pain. Say if I was to put the hot end of it against some particularly delicate part of your body." He paused and looked me up and down. Smiled. "Or hers."

This time Treasure jumped straight up, straining against the chair, and her scream was muffled only because Frank had obviously clamped his hand over her mouth.

I raged and struggled and lunged against the cuffs and all I managed to do was pull a muscle in my back and make my wrists bleed. When I had worn myself out, I quit. Treasure was crying. She just kept saying, "Please. Please. Please."

Lewis leaned forward and put his elbows on his knees. Took a last deep drag on his cigarette and crushed it out on the edge of the coffee table. "I got your attention now, Reverend? You listenin' real good?"

Tears of frustration and rage ran down my face and dripped off my chin. They made me feel even weaker and more humiliated than I already did, if that could be possible. "Yes. Yes, please."

"I'm only gonna say this one more time. I don't like repeatin' myself, but I'm goin' out of my way because you're a man of the cloth. Now you listen really carefully and try to remember and then you go down the road and you convince that old fart constable, okay?"

"Yes. Yes, I'll tell Ray."

"That's good. Now here's what you're gonna tell him, Reverend: Leave . . . it . . . alone. You got that?" His face was an inch from mine. He smelled like garlic, bacon grease, and Aqua Velva. "No one gives a damn about that old hillbilly that killed himself. Killed himself, you got it?" He tapped the gun against my forehead with each word. "You . . . got . . . it?"

"Yes. I've got it."

He stood up and called into my bedroom. "Bobby, you ready?" Some more crashing and banging came from the bedroom and then Bobby said, "Yeah, I guess."

Lewis surveyed the room and nodded. "Well, okay then. Let's go." He looked down at me. "You'll remember now, won't you, Reverend?"

I nodded, ashamed to look him in the eye.

"Because the next time I won't just play with you like I did this time. Next time, I'll kill you and the lady here. And you know what? I'll have fun doin' it."

I just kept nodding.

"Okay, then. Sleep tight."

I felt a pin prick in my arm and turned to see big Frank smiling at me as he depressed the plunger on a hypodermic needle that was buried in my bicep. I started getting dizzy almost immediately and felt my eyes get heavy. The last thing I heard before I blacked out was Treasure crying, saying, "No. Please, don't." And then I was out.

"Well, can you get 'em off?"

"Yeah, but it'll take me a minute or two. Okay?"

"Okay, fine, Darnell. Just get the damned things off, will ya?"

I felt something tug at my arm and fumble at my wrist and, then a click and the pressure was off and my left hand was free. The blood began to flow back into my hand and it burned and itched. Drops of blood dripped down the back of my hand from where my wrist was torn and raw.

Treasure was sobbing.

"She's movin' too much, Ray. You gotta hold her still or I can't get it."

"Treasure, honey, just hang on. We'll have you outta them things in a minute, okay? Just hang on."

The pressure on my right arm eased up as Treasure leaned back in her chair. Another click and my right arm was free. My ankles were still fixed to the legs of the chair and now I realized that a blanket had been laid over my lap.

I opened my eyes and closed them again immediately. The light in the room tore through my head like zigzag lightning. I groaned.

"Dan?" It was Ray.

"Mmm."

"Just hold on there, buddy. We'll have you outta this mess real quick. Come on, Darnell, will ya?"

A minute and two clicks later and I was free. I tried to stand up but sagged forward and Ray caught me and eased me onto the couch approximately where Lewis had sat. The old nylon upholstery scratched my back and butt but felt great.

I opened my eyes again in time to see Naomi helping Treasure out of her chair, catching a blanket as it fell from her shoulders, and easing her toward my bedroom. The blood from her nose had run down over her mouth and chin, and dried. There were bruises on her upper arms, and she walked with the shuffle of the abused and defeated. When the blanket slipped I noticed a round bruise high on the right cheek of her butt about the size of a half-dollar and then realized that it wasn't a bruise but a tattoo of a sleeping kitten. A remnant from those wild young days in Cincinnati. I felt so sorry for her.

Naomi draped the blanket around Treasure's shoulders and they disappeared into my bedroom. I could hear Naomi's voice, soft, warm, and consoling. The tap water in the bathroom went on.

Ray handed me a zip-lock plastic bag full of ice cubes and a cup of hot tea just as May June came through the front door with her granny-woman kit slung over her shoulder. Ray nodded toward the bedroom and she went in without saying a word.

I put the ice gently against my head and sipped the tea. They both felt wonderful. Feeling a little invigorated, I delicately stood and wrapped the blanket around my shoulders, doubling it over in front of my chest. That was all the movement my head would allow, so I sat back down.

"Naomi found you," Ray said, sitting on the other end of the couch and turning to face me. "She come and got me. Mother stayed behind and called Bless and Darnell, then she gathered her things and come up."

"Darnell picked the handcuff locks?" I asked.

Ray nodded. "Picked them with an old fingernail file and a little tiny screwdriver he keeps just for doing locks."

"There were three of them, Ray," I said.

"You don't need to talk about it right now," he said. "We can do this tomorrow."

His gentleness infuriated me and made me feel like crying at the same time. Never in the big, bad city had anything like this ever happened to me, not so much as a picked pocket or a stolen hubcap. I'd lived in the city most of my life and never even seen a rat until I moved to the country. Now I'd seen three of them. The two-legged kind.

"I felt so . . . so useless," I said, my voice breaking. "He just kept hitting her and I didn't know what—"

"It's a hard thing for a man," Ray said. He patted my knee.

I fought back the tears. "Lewis, Bobby, and Franklin-likes-to-be-called-Frank," I said. "No last names." I described them. "They weren't from around here. They didn't have accents."

"Funny," Ray said. "I always thought it was you northerners who had the accents until I was in the Army. Then I learned that it was us rednecks that talked funny."

We sat there for a few minutes. Listening to the murmur of the women's voices coming from the bedroom. Ray took my tea mug and refilled it. Brought it back to me.

"What about Crazy George?" I asked.

Ray shrugged. "High as a kite. Probably cocaine and cheap whiskey. I left him in the jail to come down. We'll talk to him in the morning. Elias knew him."

Elias Knowly was the big bubba who served as chief deputy to sheriff William B. Fine. Naomi had dated Elias in high school, and he still carried a considerable torch for her even though he was married and had kids. He was as honest and decent as the day is long and I liked him even though he was ambivalent about me.

"Elias? He knows Crazy George?" I asked.

"Knows about him," Ray said. "Seems he's kind of a legend with the kids in town. They go out to the junkyard and torment him when they're bored. The kids, not Elias."

"Nice."

"Yeah. Eli says they've run him in a couple o' times. Always high. But they can't find his stash in the junkyard and they don't much like the idea of lookin' for it in all that crap." Ray lit a cigarette and leaned back on the couch, resting his head on the back, looking at the ceiling.

"Where's he get his drugs?" I asked.

Ray shrugged. "Who knows? Cocaine's easy to get, you know where to go and who to ask. Probably grows his own weed there in the junkyard—and now I think of it, he probably laces it with angel dust. He's got that wild look about him." He blew smoke at the ceiling. "None of this makes a damned bit of sense."

"Why'd they come after me?" I asked, leaning back and looking at the ceiling with Ray. There was a cobweb in the corner and some small cracks in the plaster.

"And why all this trouble over some dogs?" Ray added. "I mean, they're valuable and all, but, lord, they're just dogs." He closed his eyes and massaged the bridge of his nose.

"These guys didn't strike me as doggers, Ray."

"Oh, they ain't. They don't give a damn about no dogs. It's the money. Anytime you got big money involved you can just about count on it drawin' in nasty types from all over. They came after you because you're an easy target. Preacher's not liable to have a gun under his pillow." He chuckled to himself. "I heard this ol' boy one time say that the answer to ninety percent of all 'why' questions is either money or poontang. Whataya think?"

I smiled at the ceiling. It hurt my head but it felt good, too. "Why'd you rob the bank, Tom? Why'd you leave your wife and family, Dick? Why'd you quit your job, Harry?" I nodded. "Yeah, it works for me."

"Well, if you're laughin' you must be okay," May June said, coming out of the bedroom. "Let's have a look at you."

I took the bag of ice off my head and she shined a little flashlight into my eyes. "Hmm," she said, breathing through her nose. She prodded and poked around, but as always, her hands were gentle and reassuring, confident and strong. "Well, I'd say whoever done this knew exactly what he was doin'. Probably done it a time or two before. Just enough to put you out without doin' too much damage. Probably have a headache in the morning."

"I already have a headache," I said.

She looked at Ray. "What time is it, Dad?"

"Two-twenty-one," he said.

She looked at me with a what-did-I-say expression.

"How's Treasure," I asked.

"Well, she's bruised up a mite. I'd say them was some pretty strong hands what done them things to her, but they was educated hands, too. The kind what know how to cause pain without leavin' any lastin' marks. Nothin's broken 'cept her lip and her pride. I s'pect I could say 'bout the same fer you?"

I nodded and felt my brain banging around inside my skull. She picked up my hand with the ice pack in it and placed it gently back on my head. "Keep that there a spell," she said.

"Treasure," I said, again. "Did they. . . ?" I let it trail off.

"Naw. Beat her up and probably did some other things to hurt her. But they didn't molest her. I mean, they didn't rape her. I guess what they did was molestation enough." She looked around the house and only then did the devastation really hit me. There was nothing breakable that wasn't broken. Anything that was upright or neat before, was now on the floor, smashed, crumbled, and destroyed. "What were they lookin' for?" she asked.

I shook my head again. "Nothing. They were just being mean. Destroying for the fun of it. Pain for its own sake."

"My, my, my," she said, shaking her head in sympathy with my own.

"They must have had themselves a real good time," Ray said. "How about the church?"

"They didn't go in there while I was awake," I said. "They didn't even open the door to my office."

Naomi came out of the bedroom carrying a couple of sheets and a pillow and some clothing for me. She looked at me with tears ready to burst from her eyes, and finally she leaned down and kissed me on the forehead and laid the things next to me on the couch. She put her hand on my cheek and said, "I'll come over and help you in the morning. We'll talk."

She and May June left. Ray walked into the kitchen and came back out with his shotgun. "Thought I'd just stay and keep an eye on things," he said, settling into my reading chair.

"You think they'll be back?" I asked.

"Nope."

"Well, what are you—"

"Just makes me feel better to be doin' somethin'," he said. "Go to sleep."

I made the couch into something like a bed and laid the ice pack on the floor. I figured that any leakage couldn't do any more harm to the place than the three two-legged rats had made. Screw it.

Ray sat in the dark, smoking, looking out the window. I was glad to have him there. Tomorrow we'd talk to Crazy George. Did he know anything about Lewis and Bobby and Franklin-likes-to-be-called-Frank? How did he get the dogs? What was so important about those beagles that someone would kill Calvin Haines for them and then let George sell them for $100 apiece?

And what did Naomi want to talk about? Well, let's see, there was the wreckage in the parsonage and the attempts on my life and the beating that Treasure had received. But I didn't think that was what she wanted to talk about.

"We'll talk," she had said. I hate it when a woman says, "We'll talk."

Blessing Haines Keifer showed up about a half hour later. Ray quietly took her into my bedroom and he came back out alone. She slept in the same bed with her sister and they were both gone when I woke up at about ten o'clock the next morning. Ray was making coffee in my miraculously undamaged Mr. Coffee machine.

CHAPTER 15

"YOU LOOK LIKE HELL," Ray said, glancing over his shoulder as I came into the kitchen. I had managed to pull on the T-shirt and jeans Naomi had brought out to me the night before.

"Thank you. Good morning to you, too."

He tossed me a wet dish towel. "At least wash your face before you sit down at the table. You'll put me off my feed lookin' like that." He turned back to the stove and stirred a ten-inch skillet full of scrambled eggs. "You feel like eatin'?"

"Just coffee." I ran the dish towel over my face and head. Its damp coolness felt good and helped wake me up.

Ray nodded at the coffeepot. "There ya go." He sat at the table and ate the eggs out of the skillet with the fork he'd used to stir them.

I poured a mug of coffee, added milk and Sweet'n Low, and sat opposite him. He had managed to put some order to the kitchen. Swept up the broken stuff and closed the cabinet doors, mopped up most of the food that had been dumped out of the fridge. My head ached and my back and neck were sore, but that could have been as much from sleeping on the couch as from the ordeal at the hands of Pinchface Lewis and his friends.

"Where is everyone?" I asked, cautiously rolling my head, trying to loosen my neck a little.

Ray answered around a mouthful of scrambled eggs and Wonder bread. "Treasure and Bless left about eight. Naomi stopped by but said she didn't want to wake you up. Said she'd call you later." He considered his breakfast, went to the fridge and came back with a bottle of catsup, splashed some on the eggs. My stomach did a cartwheel.

"How'd she seem?" I asked.

"Naomi? Fine. Same as always. You know Naomi. Worried about you but, other than that, she's fine."

"Not mad?"

"Mad? Naw, hell. Why would she be mad?"

"She said she wanted to talk to me."

His fork stopped halfway to his mouth. "She did?"

"Last night, right before she left. She said she'd be down this morning to help me clean up and we could talk." I sipped some more coffee. It was starting to wake me up.

"What did she say, exactly?" Ray asked, chewing slowly.

"She said, 'We'll talk,'" I said.

Ray laid his fork down and pushed the nearly empty skillet aside, started his cigarette ritual. When he had his Camel going, he said, "We'll talk, huh?"

I nodded.

Ray nodded.

"We had our clothes on when those guys arrived, Ray. I didn't invite Treasure over. She came by to drop off my honorarium for the funeral and she seemed like she needed to talk. We talked here at the table and then those goons busted in and made us strip and beat the hell out of her and scared the crap out of me." I drank some more coffee and managed to slop it on my T-shirt. "Damn!"

Ray nodded some more. Lit another cigarette from the butt of the first, laid the pack on the table. Sipped some coffee.

"I guess I should tell that to Naomi, huh?" I said.

"I guess," Ray said.

I pulled a Camel out of his pack and lit it. We sat there for a few minutes, smoking, drinking coffee. The sun was out and a cardinal was singing outside the kitchen window like nothing had gone wrong at all.

I stubbed out the cigarette and sighed. "So what do we do now?" I asked.

Ray sloshed the dregs of his coffee around and looked at it. "Well, first of all, you go take a shower and put on some real clothes while I make some more coffee. Then you find your pipe so I don't have to share my cigarettes with you. Then you come back in here and sit right back down there and drink another cup o' this fine brew."

"Then what?" I asked, getting a little impatient with his recitation.

"Then," he said. "We'll talk." He smiled.

Showered, shaved, and dressed, my pipe full of Borkum Riff, my mug full of coffee, I sat once again across from Ray and told him the whole story of the night before. He was a good listener, not interrupting, but taking notes and nodding his head to give me encouragement.

Then when I was finished, he asked questions.

What did they look like, exactly? What were they wearing? How did they talk? What words did they use, precisely? What did the gun look like? Big? How big? What color? Revolver or automatic? Where did they stand? How did they move? Who did what, when?

Then he started back at the beginning and did it all again, probing, pushing, tweaking my memory. I never knew how amazing the human memory was. I remembered things I didn't realize I had remembered. I didn't even realize that I had seen or heard some things so I could remember them.

Like: They had arrived in a car, probably big. I hadn't heard the engine noise, but I had heard one of the doors chunk closed. Like: Lewis walked with a slight limp and Bobby was left-handed. Like: Franklin had a raspy voice and a missing eyetooth on the right side of his mouth. Like: Lewis dressed and smelled like a cheap hood but he lit his cigarette with one of those expensive cigarette lighters. Things like that.

Finally, Ray stopped asking questions. He leaned back in his chair and flipped through his notebook. Started his cigarette ritual again. "Why you?" he asked to the room.

"Like you said last night. I was easy," I said.

"Yeah, maybe. But I'm the investigator here. I'm the cop. So why'd they come after you instead of me?"

"Maybe they thought I would be easier to intimidate," I offered.

"Were they right?"

"Yeah."

He shook his head. "Nah. I woulda done the same thing you did in those circumstances. You lived through it, you did the right thing. It don't figure, though. If they wanted me to drop the investigation they shoulda come after me."

"They're not rocket scientists, Ray," I said. "Maybe they're just some dumb toughs who came down here or were sent down here from . . . wherever . . . and reached out to the first target of opportunity that came their way."

"And that's another thing," Ray said, standing up and putting his notebook in his shirt pocket. "Where the hell'd they come from?"

"Up north somewhere?"

He shrugged. "Maybe. Not havin' an accent don't mean a lot. When you lived in Louisville, you ever hear a local TV newscaster with a hillbilly accent?"

I agreed that I hadn't.

"Or a radio announcer?"

"Maybe on a country-western station."

"Lots o' people in this state don't have southern accents. Them what do, some work hard at losin' it. It don't take you far in the city 'less you're a lawyer or a preacher or a car dealer."

I sat and he stood. We listened to the cardinal. We smoked.

"It just gets muddier and muddier, doesn't it?" I asked.

Ray nodded. "Get your jacket," he said. "Let's go see if Crazy George can clear the waters a bit."

Elias Knowly, the chief deputy of the Durel County Sheriff's Department, is a big beefy guy who, at first glance, looks like he would just as soon tear your head off as say hello. He stands about six-foot-three-inches tall and probably weighs in at about 230 or so. He played running back on his high school football team and a knee injury stole his chance at college ball, so he went to the state police academy and came home to keep the peace in his home town. His chest and biceps stretch his uniform shirt, and his short dark hair is always parted as straight as an arrow. He smells like Old Spice and Listerine and leather, and every woman in Perry has a crush on him except his wife, who is fat and ignorant and vulgar. She wasn't always like that. Naomi says it's a hereditary thing.

Eli is as sweet a man as you would want to know, and after a brief conversation you realize that his face is an open book. He worships the water Ray Hall walks on and he couldn't tell a convincing lie if his life depended on it.

I knew something was wrong the minute we entered the Sheriff's office in the back of the county courthouse. I could see it in Eli's grim countenance.

"It ain't my fault, Ray." That was the first thing he said.

"What ain't your fault, Eli?" Ray said, but I think we both knew, or at least suspected.

Elias's shoulders sagged and he looked at his shoes. "He ain't here."

"Who . . . you mean George? George ain't here?"

Elias nodded without looking up.

"Well . . . what the hell, Eli?" Ray asked, more in exasperation than anger.

"Sheriff came in early this morning and said we had to cut him loose. Said we didn't have anything to hold him on, on accounta you didn't fill out any papers or nothin'." He looked up and shrugged.

Ray slapped the counter in the bull pen and a couple of deputies looked up from their coffee and donuts and just as quickly looked back at them again. "Damn it, Eli. I just wanted to ask him some questions. I didn't want to give him the chair." He looked around, a splotch of red creeping up his neck. "Where is that little peckerwood?"

Elias seemed to know instinctively that Ray was talking about the sheriff, not George. Even as second cousins, Ray and Sheriff Fine had little affection for each other, despite the fact that the sheriff thought he owed Ray a job as constable. Ray had saved his life when, as teenagers, they had gone swimming in an abandoned stone quarry. Elias looked around the office and spoke softly. "He's gone. Said he was goin' to Corbin this afternoon and said he won't be back till tonight. He's got a sheriff's meetin' tonight and they usually play poker after the dinner."

Ray ignored the NO SMOKING signs all over the office and lit a Camel. Finally he sighed, pointed at the deputies eating donuts, and said, "Well, get a couple of those good-fer-nothin's and come on. If we gotta chase George outta that junkyard, we sure as hell ain't gonna do it alone."

So Elias brought three deputies in two squad cars and followed us out to the junkyard. It was good that they came along. It saved them time, in the long run.

We found George immediately upon arriving at the junkyard. He was lying face down in the mud outside the office shed, about thirty feet from the door.

The deputies and I fanned out behind their cars and Ray walked slowly toward the body, carrying the sawed-off pump shotgun from Elias's squad car in his right hand. When he got to the gate he racked a shell into the gun and leveled it at the shed.

"Don't expect there to be anyone still around," Elias said quietly at my side. "But you gotta be careful." I didn't think he was explaining things to me as much as he was reciting the SOP of the sheriff's department for his own benefit.

Ray walked as though he was negotiating a minefield, taking one step at a time, watching for any kind of movement from the shed or the piles of cars and trash in the yard. When he got to George he stopped and held the shotgun in one hand, still aimed at the decrepit old building. He fumbled around George's head and neck for a moment and then yelled without turning his head.

"He's dead." He glanced at the body and back at the shed. "Looks like a shotgun. Big shot. Tight pattern. Two, maybe three rounds."

Elias blew out a breath. "Pump or semiautomatic," he explained to me. "Shot him three times before he hit the ground." He hollered to Ray. "I'm comin' up."

"Come ahead," Ray yelled back. "Go right."

Elias made some hand motions to the other deputies and said to me, "Stay here and keep your head down." Then he and the deputies all moved at once, zigging and zagging, in and around each other in the yard. They all seemed to be moving in a crazy, prearranged maneuver that was designed to look like random movement but got them to exactly the place they wanted to be. I wondered how many times they had practiced this routine. Ray walked straight toward the front door of the shed, the shotgun aimed forward at waist level.

Ray and the deputies reached the shed within about two seconds of each other. Ray didn't even hesitate, he just kicked the door down and walked in. About thirty seconds later he emerged with the gun in his right hand, pointing at the ground. He walked straight to Elias's squad car and got on the radio. "Marge, this is Ray Hall out at the junkyard. Get two ambulances out here real quick, okay?" Something squawked over the radio and he listened. "No, none of us. But we got one dead and two hurt real bad so don't ask any more questions, okay? Just get the squad down here fast as you can."

Elias came running from the shed up to the squad car, flustered and breathing hard. "Damn, Ray. You're supposed to use the codes. Now everyone with a scanner knows where we are and what we got goin' on."

Ray gave Elias one of his looks. "Everyone with a scanner knows the codes, Eli. How bad you figure them Feuchs boys are?"

Elias shook his head. "Someone sure gave them an ass whippin'. Trent looks like his jaw's broke and his nose and maybe his collarbone. His face is beat to a pulp. Floyd's got a couple busted ribs, probably a concussion, and I think both of his hands is broke. Geez, Ray."

"You find their weapons?" Ray asked.

"Yeah," Elias said. "Dumb peckerwoods. Thought they was gonna finally get to use their rat killers and someone just took them away from them and got pissed off all over their heads."

Ray nodded and lit a cigarette while we waited for the ambulance. "Went canoein' with a couple good ol' boys when I was in the Army. Up in Minnesota. The outfitter told us there was some bears botherin' some of the campsites and which ones to stay away from. This one old boy I'm with, he pats his hip and shows the outfitter this .38 six-shooter in a holster on a western belt. Well, the old outfitter, he looks at that gun and he says, 'Son, you use that thing on a bear, be like yellin' "redneck" at a Klan rally. It's stupid, it pisses someone off, and it's likely to get you killed.'"

"You think someone said somethin' out of line, Ray?" Elias asked. The story had gone right by him.

"What I think is that Trent and Floyd didn't bring a big enough gun." He looked at me. "What d'you think Reverend?"

"I don't know that there is a big enough gun," I said, thinking about Franklin-who-liked-to-be-called-Frank—the guy who had beaten Treasure the night before.

"Who the hell are these guys?" Ray asked aloud over the roar of the Jeep. "What's their game? They beat up Treasure to scare you so you'll convince me to stop lookin' into Calvin's death. They kill George but they leave Trent and Floyd alive. Barely. They call you on the phone to warn you off. They cut the brake line in my Jeep—yeah, I forgot to tell you—it was cut. They go to all this trouble for some dogs, but they never ask anything about the dogs, and they don't even seem to know I have 'em."

"I'm staying with the hired muscle theory," I said. "Maybe they just do what they're told and don't think too much about it."

Ray tried to light a cigarette in the Jeep, failed, and flung it over his shoulder. We were headed back to Baird, Ray to think and me to clean the parsonage and work on my sermon for the next day. "They're not from around here," Ray said. "None of the deputies can recall seein' anyone looks like 'em in this county."

"No accent," I said, remembering.

"City," Ray said.

"Which one?"

Ray shrugged. "Louisville, Lexington, Cincinnati, Knoxville, Charleston, Nashville, Frankfort. Who the hell knows? We find out who they are, we'll find out where they're from."

I remembered something I'd read in a mystery novel. "Find the who and the who will tell you why."

"What?"

"Just thinking," I said.

"Yeah, me too."

When we got back to Baird, May June was directing a work crew at the parsonage. She had rounded up the Carmack twins and their plump, pleasant wives and several other members of the church and she had them hauling trash out of the parsonage and throwing it in the back of Walter Rudepohler's dump truck.

I climbed out of Ray's Jeep just in time to see John Rudepohler, Walter's bearded brother, hauling my broken nineteen-inch television set through the door under one arm. Under his other arm was the CD player my kids had given me. Something in my chest seemed to crack and the air went out of me.

I sat down on the porch and tried to breathe. Normally I'm not very attached to things I own. Since I moved to Baird I had tried to travel light, staying a nice, safe distance from my possessions. Something gets broken you just repair or replace it. No problem.

Last night I had been so worried about Treasure and so devastated by the humiliation those three guys had visited on me that I hadn't really thought about my property. Now I was watching people haul it out and throw it in the bed of a dump truck and I think I could have handled even that, except for the CD player. That, my kids had given me. It wasn't just a thing.

Ray was kind enough to sit down silently beside me and light a cigarette without saying anything.

"Damn it," I finally said in a sigh. The sudden depression had passed, along with the embarrassment and humiliation of being violated by bullies. Now it was replaced with a cold, smoldering anger. I hated those guys.

"It's just stuff, Dan," Ray said.

"It's *my* stuff," I reminded him.

"We'll help you replace it."

"My kids gave me that stereo," I said. "How are we going to replace that? The way they must have saved to buy it? The expectation in their faces when they watched me unwrap it? The joy in their voices when they showed me how to work with all the dials and switches? How are we going to replace those things, Ray?"

"You got a right to be mad," he said.

"Damn right I do."

"Well," he groaned, standing up. "I guess we're just gonna have to find them boys and knock some respect into 'em. Get 'em to tell us what this whole thing is all about."

"How? Where do we start?" I asked, depressed and doubtful.

"Don't know," he said. "I'll fret it over dinner and let you know when I think o' somethin'." He looked up at the steeple under repair. "You gonna come down to the diner for supper?"

"No, he ain't. He's gonna eat what I cook for him and then he's gonna let me give him a back rub." I looked over my shoulder to see Naomi standing in the door of my parsonage. She was wearing blue jeans and a dark blue T-shirt under a blue and gray flannel shirt which hung open. She had the sleeves of the flannel rolled up and her hair was pulled back under a blue bandanna. She had dirt smudged on her face and she looked wonderful. Whatever had broken in my chest started to mend and heal and warm at the sight of her.

"Oh, well, if you're cookin' maybe I'll eat down here," Ray kidded. He prodded me with his elbow and said in a stage whisper, "She don't cook for just anyone, you know."

Naomi came out the door and pushed Ray out of her way so she could sit down next to me. As she came, she called over her shoulder, "May June, Ray's pickin' on us. Make him go home."

May June poked her head out of the door and looked at Ray. "Don't be a pain, old man. Go on home and I'll make you some supper." Ray winked at us and started to leave but she stopped him. "Don't go empty-handed. Here, take this." She handed him a beer case full of cleaning products, rags, and rubber gloves. Then she herded everyone else out of the house and off the porch.

They all greeted me as they went, using the one-word greeting that was common among mountain folk and seemed, according to the inflection they used and the tilt of their head, to speak volumes.

This time, their heads were up and they looked me in the eye. Their eyes seemed serious but hopeful. The men shook my hand and the women hugged me.

"Reverend."

"Reverend."

"Reverend."

And so on, all filing past me, silently expressing how sorry they were about what had been done to my things, and assuring me with their presence that, to the degree that they could make it so, things would be put right.

When they had all gone, Naomi took my hand and led me into what was left of my home. The shelves were set back up and the books were lined up on their ends, neater than they had ever been. The broken lamps, which had come from the Mountain Baptist Children's Home across the road, had been replaced with exact duplicates. Likewise the furniture which had been broken. The only furniture in the house that was mine was a recliner, the bed, the Mr. Coffee, and the microwave oven. They were relatively intact. In the kitchen, the food had been cleaned off the walls and the refrigerator had been restocked with more food than I had bought in the previous eight months. The broken dishes had been replaced with a mishmash collection of spares from my parishioners' kitchens.

"I'm roasting a chicken," Naomi said, looking in the oven. "May June cleaned the cobwebs out of here and it looked so nice I just had to cook somethin'." She smelled like shampoo and lilac and Pine-Sol. She put her arms around my waist and backed me up to the counter. Looking up into my face, she kissed me on the chin.

"What about your clients?" I asked.

"I'm takin' the day off," she said.

"The whole day?"

"I got an appointment at eight tonight. . . ."

"Ah."

"We got all afternoon, Dan. Go take a shower. Then we'll eat."

"And talk?" I asked.

"Yeah. We'll talk, too."

She came to me in the shower. She washed my back and my chest and, well, eventually, everything. I tried to reciprocate but she wouldn't have it. Without a word, she soaped her own body and then used her body to soap mine again. When we were both cleaner than angels she led me out of the shower, patted me dry with a big fluffy towel, and took me to bed. She took charge there as well. Assertive and gentle, demanding and insisting and forgiving and more beautiful than any woman—any person—I have ever known.

We weren't exhausted and out of breath afterward. There was no sweating and shouting. We were together again, though. Connected. Fulfilled. The universe had tilted when I found Calvin Haines, and started tumbling when those three guys broke into my house. It completely flipped over when Ray and Elias and I had found Crazy George, dead in the mud of the junkyard. Now it was starting to settle back into its track again, lined up and level as it was supposed to be. The cardinal, which was back outside the kitchen window, was letting the world know that he belonged there.

We lay beside each other, Naomi's head in the crook of my arm. I decided to be the first to break the silence. "Is this when we talk?" I asked.

She stretched and rolled toward me, put her arm across my chest. "I guess so."

"She came here to drop off my honorarium for the funeral," I said. "She was hurting and we talked for a while. We had our clothes on when those guys arrived. I don't know why they made us strip, but it wasn't my idea and I sure as hell didn't get a kick out of seeing Treasure Haines naked and bleeding." There. I said it all just the way I had rehearsed it in my mind. Maybe a little heavy on the indignation, but otherwise effective, I thought.

"I know," she said. She yawned. Played with the hair on my chest. A few moments passed.

"You know?"

"Yeah. Treasure told me. Last night."

"Treasure told you."

"Yeah. She was bruised and bleeding and crying. But she was worried about you. She's somethin'."

"She came on to me out at the farm the day before the funeral," I said. I don't know why I said it. Confession is good for the soul?

"And you were flattered," she said. "You know she's got a tattoo of a lion on her butt?"

"I thought it was a kitten. I only saw it from across the room."

"You think I should get one?"

"No."

"Me neither."

This was absolutely the weirdest pillow talk I'd ever had.

"How you feelin'?" Naomi asked after a few more minutes.

I gave it a few moments' thought. "Better," I said.

"But still hurtin'," she said.

"Yeah."

"Still scared."

"Yeah."

"You found Mr. Haines and you handled it and you stayed on top of things even though you were feelin' down and missin' your kids. You went with Ray to tell Bless about her daddy and you were competent and professional. You helped Ray find Crazy George and bring him in and you did a funeral that was good and inspiring and you did it under difficult circumstances. And Treasure Haines gave you a tumble and you felt attractive and masculine." She propped herself up on one elbow and looked down into my face. "Then those three guys broke in here and took it all away from you. Stole it from you."

I just nodded.

She laid her head on my chest. "I had a girlfriend in high school was raped by her daddy's best friend," she said. "She didn't think she could tell her daddy. Thought he wouldn't believe her. So she came to me. We'd sit and talk for hours, her and me. Sometimes she'd just cry. She had all these feelin's but she didn't know how to sort 'em out, how to talk about 'em. I wasn't much help, bein' just a kid myself." She sat up a little in the bed and leaned against the headboard and I snuggled up next to her. She laid her hand on my head and played with the hair on the back of my neck.

"You need a haircut," she said.

I didn't say anything.

"After a while I couldn't stand it no more. I didn't know what to do so I told her she had to talk to someone. Someone who would know how to handle things. We finally decided on Reverend Mayhew. He was the circuit rider that served this church and the ones in Henderson and Kern's Pass.

"I went with her on Sunday afternoon after services. I was a Baptist back then but Daddy didn't go to church and Momma let me go with my friends to their churches sometimes. So we came here right after lunch and we went to services and then we went to see Reverend Mayhew. He always preached here in the afternoon.

"Well, it took her a while, but she finally got the story out. Cryin' and sobbin' and talkin' in little bits and spurts. But she got it all out. Reverend Mayhew was this big old guy, big as Ray with a barrel chest and a beard like the Amish wear and this baggy old suit that he wore all the time. He was kinda scary but you always knew that he was in charge. He didn't brook nonsense nor suffer fools gladly, my Daddy used to say. If there was a right thing to do, you just knew that he would know what it was. Do you know what I mean?"

I nodded against her stomach. "Charisma," I said. "Natural leadership ability. You don't know why you follow a person like that but you can't really help yourself. You just follow him. When he enters the room the air changes."

"That's it," she said. "Well, his eyes got about as big around as this pillow here. Then you could see him getting control of himself. He gets up outta that pew he was sittin' in and he comes over and sits next to her and he takes her in his arms like she's a little broken thing and she just falls to pieces right there. I never saw anything like it in all the weeks I'd been talkin' with her and not since, either.

"When she finally dried up he cupped her chin in his big ol' hand and he looked into her eyes and he says, 'Darlin', that man stole somethin' from you. Not from your daddy. From you. Now I'm gonna ask you to trust me to get it back for you. Can you do that? Can you trust me?' I never forgot those words."

Now I was sitting up, looking at Naomi. Tears were coursing down her cheeks but her voice was still steady.

"He told her to stay in town and wait. We went over to the store and had a Coke and then we came back here and we prayed and we talked and we waited. It felt like forever but it was probably only a couple hours. When Reverend Mayhew came back he had her daddy with him, and her daddy come runnin' down the aisle of the church and swept her up in his arms, him cryin' like a baby. He took her home with him, and Reverend Mayhew thanked me for bringin' her to him. Said it was the right thing to do and I was a good friend to her when she needed a good friend."

"What happened to the guy?" I asked. "The guy who raped her?"

"They killed him."

"Lord."

"They were hill people, Dan. We didn't have a constable then, Ray was workin' in the mines. The sheriff, if they'd taken the trouble of goin' to him, wouldn't have done nothin'. They exacted justice the only way they knew how."

I sat up and looked at her. "The minister?"

"Oh, I don't know that he pulled the trigger, but he was there. He went and told her daddy and her brothers and he went with them to face down the man that raped her. And when that man came outta his house he stood there on the porch and he laughed. Said she was a whore who asked for it and had been askin' for it for a long time. He said she wanted it and the only thing he was guilty of was givin' her what she wanted. And then they shot him dead right there on his porch. And him her daddy's best friend. Some of this I learned from my daddy, who learned it from her daddy. Some I learned from her. She said they told her the whole story."

"This girl," I said. "Do I know her?"

She slapped me on the arm. "It ain't me! Good lord, is that what you thought?"

"I just—"

"No, you don't know her. She's married now and livin' in Perry with her husband and three kids. He drives a truck and she and I still have lunch together sometimes." Naomi got out of bed and began getting dressed. Watching her get dressed was almost as much fun as watching her get undressed. "She talked with Reverend Mayhew every Sunday for nearly a year. Just the two of them. If it had been anyone else I would have been jealous, but you just couldn't be jealous of Reverend Mayhew."

"He must have been something," I said.

"Oh, he was. I felt like, if God was to walk this earth, he would look and act like Reverend Mayhew. And I was a Baptist."

I sighed, trying to picture the big old mountain preacher. "Where are the Reverend Mayhews of this world when you need them?" I wondered aloud.

Naomi sat on the edge of the bed. "Dan," she said. "Those men took something from you. I don't know what it was and maybe you don't either. But you know they took it. I wish I could go to Reverend Mayhew right now and ask him to help you get it back, but he's dead and buried ten years, now. I think you gotta get this thing, whatever it is, back for yourself."

"I have to kill them?" I asked, only half joking.

She didn't laugh. "I don't know. Only you know that. But I'll tell you what I do know. I've seen the people in this community when you are in that pulpit and I've watched their faces when you walk into a meeting. You're their Reverend Mayhew, Dan. Risen from the grave and big as life. They feel the same about you as they did about him. If there's a truth to be known, they're sure you know it. If there's a thing to be done, they're sure you'll tell 'em what it is. They believe in you and trust you. They'd follow you to Hell if you asked 'em."

"But?"

"But you gotta get your thing back first. Whatever them boys took from you. And you need a Reverend Mayhew to help you."

"Who. . . ?"

"Ray Hall. Go to him. Tell him."

CHAPTER 16

CONSIDER HOW MANY ARE MY ENEMIES, and how they hate me with cruel hatred. O guard my life and deliver me; do not let me be put to shame, for I take refuge in you. May integrity and uprightness preserve me, for I wait for you.

Naomi's roasted chicken was picked clean, the carcass in the freezer compartment of my fridge where, Naomi insisted, it would keep until I decided to use it for soup stock. I didn't have the heart to tell her I wasn't sure what soup stock was, much less how to make it.

The dishes were washed and put away and the house smelled of Pine-Sol and chicken. With all the broken things taken away, the place seemed almost too neat, too spare.

Naomi had gone back to Perry to do somebody's income tax return. Back to the numbers she loved almost as much as she loved me. I already missed her, but it wasn't that painful kind of missing that I had for my kids. It wasn't loneliness. I didn't feel like I was empty without her around, exactly. I just felt like there were a few more things I wanted to say to her and the time had run out before I could say them.

I think of that feeling now and wonder if it isn't really a good thing. I wonder if it isn't something we should cultivate with the people we love. Maybe we should plan time apart so we can build up a stack of things to talk about when we get together again. And then, when we get together, maybe we should part again, just before we get to the end of the stack. I don't know. I've counseled a lot of couples who have told me that they just don't have anything in common with each other anymore and thought they should get a divorce over what amounted to a lack of things to talk about.

Anyway, that's what was going through my mind while I sat in my office, looking down at my Bible, trying to focus on the passage that it had fallen open to—what I had begun to think of as the Calvin Haines passage. Psalm 25.

"O guard my life, and deliver me; do not let me be put to shame, for I take refuge in you." Verse 20.

The psalmist is talking to God, but all I could think of was Reverend Mayhew. Naomi's friend had taken refuge in him. He had

— 142 —

guarded her life and delivered her. He had not let her be put to shame. Lord, what a man he must have been. Naomi had said that I was like him but I couldn't see it. They didn't make Reverend Mayhews anymore. Where the seminaries had once made Reverend Mayhews, they now made . . . what? Well, whatever it was, it was politically correct, sensitive, well-read, empathetic, and largely ineffective. I thought about most of the ministers I had known over the years as colleagues and I wondered how anyone could ever take refuge in any of them. It was sad.

I wondered in whom Treasure Haines took her refuge. She had suffered more than I had at the hands of those three goons. To whom would she go for comfort? Who would guard her life and deliver her? I surely hadn't. I had let her be put to shame. So to whom would she go? Durel County wasn't her home anymore. Would she go to Blessing? If her father had been alive, would she have gone to him?

I thought about her standing in the kitchen of her father's house, crying over the Barq's grape soda in the fridge. Yes, she would have gone to her father. She had loved him and he had loved her. Not like I loved my kids, still hugging and kissing them when they were teenagers, laughing at their jokes, and not being too shocked by their language or their music. He was too old and too Appalachian for that kind of love. But in his own quiet, strong way, he would have loved her. One of the last things he had written on the legal pad next to his telephone had been her name.

Funny. What would make me think of that? Sitting in my study, looking down at my Bible, free associating over a cup of coffee and it just popped into my head.

And then I saw it. That is, my conscious mind saw it. Obviously my subconscious had seen it a long time ago and had just now decided to relay the message to the front. It was a lined, yellow piece of paper, folded into quarters and sticking out above the pages of my Bible along with all of the other little ribbons and bookmarks. I tugged it out and, sure enough, it was the rubbing I had taken off the legal pad beside Calvin Haines's telephone the day I had met Treasure at the old farmhouse.

I opened it and spread it out on the desk, tried to make sense of it. Mostly it looked like doodles. Squiggly lines running across the page, overlapping each other like those Palmer Method exercises you used to do in grade school so your cursive handwriting would look exactly like everyone else's. A few words were hidden in the squiggles. And a few names. Treasure. Blessing. Some names I didn't recognize if, indeed, they were names. There were some stick figures in the wide blank space at the top of the page and some stick animals along the left side, in the margin. And there, in the middle of the page, as bold as a beacon, was a number. Ten digits.

I called Ray.

"A credit card number?" I asked.

Ray gave me one of his looks. "Cal Haines never owned a credit card in his life. Most hill people still don't believe in 'em. The older ones don't anyway. Some of the younger ones get 'em and get in trouble with 'em sometimes."

"Maybe one of the girls," May June said.

Ray and I were sitting at the counter in the diner and May June was leaning over, trying to read the yellow sheet upside down from the other side. Ray took his wallet out of his pocket and extracted a Visa card. He caught my eye. "I moved outta the hills a long time ago. I got a library card, too. Wanna see?"

"I'll take your word for it."

He examined his Visa card for a moment, then said, "Sixteen digits."

May June frowned. We all sat there looking at the number, thinking. May June did something with her fingers, ticking them off against her thumb. Her eyes popped open. "It's a phone number," she said. She picked up the old rotary dial telephone from beside the cash register and laid it on the counter. "Try it."

Ray looked at the number. Considered it, then picked up the phone and began to dial.

"You've got to dial '1' first," May June said. "Them first three numbers is the area code, I'll bet."

Ray sighed, depressed the button, and started again. He listened. He raised his eyebrows. He hung up. He started his cigarette ritual.

"Well?" May June and I said simultaneously.

"Treasure," Ray said. "Her answering machine. Back in Cincinnati, I guess."

May June and I looked at each other. We looked at Ray. May June refilled our coffee mugs. "He called Treasure right before he died?" May June asked.

"We don't know when he called her or if he did," Ray said. "He coulda written that number on that pad anytime."

"Still. . . ," May June said.

"Yeah," Ray said. "Still."

"What?" I said.

Ray sighed. "I don't know what. But I guess tomorrow I'm gonna go out to Calvin's farm and have a look around like I shoulda done in the first place and see what I can see."

"I'll come along," I said.

"You gotta preach tomorrow," Ray said. "Or you gonna give up the pulpit and be a full-time deputy constable?"

I didn't know what to say. Naomi had said I should go to Ray Hall and tell him how I felt. Now I didn't know if I could. How do you talk about being violated and humiliated like that? Weren't real men supposed to suck it up and be tough and move on? And how was I supposed to—

"You okay, Dan?" May June asked. "You're lookin' a little pale and pensive?"

I looked at May June and her face was so open, her eyes so kind, that the dam broke. I told them. I just let it all flow out of me—the pain and the humiliation and the depression and the rage. And I told them about what Naomi had told me, about getting my thing back.

"You're mad," Ray said. "And it ain't just the furniture."

"And you're still a little bit scared," May June said.

"Yeah," I admitted. "I'm scared of those three guys and what they've done and what they could still do. And I'm scared of my own feelings, what I'd like to do to them. They'll come back, Ray. We won't back off like they want and they'll come back."

"You wanna stay here with us?" May June asked.

I hadn't realized until that moment that that was exactly what I wanted. I didn't trust my voice so I just nodded.

"You can stay in Ray Junior's room," May June said.

I looked at Ray and he nodded. Ray Junior had died in Vietnam. His room was kept exactly the way he had left it. Naomi had been allowed to use it last summer, when she was recovering from a minor car accident. Later she had told me that she felt like she was sleeping in a church.

"Thanks," I said.

Ray said, "It's okay." He nodded again, like he was confirming something in his own mind, but he didn't say anything else. After a moment he pushed the phone over to me. "You gonna get someone to fill the pulpit for you?"

I suppose that, in the back of my mind, I had been working on this problem all afternoon because I knew instantly whom to call. May June found the number for me, and the Reverend Doctor Jerome Bretz picked up on the first ring in his office at the Mountain Baptist Children's Home across the road. As always, he was working late.

"Reverend Thompson," he said, in that formal way he had. "It would be my pleasure to stand in as your second. As a matter of fact, this comes as something of an answer to a prayer." He had just a hint of a southern accent.

"Is that so?" I said, not knowing what to expect.

"Indeed it is," he said. "This is such a small village, word of your troubles has made its way to this office. I did not wish to presume, but just this morning in my devotional time I asked the Lord to guide me in how I might respond to you in the same spirit of Christian charity and hospitality you have offered to me. It looks as though, with this call, my prayer has been answered."

"Oh, well—"

"No need to thank me. It's the least I could do. Don't give it another thought. Good night." He was gone.

I replaced the receiver on the telephone and Ray spoke what I was thinking. "He's an odd little duck, ain't he?"

"I didn't tell him what time," I said.

"It's on the sign in front of the church," May June said.

"Oh, right."

"Strikes me as the kind of man who never uses two words when a hundred will do," Ray said. "And a little, well, tight, I guess I'd call it."

Yes, *tight* was just the right word to describe the bespectacled, stooped little man who now ran the Mountain Baptist Children's Home with singular seriousness and determination. "I think that under all that erudition and formality, there beats the heart of a good Christian bureaucrat," I said.

"Erudition. That means book learnin', Mother," Ray said to May June.

She smacked him over the shoulders with a dish towel. "I know what it means. You're gettin' mean now. You better go to bed. Come on, Dan, I'll get you settled in your room." She paused a moment, nodded once, and then moved on up the stairs to the apartment.

"I'll turn off the lights and lock up," Ray said. "Be up in a bit."

I was sitting in a rocking chair, smoking my pipe and watching the news on a Lexington station, when Ray came up the stairs into the apartment. As apartments go, it was pretty spartan. A living room with a little galley kitchen, two bedrooms, and a bathroom. The bathroom had one of those old, claw-foot bathtubs with a shower curtain that wrapped around it on all sides. The shower head hung straight down from the ceiling in the middle of the tub and was as big as a dinner plate. The only modern thing in the apartment was the television. It was big, maybe thirty inches, and they had a small satellite dish on the roof of the building.

Ray came in and dropped a gym bag on the floor next to my feet. "Mother go to bed?" he asked.

I nodded that she had.

"I called Elias. He said he'd put a deputy on Treasure and Blessing.

Naomi is staying with Percy and Gloria Mills, and a deputy will keep an eye on them, too. Probably wasn't necessary, but better safe."

I nodded again. "Thanks, Ray."

"I went up to the parsonage and had a look around," he said. "Brought you some clothes. You might want to check them out. Make sure they're okay."

"They'll be fine, Ray. Thanks. And thanks for letting me stay with you. I feel kind of silly, now that I'm doing it." I did, too. But I felt safe.

Ray shook his head. "No need for that. May June would have insisted if you hadn't asked."

"Really?"

"Sure. She's got a soft spot for you, you know. Couldn't stand it if somethin' happened. I don't know why. You wanna check them clothes out." He stood in the center of the floor, staring at the television, jingling the change in his pockets. Ray usually looked right at you when he talked.

I unzipped the bag and looked in. Underwear, socks, shaving kit, a couple of shirts, and a gun. I just looked at it lying down there in the bottom of the bag like an ugly, black, deadly monster from some faraway galaxy.

Ray stooped next to me and looked into the bag. "Colt Python," he said. "357 Magnum with an eight-inch barrel." He reached into the bag and pulled the gun out, holding it around the trigger and cylinder. He pointed at it with his other hand as he spoke. "Double action. That means you just point it and pull the trigger. Kicks like a son of a bitch, so use both hands just like you see on the TV cop shows."

"Is it loaded?" I asked, not taking my eyes off of it.

"Five rounds. The top chamber is empty so it won't go off if you drop it or catch the hammer on something. Just pull the trigger and it'll shoot fine. You ever fire a handgun before?" He handed it to me. It was heavy and it fit my hand comfortably. I know this sounds dumb, but it felt, well, masculine.

I nodded. "When I was a kid. My uncle had a twenty-two target pistol. We used to shoot at tin cans."

"Revolver? Like this?"

"Not this heavy," I said. The Python must have weighed two-and-a-half or three pounds. It was a little slippery from the gun oil. It even smelled masculine. Like wood and metal and oil and cordite.

"Well, the principle's the same," Ray said. "Only difference is that your uncle's twenty-two was a target pistol. This gun's got only one purpose, Dan. It's for killin' people. NRA can go on all it wants to about targets and huntin' but this gun's a man killer. You have to point it at someone, you point it at the biggest part of his body and you pull the trigger three times at least.

I brought the gun up in front of me with a two-handed grip just like my uncle had taught me.

"If you have to use it you'll be stressed and you'll feel hurried, but don't be. Just seein' you with this thing will give a man pause. That'll give you time to level it and squeeze off three rounds. Hell," he snorted. "The noise alone will probably kill 'em."

I sighted down the barrel and closed my left eye to look over the sights. I was aiming at the anchorman on the television.

"Don't try to aim. If you're far enough away to aim you'll probably miss anyway. Just point it and shoot. It'll stop a horse." We both stood and I let the gun hang at my side, beside my leg.

"Put it in the bag," he said. "Keep it beside your bed. If they come tonight, they'll come loud. That's their style. You hear someone stumblin' around tryin' to be quiet it'll be me gettin' up to take a leak. Don't shoot me."

I put the gun in the bag and noticed that all of the clothes in there with it smelled like gun oil. There was a box of cartridges rolled up in an undershirt. I called out quietly to Ray as he walked toward his bedroom. He turned and lifted an eyebrow.

"I thought all you carried was that little single-shot shotgun," I said. "I thought you didn't own a handgun."

"I don't," Ray said. "That one belongs to Elias Knowly."

"Eli?"

"After he heard what happened to you and then saw what was done to the Feuchs boys, he sorta insisted I take it. Said he'd get another one from the locker at the office." Ray smiled and shook his head. "He worries about me." He started into his bedroom and stopped and came back. "I got a shoulder holster and a belt holster. You can use either one if you want."

"I'd feel silly," I said. "Besides, how would that look? The preacher packin' heat?"

He shrugged. "Them Feuchs boys looked pretty silly, too, lyin' all over their shed in pieces." He started away and came back one more time. "Don't tell May June," he said.

I nodded, but he was finally gone. Closing the bedroom door behind him. I could hear his and May June's voices in mumbled conversation beyond the door. She giggled and then it was quiet. I turned off the television and went to bed.

I slept fitfully. The bed was twin-size and it was too short. The pillow was wafer thin. The room was a shrine to Ray Junior—trophies, model airplanes, pictures, baseball cards. I jumped awake at every creak and groan of the building. And there was this huge gun in a gym bag about a foot from my head.

They didn't come that night.

I woke up to the sounds of thousands of scampering little feet. Well, that's what it sounded like. It turned out to be twenty little feet clicking and clacking around on the hardwood and linoleum of Ray and May June's apartment. The Wishbone/Trueblood beagles had arrived.

They bounded into my room with May June's encouragement. "Go on. Go on in there and wake him up. He's in there sleepin'. Go on in and get him up. That's it."

In they came, sliding, skidding, bounding over each other, then up onto my bed. They licked my face and each other, then, satisfied that my face was clean, they turned around and stuck their butts in my face and sniffed every available surface of the bed. All of them but one.

I heard a little whine from below and beside the bed and rolled over, nearly dumping a couple of pups off. Down on the floor was what had to be the runt of the litter, looking up at me with a pitifully expectant expression on his face. I picked him up and put him on my chest so he could be with his siblings and he immediately slid off my chest onto the bed and tried to snuggle into my armpit.

"Oh, yeah. He's gonna be a real go-getter," Ray said from the door. "Full o' piss and vinegar, that one."

I pried the pup from my armpit and put him on the floor where he began wailing and crying as though the end of the world had come. It was heartbreaking, so I gathered his family and put them down there with him. They sniffed around for a few seconds while I sat up on the side of the bed, then they scampered out through Ray's legs, into the living room.

"Coffee's on," Ray said. "You want some breakfast?"

"Cereal?"

"Wheaties and Frosted Flakes," he said. "Maybe some Raisin Bran."

"Let's eat," I said.

"It's rainin'," he said.

"Of course it is," I said. From across the hills came the sound of a church bell, calling worshipers to church. I said a little prayer for the Reverend Doctor Jerome Bretz.

I came to the kitchen in jeans and T-shirt, my hair standing on end and my mouth feeling raw and pasty. My eyes felt like they had been sandpapered.

"You look like hell every morning," Ray said. "It wasn't just yesterday. Naomi ever see you like this?"

"She thinks it's cute," I said.

"Love's blind."

"May June gone to church?" I asked, to change the subject.

Ray nodded and plopped a bowl, a box of Frosted Flakes, a carton of milk, and a mug of coffee on the table. I sat, sweetened the coffee, and dumped in some of the milk. Filled my bowl with cereal and splashed about a tablespoon of milk over the top.

"Darnell came by and dropped off the pups for safekeeping while he and May June went to church," Ray said.

"What are you going to do with them?" I asked.

"Ah, just let 'em run around the apartment, I guess," he said, shrugging and watching the dogs scamper around the living room. They seemed to be fascinated with the fringe on the couch.

"I mean later," I said. "When this thing is all cleared up."

He sat down opposite me at the little table for two. "I guess legally they belong to Treasure and Bless. Part of Calvin's estate. I'll probably just give 'em back to them and they can sell 'em."

"What about Darnell's pup?"

"Well, I don't know what the law says about a thing like that, but the way I figure it, that pup is his. He paid for it in good faith. I imagine the girls'll see it that way, too. They're good people."

One of the pups started screaming and crying like he was dying, and Ray and I both looked over to the couch. The runt had one of his teeth caught in the couch fringe and couldn't get loose. I went over and unfastened the loop from his mouth and set him off toward the rest of the pack.

"There you go, Gideon," I said. "Free at last."

"Gideon?" Ray asked as I resumed my seat at the table.

"In the Old Testament, remember? He was 'the least of the brethren,'" I said. "Did you notice that all of the pups are males?"

Ray nodded. "It's uncommon, but not unheard of. They won't bring as much at sale as a breeding female, but they're still valuable."

"I wonder if the registration papers are at the farm," I mused.

"Well, if you ever finish your breakfast we'll just go on up there and find out," Ray said. He stood and started cleaning up the breakfast mess.

"I showered and shaved and got dressed in yesterday's jeans, a clean T-shirt, and one of Ray's flannel shirts, open and out. My high-top basketball shoes were the only ones I had, but they were fine. By the time we were ready to leave, the rain had stopped and the sun was peeking out through the clouds.

Ray left a bowl of water and a bowl of milk for the pups, who immediately pounced on the milk. All except for Gideon. He stood at the top of the stairs and cried as we left. The little wails pierced the quiet of the empty diner.

CHAPTER 17

CUT-THROUGH VALLEY looked much the same as it had five days earlier when we had left, after burying Erasmus Wishbone and Marietta Trueblood. The rain had rinsed the dust out of the air and off
the buildings, and by the time we pulled up in the front yard, the
house, the barn, and all the outbuildings shone like new.

The Haines sisters had taped a piece of cardboard over the win-
dowpane I had knocked out of the door and Ray punched it out of
the frame and reached through to let us in.

Inside the house, everything remained as it had been the day I
met the sisters to talk about the funeral. We had sat in the living
room, me in the rocker, Blessing on the couch, and Treasure in
the big wing chair. Our soda bottles were in the trash can in the
kitchen. The dining room table was still piled high with the stuff
that Calvin had collected there.

Ray stood looking at the big table and the six chairs which surrounded it, the bare spot where Calvin sat to do whatever it was
he did. "I guess this is as good a place to start as any," Ray said,
spreading his hands before him.

"What are we looking for?" I asked, feeling overwhelmed by the
mess.

Ray shrugged. "I don't know. A trail, I guess. Somethin' that
leads away from here and into the city. Somethin' that will lead us
to Lewis and Bobby and Franklin-who-likes-to-be-called-Frank."

"A flag," I offered.

"Yeah. Whatever doesn't fit."

I went in to the kitchen and found some plastic garbage bags
under the sink and brought them back. I didn't intend to throw
anything away. That would be up to Treasure and Blessing. But
we did have to sort the stuff in some way and putting it in trash
bags was as good a way as any.

It took two hours to go through all the stuff stacked on the table.
There were receipts for everything from dog food to groceries to fertilizer. There were canceled checks that went back five years and
income tax returns for the same five years. (He did his own.) Calvin
was virtually guaranteed a million dollars in twenty-two unopened
junk-mail packets covered with pictures of celebrities, and he was

desired as a member of nine book and/or record clubs. He must have sent a check to a charity at some time in his life, because he was on every mailing list of every do-gooder organization I had ever heard of and several I hadn't. Media evangelists of every stripe and persuasion promised him salvation as well as books and cassette tapes in exchange for a contribution. Ray, looking through the canceled checks, said that Calvin had sent a couple of five-dollar donations to a few of the more reputable charities, but nothing big or noteworthy.

Calvin's checkbook and savings account passbook were next to his work space and they were as unforthcoming as the rest of the stuff. He deposited money in his savings account until he needed it to pay bills, then transferred it to his checking account. Ray did some mental arithmetic and figured that there were no deposits so big as to be suspicious. Everyone knew that Ras had won some big prizes, so it wasn't really surprising to see them reflected in Calvin's savings account.

Ray sat in Calvin's chair and I sat at the other end of the table. We were rubbing our eyes, smoking, and drinking the last two grape sodas from the fridge. I had taken the big handgun out of the shoulder holster under my jacket and laid it on the table.

"Not a damn thing," Ray said.

I blew some smoke toward the ceiling.

"Nothin' about dogs. Nothin' about people from the city. Nothin' about drugs, or hidden gold, or moonshine, or nothin'. Damn."

I drank some grape soda.

Ray drank some grape soda and looked around for something to put his cigarette butt in. Note to cigarette smokers: Try a pipe. If you use a lighter to fire it, you don't need an ashtray nearly as often.

"Now what?" I asked.

"Now we do the rest of the house," Ray said. He poured some grape soda over the burning end of his cigarette and then dropped it into the trash can next to Calvin's chair. When the soda hit the cigarette it sizzled for a second and I had a flash of Pinchface Lewis blowing on the end of his cigarette and talking about how painful it could be when applied to certain areas of the body. I shuddered.

"It ain't that bad," Ray said. "We just go upstairs and take it one room at a time, check out the obvious places. If he had a secret hiding place we'll never find it anyway."

We started in Calvin's bedroom. Big oak dresser and chest of drawers. Brass double bed with handmade patchwork quilts. Occasional chair with dress pants folded neatly over the back. The wallpaper was floral and delicate, not at all like Calvin. Martha must have done the decorating.

The other two bedrooms were still decorated for their original occupants. One had obviously been shared by the girls and then by Blessing and her late husband. The two twin beds had been pushed together and the legs wired to hold them in place. They were covered with a single king-size bedspread. The rest of the room was decorated for and by teenage girls. Pictures of country and western music stars were thumbtacked to the walls. Stuffed animals stood on shelves. There was a makeup table with lots of lights.

Victory's room was straight out of Jack Armstrong: sports trophies, a gun rack with a .22 single-shot rifle and an ultralight spinning rig hanging from the hooks. The twin bed was shoved against the wall, and the top of the dresser was littered with the stuff that boys carry in their blue jeans pockets: interesting rocks, penknife, cigarette lighter, baseball cards, string, Chap Stick, combs. The footlocker at the foot of the bed was full of sweaters, baseball gloves, sweatshirts, and high school yearbooks. The closet was full of clothing Vic had worn the weeks and months before his death. The shelf above the clothing held baseball caps, some board games and jigsaw puzzles, and a small pink Samsonite suitcase full of money.

"Well, I'll be damned," Ray said when he popped the suitcase open on the bed. The bills were neatly banded and packed. The suitcase was about three-quarters full.

"How much do you think it is?" I asked.

Ray shrugged. "Let's count it."

We did.

Twenty bundles of twenty-dollar bills. Fifty bills to the bundle. Twenty thousand dollars. Ray examined the bands that held the money in neat little packets. The teller's stamps on the bands indicated that the money had been counted at a Lexington bank. Ray stood by the bed and started his cigarette ritual. He started to say something, then thought better of it and closed the suitcase instead. He picked it up and headed out of the bedroom and down the stairs. He went into the kitchen and put the suitcase on the kitchen table, opened the fridge and took out two Coors bottles, handed one to me, pulled out a chair, and sat down. So did I.

We drank. We smoked. We looked at the suitcase. I had no idea what I was supposed to be thinking about, but Ray seemed to so I left it to him. I wondered how Treasure was. I thought about Naomi and counted the days until April 15 when she would return to her cabin on Mt. Devoux, and wondered that I was probably the only person in America who was anxious to see that date arrive. I realized I was hungry and rummaged through the kitchen pantry to see what I could see. I found some sardines and saltine crackers, a can of Planters peanuts, some beef jerky, and a bag of Oreos. There was some trail bologna, hard salami, hard-boiled eggs, and cojack cheese in the refrigerator and it all seemed okay. The bread in the breadbox was moldy, so we had to settle with the crackers. I spread the little feast out on the kitchen table, opened a couple more beers, and ripped some paper towels off the roll by the sink. Hey, who says a throw-together meal has to be meager?

Ray continued to think while he ate. Directly he got up, went into the living room where he had thrown his jacket over a chair, and came back with my rubbing on the yellow legal paper. He sat it in front of him and studied it while he ate. I moved around beside him so I could see it too, being careful not to let any of the oil from the sardines drip on it.

Nothing had changed on the paper. Same squiggles. Same phone number. Same names. Same stick people and animals in the margins.

"Phone work?" Ray asked.

I picked it up and heard the dial tone, nodded.

"Call Treasure. She's probably at the diner with Bless. Ask if either of them knows why their dad would write German on his notepad."

I looked up the number for the diner in Calvin's phone book and Blessing picked up on the first ring. I told her who I was and asked to speak to Treasure. Treasure came on the line with a voice that sounded sleepy and sexy but was probably just weary. I asked how she was doing.

"Okay," she said. "Tired."

I didn't know what to say, so I said, "It's been a long week."

She made a laughing sound that wasn't really a laugh. "Yeah. It sure has."

"We're at your dad's place," I said.

"You are?" A little more life in her voice.

"Yes, we . . . that is, Ray . . . we were trying to find something, a clue or a lead that might give us some idea. . . ." I wasn't doing this very well.

"Did you find anything?"

For some reason I couldn't explain, I didn't tell her about the money. "Well, you know that paper I showed you? The rubbing I made of your dad's notepad?"

"Yeah," she said, like she sort of remembered it but not well.

"Well, we were looking at it again. Trying to figure out some of the things on it. Would you know why your dad would write German on his notepad?" I asked.

She paused for a moment, then said, "I didn't even know he knew German. What did he write?"

I looked over Ray's shoulder again and he pointed to a spot on the rubbing. "No," I said. "Not the language. The word. He wrote what looks like the word *German* on his pad. Does that word mean anything to you?"

Just a split second's pause this time. "No. Just a minute." I could hear her asking the same question to Blessing. Then: "Bless doesn't know anything about it, either."

"Okay," I said. I asked Ray if he had anything else. He shook his head and kept looking at the paper, sipping his beer. Back into the phone, I said to Treasure, "Well, take care of yourself. I'll let you know if we find anything else."

"Okay," she said. "Thanks for calling. And thanks for sending those deputies to look after us."

"No problem."

"Bye," she said.

"Uh, Treasure?" I said. One other question popped into my mind. "When was the last time you talked to your dad?"

"Oh, gee," she said. "Christmas? Yeah, I guess it would have been around Christmas. I didn't get down for Thanksgiving and I called then. He was expecting me to make it for Christmas and then I found out that I wouldn't be coming then, either, and about three or four days before Christmas I called him. He wasn't happy."

"Okay," I said. "Thanks again."

"No," she said. "Thank you, Dan." She hung up.

I cradled the phone and told Ray what she had told me about not talking to her father since Christmas. "And she says she called him," I added. "So why would he write her number on the pad?"

Ray shook his head but didn't say anything. He stood up, still looking at the paper, and walked through the house to the front porch. He stood there, looking out over the yard, the barn, and the rest of the farm. I stood next to him and lit my pipe. Glanced at the page again, through the cloud of smoke. It was the smoke that helped me see it, I think.

Through the blue-gray cloud I couldn't make out the words or numbers. Only the stick figures in the margins stood out, so I let my mind focus on them for a moment.

"Ray, what are these?" I asked, pointing to the animals.

"Birds, I guess."

"What kind?"

"Turkeys? I don't know."

"Ducks, maybe," I said.

"Maybe."

"You know how I found this paper again after I forgot about it?" I said.

"Yeah, in your Bible," Ray said. "You told us last night."

"Yes, but it was a little more complex than that. I was thinking about Calvin and looking into my Bible at a verse he had quoted to me. Then I looked back down at my Bible and there was the edge of the paper, sticking out from the pages."

Ray finally looked at me. He was lost. "Yeah."

"What I think happened," I said, "I think I saw the paper peeking out of the pages but it didn't register in my conscious mind that I had seen it. It was like one of those subliminal suggestions they used to put into movies. *Buy popcorn!*"

Ray nodded. I think he was beginning to follow me. "Have you been reading books again, preacher?"

"Several, in fact. They're real big on psychology and stuff like that in seminary." I looked back down at the page in his hands. "There's a whole field of psychology that deals with handwriting and what it tells about the subconscious, or rather what the subconscious tells about a person through his or her handwriting. The people who study this, some of them think that doodles tell even more than handwriting."

I pointed to the stick figures and the animals. "So what was on Calvin's subconscious mind when he made those drawings?" I said.

Ray turned the page this way and that. "Turkeys? Ducks?" He turned and went back into the house and sat at Calvin's chair at the dining room table where I had originally found the pad. He looked straight ahead and out the window across the table. Finally, his gaze froze. "Chickens," he said. He stood, walked out the front door and across the yard to the old chicken coop.

The building was devoid of chickens. There was plenty of evidence of their having once been present, though. Chicken feathers, chicken crap, chicken smells. The little building was about fifteen feet long and ten feet wide. One side was lined with boxes that were used as nests, two rows of them, one above the other with ramps running up to them. The other side had one row of nests about five feet off the floor. Below them were nine little openings with ramps heading down into the chicken yard.

We walked through the building, looking at everything. I sneezed three times in quick succession and Ray handed me a clean bandanna from his pocket. The light was dim, but we could see well enough because sunlight streamed through the open door and hundreds of little holes and cracks in the walls and ceiling. The dust that we stirred up sparkled in the sun's rays.

"You see anything?" Ray asked when we had walked from one end to the other.

I shook my head, holding the bandanna tightly over my nose and mouth.

"Worth a look," he said. "Maybe we should check the other sheds, too."

I nodded.

We started back down the coop to the door at the end and Ray stopped beside the door. A wooden feed box with a hinged top sat just off the floor, affixed to the wall. Ray opened the top and we looked in. A small wrinkled brown paper bag was all that was in it. Ray opened the bag and poured the contents into his hand. Photographs. Fourteen of them.

Twelve had been taken with an inexpensive thirty-five-millimeter camera with a small insufficient flash attachment. The center of each picture was slightly overexposed but clear. The image faded to black, however, around the perimeter.

The other two pictures were faded Polaroids.

The twelve thirty-five-millimeter pictures were of barrels. They were probably fifty-five-gallon drums. In some of the pictures the drums were upright. In some they were on their sides. Some were tightly sealed. Others were broken open and some kind of powder was spilling out all over the ground. There were stamps or placards or signs of some kind on some of the barrels, but the pictures were of such poor quality that they were impossible to read. The skull and crossbones, however, was obvious and clear.

The two Polaroids were considerably older than the other pictures. They were faded and the color was washed out, turning brown. They were curled at the edges, cracked and dried. In one picture a fat man in a suit was sitting on a chair. His comb-over hair was disheveled and his tie was pulled loose and he was holding a drink of some kind in his left hand. His right arm was around the waist of the young girl who was sitting on his lap. She wore only panties and a pouty expression, her smallish breasts pressed against the fat man's cheek. The other Polaroid was of just the girl. She was maybe nineteen or twenty years old, naked, lying on a stage between two brass poles with her legs spread and in the air. Her face could be seen clearly as she looked seductively into the camera lens through the V of her legs. She wasn't smiling in either picture. Even at that young age Treasure Haines knew that a smile would mar the striking beauty that seemed to center itself in her eyes.

"Treasure," I said, as much to myself as to Ray.

"Mmh," was all he said.

He shuffled the pictures in his hand and looked at the barrels again, going through them one by one.

"Can you make out what they are?" I asked.

"Nope. But I know where they are," he said.

I waited. He shuffled through them some more, slowly, looking at each one, nodding to himself. Finally he stepped out of the door and into the sunlight again. He looked up into the hills behind the barn.

"What?" I said.

"Coal mine," he said. "They're in a coal mine. An old one. Probably Calvin's." He put the pictures in the pocket of his jacket and started off toward the toolshed. "Run up to the house and see if you can find some flashlights or lanterns. I'll check the shed. You ever been in a coal mine before?"

"No," I said.

"You'll love this," he said.

The mouth of the mine was about twenty feet tall and fifteen feet wide. It looked like the opening of a cave, and cool air wafted out of it. Some thirty feet from the opening, two small iron railroad rails emerged from the darkness and ended abruptly at a pile of coal and rock about the size of my Volkswagen. Ray and I stood in the sun, looking into the darkness, smoking and shuffling our feet.

I had found a six-cell flashlight in the house and Ray had brought two twenty-minute road flares from his Jeep. He flipped his cigarette into the grass and sighed. "Well, here we go. We'll use the flares and keep the flashlight for later if they burn out. Stay behind me."

Just a few feet into the mine the temperature dropped about ten degrees and goose bumps popped out on my arms. Ray struck the flare and the interior was filled with orange light. I kept thinking about gas pockets and widow-makers.

The main shaft had a flat floor and the ceiling was about seven or eight feet high, with ten-foot-by-ten-foot rooms dug off to the sides. Ray said these were dig sites, places where the family had dug for coal, shoveling it into carts that would move up and down the main shaft on the tracks. A miner would use a small piece of dynamite to blast out the rock and coal, scoop it into a cart, push the cart out into the sun, and sort it into the piles we had seen outside the mine. Miners had to pay for their own dynamite, though, so the poor ones had to use a pick ax.

Fifty feet or so into the mine, the floor of the main shaft began to slope down at about a twenty-degree angle. Pushing a cart full of coal and rock up that incline, slipping and sliding on the wet floor of the mine, would be nearly impossible. Ray said they would use ropes to pull the cart up the incline, sometimes using pulleys and sometimes using a pickup truck outside the entrance.

Another one hundred feet or so and the shaft leveled off again. The barrels were at the bottom of the incline. We stood about twenty feet from them, and Ray took out his notebook while I held the flare.

There were thirty-eight of them that we could count. The ones in the rear were stacked two high, but the ones in the front were just thrown there, tipped over, yellow crystals flooding out of them. Some of the powder had mixed with the moisture on the floor of the mine and turned into a yellowish soup.

"Can you make out what's on the placards?" Ray asked.

I turned on the flashlight and directed the powerful beam at one of the barrels. The black skull and crossbones leapt off the white background of the sign and the word POISON was clearly legible. There was another piece of paper encased in clear plastic below the placard but we couldn't make out anything on it.

"What is it?" I asked.

"Poison."

"I can see that, Ray. What kind?"

"Well, just offhand I'd say it's M-E-B-S."

"What's M-E—"

"Methyl ethyl bad stuff."

"Ah."

Ray put his notebook in his pocket and took the flashlight from me. The shaft was starting to fill up with smoke from the flare. "When that goes out we'll just use the flashlight," he said. "Startin' to stink in here. Stay here, I'm gonna see just how bad this bad stuff is."

He walked toward the barrels, tiptoeing around the spilled contents. "Didn't bring any rubber gloves with you by any chance, did ya?"

"Sorry."

"I don't know why I deputized you," he said. "You're wors'n that pup you named." He chuckled.

"Gideon."

"Whatever."

He was standing at the barrels now. He took his old Barlow pocketknife out and slit the clear plastic and removed some papers. He fumbled with them, the knife, and the flashlight for a couple of seconds and nearly dropped the flashlight in the stuff on the ground. I caught my breath but he managed to get back to me, his load intact. He unfolded the papers while I held the flashlight and we both looked at them.

"Well, it's bad, but not as bad as I thought," he said.

"What's Kyler's PQ?" I asked.

He pointed further into the body of the invoice. "Paraquat." I guess my face betrayed my ignorance. "It's a herbicide. Weed killer," he said. "It's illegal. People used to use it to kill the vegetation in a field for no-till planting. Government used it to kill marijuana fields. Sprayed it from airplanes and helicopters."

"How dangerous is it?" I asked.

Ray shrugged. "Depends. You spray it on a plant, the plant dies, it falls down, the dirt neutralizes the paraquat."

I waited. There had to be more.

"Only a couple of problems with it," Ray finally went on. "Takes a couple of days for the dirt to neutralize it. What if it rains before the dirt can kill the poison? The bad stuff runs into the rivers and lakes. Kills the fish and the animals and poisons the humans who swim in it or drink it. Or if it gets into the water table, same thing. Also some of it is bound to land on humans. It can poison you through inhalation, consumption, or absorption. Nose, mouth, or skin."

"Lord," was all I could think of to say.

"The last straw was when the government sprayed it on marijuana down in South America. Plants died but the growers chopped them up and sold them anyway. Then we had all these middle-class American kids smokin' that crap with poison sprayed all over it. Nice, huh?"

"Ray?"

"Some folks say they got what they deserved they smoke dope. It don't seem right, though. Go blind, eat away your brain, screw up your sex life. Maybe even kill you."

"Ray, should we be standing here?"

He looked at me as though the thought had just occurred to him. Then he smiled and said, "I reckon not. Besides, we got places to go."

"We do?"

"Yep. We found our *German.*"

"We did?"

He pointed at the delivery invoice from the barrel again. Typed across the bottom was: "Consigned to Gorman Disposal, Inc. for disposal." The date of the consignment was stamped beside the phrase and there was a signature of the Gorman Representative who had received the shipment. A. G. Gorman.

Gorman, not *German.*

CHAPTER 18

MAY JUNE ALWAYS CLOSES THE DINER after lunch on Sunday, so we had it all to ourselves when we got back to Baird. The wind had picked up and more clouds had rolled in as we drove home. It was getting cold and it looked like the morning's rain was coming back for a return engagement.

May June slid mugs of coffee in front of us and took a seat on the stool next to me. "So what'd you find?" she asked, sipping her coffee. Ray and I emptied our pockets on the counter and Ray organized everything in a neat little grouping.

"Well, we got paraquat in the mine," he said, touching the invoice. "Was supposed to be burned or whatever they do with it, but it wasn't. They dumped it in Calvin's coal mine instead. Company called Gorman Disposal."

He took the photographs of the barrels out of their brown paper bag and laid them out one by one. "And we got pictures of the barrels." May June leaned over and looked at the pictures, peering down her nose through her reading glasses.

"And we got a whole pot load o' money," Ray said. He hoisted the little suitcase from the floor and plopped it on the counter. "Twenty thousand dollars, all totaled. From a bank in Lexington.

"We got some evidence that Calvin knew about all this because he's got the name of the disposal company written on his doodle pad." Ray unfolded the rubbing I had done and pointed to the name we had mistaken for *German.* "Gorman," he said.

"And we got these." He reached in the rumpled brown paper bag and pulled out the faded Polaroids of Treasure Haines, laid them on the counter.

May June picked them up and scrutinized them. "Oh, my," she said and laid them back down. She sighed. "So now what?"

Ray thought for a few moments. "Now we got to figure out how this is all tied together," he said. "What does this all have to do with the Feuchs brothers and Crazy George? What are those pictures all about?" He pointed at the Polaroids. "And who are those three characters been runnin' around, raisin' hell all over the county?"

"Well, I know one thing for sure," May June said, heaving herself off the stool and going around the counter to refresh our coffee. Ray and I looked at her as she turned around with the pot in her hand. "It never was about them dogs, was it?" She splashed coffee into our mugs. "You gonna ask Treasure about them pictures?"

Ray looked at the pictures again. "How old you figure these are, preacher?"

I looked at them and tried to judge their age but it was hard not to look at the subject. Treasure was younger in the photos but she was still stunning. The cheap, vulgar poses were obscene and titillating at the same time. The pictures were cheap, the poses were vulgar, but the woman was neither. She was just young. And there was something in her eyes, once you got past the other things staring you in the face, that was detached and remote. "This isn't me," she seemed to be saying. "This is just my body."

"Eighteen, twenty years," I said. "She was young when these were taken."

"You think that long ago? How you figure?"

I picked up the picture of Treasure and the fat man, pointed to the man's tie. "Look at that tie. It's got to be three inches wide and the knot is huge. Look at the lapels on his coat. I'd bet a dollar that's a double-knit suit."

May June looked at the picture again, closer this time. "You know, he's right, Dad. I remember when you wore your tie like that."

Ray nodded again. "So what's Calvin Haines doin' with two twenty-year-old pictures of his daughter actin' like a nekkid whore?"

"I doubt he had 'em for keepsakes," May June said.

"And I think we can assume she didn't give them to him," I added.

"So someone else sent 'em to him," Ray said. "And I'll bet I know who."

"Lewis, Bobby, and Franklin," I said. "It's their style. They want to go after me, they hurt Treasure. They want to go after Calvin, they threaten to hurt Treasure and they do hurt his dogs. She's the librarian at a small Catholic college. If those pictures ended up on the Internet. . . ." I didn't need to finish the sentence.

"What about that Crazy George fella?" May June asked. "Why didn't they threaten him?"

"Probably did," Ray said. "Probably tried to scare him and he was too stupid or crazy to scare so they had to kill him. I imagine they beat up the Feuchs brothers as a warning to George and it didn't work."

"So you gonna ask Treasure about them pictures or not?" May June asked Ray.

Ray shook his head. "Not until I know what questions to ask," he said.

"When will you know that?"

"Tomorrow," Ray said. "After I make some calls." He picked up his coffee mug and the stuff lying on the counter and headed for the stairs to the apartment.

"Well, what do we do in the meantime?" May June called after him.

He stopped at the bottom of the stairs and turned back to face us. "I don't know about the two of you, but I'm gonna watch '60 Minutes.' You got any of that cherry pie left, Mother?" He started up the stairs.

May June looked at me and shook her head. "No. But there's some ice cream in the freezer. Golden vanilla, I think. And I got some o' that thick Hershey's fudge sauce."

"That'll do."

I stayed with Ray and May June that night and slept with the big handgun on a nightstand next to my bed, under a towel so May June wouldn't see it.

By eight o'clock Ray and I were eating scrambled eggs, fried potatoes, pork chops, and biscuits at the counter in the diner. By nine we were on the road to Perry. The roads were wet and the air was cold, but the clouds were breaking up and the sun was peeking through again.

Elias Knowly was waiting for us with cups of coffee when we got to the police station. "I done what you asked, Ray. Sheriff Fine says do whatever you say, so long as it's legal, and don't bother him with it."

"He around?" Ray asked.

"No, sorry. He's having brunch with Mr. Deaver and a couple of the city council members," Elias said. He shrugged.

"Figures," Ray said. "What you got for me, Eli?"

Elias hitched up his gun belt and, with a little pride in his bearing, led us into a conference room. There were several file folders laid out on a big table. "Here's the autopsy report on George. It was like you said. He was killed with at least two rounds from a shotgun at close range. Probably no more than six feet away, Doc says."

He pointed to the other folders one by one. "Calvin Haines's phone records for the past month. They only show long distance, Ray. Sorry. Local calls still aren't recorded. Then we got Calvin's bank records here. Only the one bank. The other six banks in the county say they don't have anything for him. And we're waiting for a fax from the Lexington P.D. You were right. They heard o' Gorman before. Got a bunch of stuff on him. Should be here anytime now."

Elias looked at me. "We just got a fax machine last February. Sometimes those brunches the sheriff goes to pay off, I guess." He winked and left us to our files.

"Gets a fax machine and all of a sudden he's a smart-ass," Ray said, but there was a smile in his voice. He was thumbing through the autopsy report. He tossed it down and picked up the bank records. "Calvin's got a safety deposit box."

"We need a court order to get into it?" I asked.

Ray shrugged. "Probably. We'll get one just to be safe." He picked up the phone records. Grunted.

"What?"

He laid the file on the table and ran his finger down the columns as I watched. "Says here that Calvin only called three long distance numbers the week before he died."

I recognized one of the numbers immediately. It was the one on my rubbing: Treasure's. "He called Treasure the Wednesday before Easter and then again on Easter night," I said.

"Uh-huh," Ray said. He reached into a brown paper grocery bag he had brought and came out with the rubbing, compared the numbers just to be sure. "Yeah, that's who he called." He emptied the bag on the table and sorted through the papers. When he came to the invoice from the barrel he stopped and held it next to the phone records. He recited a number from the invoice and ran his finger down the column in the file again. "And he made three calls to Gorman Disposal. One on Monday and two on Tuesday before he called Treasure."

I looked over his shoulder again. "There's one other number on Friday," I said. "Local area code."

Ray nodded. "A toll call but not out of the area code." There was a telephone on a sideboard along the wall, along with a coffeepot and some Styrofoam cups. He picked up the phone and put it on the table and began dialing the number on the phone bill.

"Connie? Yeah, this is Ray Hall. How you doin'? Oh, 'bout as well as can be expected, you know, for an old fart. Say, Connie, I need to talk to you again 'bout this little thing, nothin' urgent. I was wonderin' if I could. . . . No, that'd be fine. I'll be in town this afternoon. What say I buy you a cup o' coffee at the police station. Okay, 'bout one, then. Thanks."

He replaced the receiver and smiled at me. "Conrad Foley. That lyin' son of a bitch."

Elias stuck his head in the door. "Your fax is comin' in from Lexington, Ray."

We walked out into the bull pen and leaned over the fax machine as it spewed out papers slowly into a tray. When the bells and whistles indicated that the message was complete, Ray picked up the papers and leafed through all five of them one by one. On the last page, which would have been the first one out of the machine, he stopped and nodded his head. "Reverend Dan Thompson, meet Mr. Artus Gorman, chairman and C.E.O. of Gorman Disposal, Incorporated."

The printed black-and-white photo was not a very good reproduction but it was clearly recognizable. The head was balder and the body fatter than before, and the tie was narrower, the lapels more conservative, but it was the same man who, twenty years earlier, had smiled for another camera while Treasure Haines pressed her breast against his face. His companion wasn't a naked female in this picture. It was a lawyer. The picture was of Gorman sitting at a table, testifying before the Kentucky state legislature, swearing to them that he was disposing of toxic waste safely and efficiently. The city of Lexington, he assured them, was in no danger whatsoever.

Ray was looking through the rest of the pages. "Suspicion of extortion, racketeering, money laundering. Also suspected of being involved in drugs, prostitution, distribution of pornography, and illegal alcohol sales. No evidence. No arrests. No convictions. He's careful." Ray handed me the page of notes from the Lexington P.D. Organized Crime Unit. "Oh, and it also says he has three sons by three different wives. Want to take a guess as to their names?"

"Lewis, Bobby, and Franklin," I said.

"Who likes to be called Frank. Bingo." Ray sighed and walked back into the conference room. A green chalkboard was fixed to the wall and he went to it, started writing. In one box at the top he wrote "Gorman Disposal." Then, under the title, he wrote "Artus" and under that, "Lewis, Bobby, Frank." At the bottom of the board he drew another box and wrote "Calvin Haines." Two arms jutted off to the side of Calvin's box, and to each he added a box, one for Treasure and one for Blessing. He connected Calvin's box to the Gorman box with a vertical line and did the same with Treasure's box. Down each side of Calvin's line he added other boxes: "Crazy George," "Dogs," "Conrad Foley," "Money."

He stepped back and crossed his arms across his chest, admiring his work. "Now all we have to do is figure out how the hell all these are connected." He took the photographs of the paraquat barrels and used thumbtacks to fix them to the frame around the chalkboard, looked back at the board, and wrote the word *paraquat* over the line connecting Calvin and Gorman Disposal. "Yeah," he said.

"Gorman was dumping paraquat in Calvin's mine illegally and paying Calvin for his silence," I said. I looked at the pictures. "Calvin got greedy and started to blackmail Gorman. Gorman responded with pictures of Treasure, and Calvin upped the ante with his own pictures of the barrels." I stopped, trying to think it through.

"Keep goin', preacher," Ray said. "Sounds good to me."

"I'm trying to figure out Crazy George. How does he fit into it?"

"The dogs," Elias said from the doorway. He was leaning against the frame, his left hand in his pocket, his right hand cradling two file folders, looking at the chalkboard. "The sheriff ought to see this."

"It's all theory," Ray said. "We can't prove any of it. Whataya mean about the dogs? Ol' George was a dogger, was he?"

Eli nodded. "We did some diggin' around about ol' George. Finally found a match on his fingerprints in our files. Seems he wasn't always crazy. His full name was George Jackson Kleine. Used to be a beagler. Had quite a reputation for dog handlin'. Not much on him. Lived up on Mt. Devoux in a little cabin he built himself. Still owned the land when he died, I guess. Anyway, it wasn't far from Cut-Through Valley." He laid the files on the table. "I figure he was helpin' Calvin with them dogs o' his. He had a driver's license and there's an old Ford pickup still registered to him, probably back in that junkyard somewhere. There's his file. The other one's from Mara Lee over to the library. Everything she could find about paraquat." He moved back to the doorway, but he didn't leave.

Ray nodded and smiled. "You're quite a cop, Eli."

Eli shrugged.

"Okay," Ray said. "So Cra . . . George went up to Calvin's on Monday night to help with the dogs like he always done. He gets there and finds Calvin dead and Marietta Trueblood dead and so he grabs the pups and gets out. He don't call the police 'cause he's crazy or scared or whatever."

"Maybe he saw them kill Calvin," I said. "Maybe that's why they killed him."

"Or maybe they found out he had the dogs and just figured he saw them and didn't want to take any chances," Ray said.

Elias cleared his throat. "The Feuchs boys gave us descriptions that fit the three you're talking about, Ray. You want me to put out an APB for 'em?" Elias was the chief deputy in the sheriff's department and outranked Ray by about ten levels, but he always treated Ray with respect and deference bordering on hero worship, especially when it came to dealing with hill people. These three weren't hill people, but old habits die hard, I guess.

Ray nodded. "Yes, Eli, I do. We can lock 'em up for what they did to the Reverend here, and Treasure, and maybe for that foolishness out to the junkyard. Armed and dangerous, remember."

"I done it before, Ray," Eli said. He left the conference room to put out his APB.

"Now we wait," I said.

"No, we don't," Ray said. "I don't think them boys are gonna be so easy to find. You notice how they show up when they want to be seen and disappear just as quick? They got someplace in the county they're stayin'. A big car like the one you heard would stand out in this county. So would three strangers as peculiar lookin' as them, but we haven't heard a word. The only hell-raisin' they're doin' is with you and the Feuchses."

"So what do we do?" I asked.

Ray picked up the receiver to the phone on the table. "Well, these rats is backed up into their hole. Onliest way to get 'em out is to poke 'em with a stick." He dialed the phone, reading the number from Calvin Haines's telephone records. "Hello? Gorman Disposal? Yeah, Mr. Gorman please." He winked at me. "Well, Mr. Gorman, Senior, I reckon. This is Constable Raymond Hall from the Durel County Sheriff's office."

Ray hummed along with the hold music for nearly a full minute. His face lit up. "Mr. Gorman? Mr. Artus Gorman?" Pause. "Well, yeah, this-here is. . . . Oh, well, fine then. Sir, what I called about is, do you have three sons name o' Lewis, Bobby, and Franklin?" Pause. "Well, it's a simple question, ain't it? Do you or don't you?" Pause. "There you go. Sir, what I'd like you to do is, the next time they call you from down here wherever it is they're hidin', you tell them that they done stepped on their peckers in the wrong county and I intend to see 'em dead or in jail. Their choice. Just tell 'em that, will you?" He listened a couple of seconds, raised his eyebrows, and hung up.

"That man has a foul mouth," he said to me. He sat down and opened the file on paraquat and started to read.

"So you shake their cage and see what falls out," I said.

"Yep," he said, not looking up. "I got me some readin' to do here. Whyn't you take Naomi to lunch. Time you get back I'll figure out what we gotta do next."

"You want me to bring you something?"

"Nah. I'll just get one o' the deputies to order me a pizza or somethin'. You go on and have a good time.

So I went.

* * *

Naomi was shaking the hand of a middle-aged, bib-overall-clad client at the door and sending him on his way when I arrived at Percy Mills's office. She led me past David Mills, Percy's son, and I gave him a little wave as we went into her office. She closed the door and then wrapped her arms around my neck and gave me a huge kiss.

"Four more days," she said, into the corner of my mouth.

"What?"

"Midnight on the fifteenth we're gonna celebrate, okay?" She slipped her hand into my windbreaker around the side and under the big gun in the shoulder holster. "Is that a gun under your arm or are you just glad to see me?"

"It's a gun *and* I'm glad to see you," I said into her neck. "Ray and Elias are worried about me. The gun's their idea." I tried to slip my hand into her blouse but she pulled away.

She looked into my eyes for a moment and nodded. "Let's eat lunch," she said.

I shook off the frustration and tried to reply matter-of-factly. "That's what I'm here for."

We went to the Courtview Diner and had cheeseburgers and milk shakes and shared a jumbo order of shoestring fries that were crisp and salty. While we ate I brought her up-to-date on Ray's investigation. When we had finished the fries and slurped the dregs of our shakes, she laid her hand on mine. "You know how to use a handgun?"

I nodded.

"But you ain't never shot one at a human target, have you?"

"I know how to shoot it, Naomi. And I will if I have to. I hope I don't."

She nodded. "But deep down inside there's this little thing that keeps pokin' at you. Maybe hopin' that you get that Lewis fella in a place where you'll be forced to use that gun." She tilted her head and raised her eyebrows, not teasing me but asking for confirmation.

I nodded again. "Maybe." I took out my pipe and started fiddling with it. "It's not an idea, really. Not even a wish. But sometimes this scenario runs through my mind like a silent, home movie. He's taunting me like he did in the parsonage that night. Sitting on the couch, laughing at me and thinking I can't do anything about it, and I just casually lift that gun up from behind my back and point it at his chest. There's this one delicious moment when he realizes that the tables have changed, that I have the power now."

Naomi moved the ashtray next to my plate as I lit my pipe. "What happens then?" she asked.

"I don't know. It never goes beyond that point. I want to shoot him so bad. I want to see that bullet slam into his chest and knock him ass over appetite across the room, but there's over forty years of stuff in my mind that says violence isn't the answer. You don't just kill an unarmed man no matter how bad he is. But fear can make you forget your principles, Naomi. And I'm telling you, I'm afraid of these guys. I've seen what they're capable of and they don't do it because they're sick or desperate. They enjoy it. They like to hurt people. Now Ray wants to rattle their cage just to see what happens." I could feel the heaviness in my chest just like it happened every time I had that dream.

Naomi took some money out of her purse and laid it on the table. She stood and came around to stand beside me, bent down, and kissed me on the forehead. "My treat," she said. "Be careful, Dan. I'll call you at Ray's tonight." She left and I ordered a cup of coffee.

When I got back to the police station I walked into the conference room to find Ray sitting at the table with a cup of coffee in front of him and Conrad Foley across from him at the table. On Conrad's left was big Hank, his face still black and blue from the beating Ray had given him. On his right was a petite blonde girl of about twenty-three or twenty-four. She had her hair in tight curls like Tanya Tucker, the country singer, and she wore a western shirt and jeans. What I could see of her body was compact and well proportioned. All three of the Foleys were scowling.

"Come on in, preacher," Ray said, kicking out a chair for me. "Pour yourself a cup o' joe and have a seat. Connie here was just about to tell me why he lied to me the other day about him and Calvin Haines."

"I never lied to you. You just never—"

"Shut up, Daddy," the blonde said.

Conrad rolled his eyes and turned to her. "Girl, if any o' your brothers was to talk to me the way you do I'd—"

"I know, you'd whip their asses for 'em. You done told me that a thousand times. Now do as I say and keep your mouth shut till Rafe gets here." She crossed her arms over her chest. Conrad looked at Ray and shrugged: What can I do?

Ray smiled at me. "This-here's Loretta, Connie's daughter. She's lookin' to take over the *bidness*. She wants to wait till Rafe Trout gets here before they say anything. Rafe's their lawyer."

"You've arrested them?" I asked.

Ray shook his head. "Oh, hell, no. I just asked Connie to come in here and chat for a spell. Loretta's kinda got her panties in a bunch, though. Been watchin' too many television shows, you ask me."

"What'd you ask them?" I asked.

"Just asked Connie what that call from Calvin was about on Friday night last week. See, Connie says he hasn't seen Calvin in several months, which is technically correct. He ain't seen him. But he talked to him. I never asked about *talkin'*, though. I asked about *seein'*. So Connie's got me on that one. I didn't ask the right question."

"That's right!" Conrad said.

"Shut up, Daddy," Loretta said.

Ray sighed, put out by the interruption. "Anyway, I figured if the two of them was just talkin' about dogs, fine. Maybe Calvin changed his mind and decided to sell the Foleys a dog. Maybe that's all that phone call was about. And if that's it, fine. No harm done. We finish our coffee, shake hands, and go home." He smiled and shook his head. "But first thing I ask him about the call, Loretta here, she clams up like a, well, like a clam, and starts talkin' all disrespectful to her daddy. Won't let him talk. Like he's five years old or somethin'. So I now gotta figure it's more'n dogs that phone call was about. I gotta figure it's somethin' real serious like maybe they know more about this whole mess than I realized." He leaned back in his chair and folded his hands behind his head. "Whataya think, preacher? Am I crazy or what?"

Conrad Foley shot forward in his seat. "Damn it, Ray, I don't know—"

"Daddy! Shut your mouth! Don't you—"

"No sir! I put up with your smart mouth because you been to college and I want you to have grit so's you can run the bidness, but there ain't no call to talk to me that way in front of people." Conrad's face was inches from his daughter's.

"Daddy!"

Conrad didn't move his face when he said, "Hank, take your little sister and buy her an ice cream. Pick me up in half an hour."

Loretta's face turned crimson. "Daddy! You can't—"

"Hank! Do you hear your daddy talkin'?" Conrad said. Loretta sputtered.

"Yessir," Hank said. "Come on, Loretta." He took her by the bicep and nearly lifted her out of her seat. "Let's get a ice cream."

She sputtered all the way to the door.

"Shut the door," Conrad said as they went out. Loretta slammed it with enough force to rattle the windows. Conrad looked back across the table at Ray. "I'm sorry you had to see that, Ray."

Ray shrugged. "Kids."

"I heard that."

"Connie, all I'm interested in is those three fellers from Lexington. I want 'em for murderin' Calvin Haines and Crazy George. I don't care a fiddler's fart about nothin' else." Ray was leaning forward now, across the table from Conrad, his arms on the table, his hands folded. I lit my pipe.

Conrad Foley sighed. "I warned her not to mess with them people, but she wouldn't have none of it. Said we had to expand, diversify. Goes off to college and thinks she knows ever' damn thing."

Ray nodded. Kids.

"Well," Conrad went on. "Artus Gorman comes to us last year. Says he's heard some good stuff about the 'shine we make. I tell him we don't make 'shine, we just broker it for the hill folks. He says, whatever. Says he's got a bunch o' hillbillies livin' in Lexington, come to the big city to work in the factories and what-have-you. They get homesick, they want a little sip o' home. Wants to make a deal with me on more 'shine than I can sell in a month down here and he wants it every week.

"Well, I don't like the sound o' this guy, Ray. I'm just a hillbilly that's tryin' to be a country singer and he's a city slicker, got more angles than a bucksaw. I ask the kids what they think and Loretta gets on her high horse, says she can handle him and I should let her take it on. I tell her just to try it for one order and see how it goes. Well, it goes good, Ray. Real good! Lord, we're makin' money like nobody's bidness."

"Only he wants somethin' else," Ray says.

Conrad nodded his head vigorously. "Damn right. He says them hillbillies in Lexington want to taste more'n just 'shine. Says he needs some o' that fine mountain herb. That's marijuana. Says he's tired o' bringin' it clear across the country and wants to get some local, homegrown. Ray, you know I never messed with drugs."

"I know, Connie."

"Then he wants girls. Says he'll pay me for 'em, just like they's cattle or somethin', so much a head. His words. Says he'll put 'em in the movies. Yeah, right. I guess we know what kinda movies he's talkin' about."

Ray nodded.

"Ray, I got some girls workin' for me and Lord knows I ain't no saint. But the girls who work for me, they come to me. Lord, I've known most of them all their lives. I put 'em to work to help them out until their husband gets back in the mine or until they got enough together to build a stake. I never beat 'em and I never string 'em out. When they're ready to leave, they leave. That's the way Daddy run things and that's the way I do. Hell, Ray, I know most o' these girls' parents. Went to school with some of 'em."

"So you told him no," Ray said. He got up and refilled our coffee cups. That done, he sat down and started his cigarette ritual.

"Yessir, I did. And I told him he couldn't sell his dope down here and I told him he couldn't dump that chemical stuff o' his down here, neither, and if he did he'd have me to reckon with."

"How'd he take it?" Ray asked.

"Not good. Not good at all. Says I'm not the onliest man in Kentucky's got 'shine to sell. Says he can get it from somewheres else just as easy."

"What'd you say to that?"

"Well, hell, Ray. Here I was gettin' rich and fat with all that money comin' in. I guess you'd say I got used to it. Bought some stuff. Made some investments. You seen them horses when you was out to the farm?"

"We seen 'em," Ray said.

"They ain't cheap, let me tell ya. Losin' that bidness was gonna hurt me and that's a fact."

"So what'd you do?"

Conrad leaned back in his chair and smiled. Now he laced his fingers together behind his head just as Ray had a little while ago. "Screw 'em."

"That what you did?" Ray asked without expression.

"That's what I told 'im," Conrad said. "Told him to take his bidness and stick it up his fat ass. Oh, he made some noise about how he could make trouble for me and how he was a powerful man and all. Sent them three boys o' his down here to strut around, try to scare me."

"Did they? Scare you?"

Now Conrad Foley laughed. "Ol' Artus musta just thought he was dealin' with me and Loretta. Them boys come to the house one day and all my boys is home. They just backwatered outta there real polite like."

"You never heard from them since?" Ray asked.

"Never." He paused as if thinking. "Not till last Friday night. Even then I didn't hear from the Gormans. Ol' Cal Haines calls me up. Says he's in trouble, and he can't go to the law but he needs help. Says he'd give me my pick of them pups if I'd help him deal with some fellas givin' him trouble. I asked him who it was and he told me.

"He said them boys had been comin' around givin' him trouble and wanted some muscle to run 'em off. I told him to give me a call next time he saw them comin' up the drive. That was the last time I talked to 'im.

"When he hadn't called by Sunday I sent the boys over to talk to 'im in the afternoon. They looked at the pups and he said everything was okay. They come home and that's the last we heard."

"So them two boys of yours wasn't lookin' to buy you a pup?" Ray asked.

Conrad laughed. "Them two? I'm surprised they thought o' that excuse that fast. Hell, they never think about nothing but themselves." He got serious. "What you gonna do now, Ray?"

Ray paused a few seconds, just to let Conrad sweat, I think. Then he said: "I ain't gonna do nothin' about you, Connie. Thanks for comin' in. But I think I'm gonna have to do somethin' real serious about Artus Gorman and his family, don't you?"

Conrad Foley nodded his head seriously. "You need any help you give me a call. I don't like them fellers one bit. They're mean, Ray."

"That they are."

"You be careful, now, ya hear?" He put his cowboy hat on as he left.

"That I will," Ray said to his back. "That I will."

CHAPTER 19

AFTER CONRAD FOLEY LEFT we sat at the conference table waiting for something to happen and nothing did for nearly an hour. Occasionally Ray would walk into the bull pen and talk to the dispatcher but her answer was always the same. "Nothing unusual." No reports of a late-model Caddie—the kind that, according to the Feuchs brothers, the Gorman brothers were driving. I had drunk so much coffee and smoked my pipe so much that my mouth was raw and I was starting to get a headache behind my eyes.

Ray was yawning and shaking his head, and when after another half hour nothing had happened, he gathered all the papers and pictures on the table and stuffed them back into the paper bag, stubbed out his Camel, put on his Cincinnati Reds baseball cap, and said to me, "Come on. Let's go talk to the girls."

I didn't know what girls he was talking about, but I went anyway because I was sick of the police station and the waiting. Instead of taking his Jeep, we just walked the six blocks to the Box Car Diner.

The midafternoon regulars were drinking coffee and power smoking Marlboros at the counter, and there were a few other folks taking an afternoon break, eating pie, drinking coffee or cokes, and chatting. Blessing, in jeans and a white T-shirt, was reading a newspaper in her regular booth, and Treasure was behind the counter drying glasses with a clean but ratty dish towel, staring into space. She was wearing a black miniskirt and a ruffled blouse. Her makeup and jewelry were minimal.

Bless looked up when the front door jangled the bell as we came in. "Well, bless my immortal soul," she shouted. "Look who walked in the front door just as I was thinkin' about 'im."

"How you doin', hon?" Ray asked as he slid into the booth. He laid the brown paper bag on the table. I pulled a chair out from an adjacent table and sat down, giving myself room to cross my legs.

"Fine as a frog hair," she said. "You?"

"Can't complain. How's Treasure doin'?"

"Can't sit and rest for a minute. She's gotta be doin' somethin' all the time." Blessing called to her sister. "Treasure! Put them things down and come over here. Act like you got some manners for the love o' Mike. Two good-lookin' men come in the place and you stand there like you's Helen Keller."

Treasure shook herself back to the present, blushed like we had caught her at something, and came over to the booth and table. She pulled out another chair from the table and sat next to me with her knee touching my thigh. "Hi, Dan," she said, still embarrassed. I nodded and gave her a wink.

"Hi, Dan," Blessing mimicked. "Lord, Ray, I think she's got a thing for him. Whata you think?"

"Well, May Junc tells me he's good lookin'," Ray said. "But Naomi's got her hooks pretty well sunk in his hide, I think. It were me, I wouldn't want to tangle with that Taylor bunch. They can be pretty tough."

Blessing laughed loud enough so that the power smokers all turned to look at us. "What are you lookin' at, you old farts?" she said to them.

"Best lookin' piece o' woman flesh in Kentucky," one guy said. He was about seventy with a face like leather and knuckles the size of half-dollars. His hair was buzz cut and gray. "You ready to marry me yet, Bless?"

"Don't you know at your age sex is lethal?" she shouted back.

"Hey, if you die, you die!" he said, and they all laughed long and hard at the old joke. They had obviously performed this skit before.

"Old farts," Blessing said to Ray. "Been so long since he had any he'd have a nervous breakdown tryin' to remember what to do with it. They're nice fellas, though."

Ray nodded. "Yeah."

"So what's goin' on with the two of you?" she asked, suddenly serious. "You find the no-accounts killed Daddy?"

Ray sighed and squared his shoulders. "We have and we haven't, Bless. Here's what we figure."

He told her almost everything as he put the bag on the table and pulled the pictures of the barrels out of it. He fanned them out for her. Her daddy, he said, was letting the Gormans dump paraquat in his mine. They were paying him pretty well, but less than it would have cost them to dispose of it legally. It looked as if he had asked them for more money and they got mad and killed him. He didn't mention the pictures of Treasure and the blackmail we had hypothesized.

"Crazy ol' George was just in the wrong place at the wrong time. We figure they saw him as a loose end they needed to tie up," Ray said.

The old black guy from the kitchen came out and Ray asked for a cup of coffee. Treasure and I ordered Diet Pepsis, and Blessing took hot water with a slice of lemon.

"What about the dogs?" Blessing asked. "Why'd they have to kill them?"

"Just meanness, I guess," Ray said. "That's the kind o' trash we're dealin' with. They hurt things for the pure joy of it."

Treasure sniffed and took some napkins from a dispenser on the table. She blew her nose daintily. "I just feel so awful," she said. I put my arm around her and she leaned into me. "Poor Daddy."

"They come after Dan and Treasure because they wanted us to drop the investigation," Ray said. "Didn't want to kill anyone else—that is, their daddy didn't want them to kill anyone else. Too messy. Besides, they probably figured they were dealin' with hicks and they could scare us off."

"How you gonna find 'em?" Treasure asked. She wadded the napkin into a golf ball and held on to it.

"Elias got out an APB. We know they're drivin' a big Caddie. Probably holed up somewhere in the county. They'll have to move sooner or later. If we don't get 'em here, we'll get 'em when they go back to Lexington. The LPD is lookin' for 'em there."

Treasure nodded and dabbed at her eyes with the balled napkin.

Ray sighed again, sipped his coffee. "The thing is, we don't have no evidence of them killin' your daddy. We can arrest them for what they done to you, Treasure, hon. We can even arrest them for killin' Crazy George out to the junkyard. But all this about your daddy is just guesswork." He lit a cigarette. "It's good guesswork but that's still all it is."

Blessing sipped her hot water. She took a cigarette from Ray's pack, lit it, and looked hard at Ray. "You could let me be with them alone for a while. I can almost guarantee they'd confess after twenty or thirty minutes. Them boys yonder would be glad to help me, too. They all knew Daddy." She nodded to the power smokers, caught the eye of one of them, smiled and waved. He waved back. "Hell, that's the only reason they come here all the time. There's better and cheaper coffee at the McDonald's out by the highway."

Ray just nodded. He knew how she felt. I knew how she felt. The gun I was wearing under my arm wasn't just for protection. There was a little revenge in five of the six chambers of its cylinder.

Ray finished his coffee, stubbed out his cigarette, and stood. "We'll be in touch," he said. Y'all take care." He patted each of them on the shoulder as we made our way out. "We're gonna go see the Feuchses just to make sure they haven't left anything out. We'll let you know when somethin' breaks."

We went out through the kitchen. Deputy Merchison was eating a piece of blueberry pie with vanilla ice cream and drinking coffee from his own mug. He looked like he was about eighteen years old. He nodded to us as we went through.

"Take care of 'em," Ray said.

Merch nodded again. His mouth was too full to talk.

We spent an hour or so at Durel County Memorial Hospital trying to communicate with the Feuchs brothers, but they were groggy from the painkillers they had been given. Ray managed to confirm what Elias Knowly had said about Trent and Floyd. They had been attacked by "three ugly fellas" driving a late model Caddie. One of the "ugly fellas" was built like an ox and one was tall and skinny. The other, according to Trent was just "butt ugly with a double-barreled shotgun sawed off like the biggest, nastiest pistol you ever seen."

The Feuchses had gotten stupid and tried to put their rat killers to work, earning them a beating that they were lucky to escape with their lives. Neither had heard the shots that killed George.

Ray said it looked like the Gormans had walked out of the office shed, probably hailed George with the intention of scaring him, and when he yelled "Incoming" and started after them they shot him with both barrels.

The Feuchses said as how that sounded about right to them. They also said that as soon as they were healed they aimed to "run them city slimeballs to ground and give 'em what fer." Ray rolled his eyes and we left.

Ray called Eli from the lobby of the little hospital and was told that everything was still quiet. All of the main roads out of the county were covered, though. The Gormans were trapped inside the county.

"That Eli's a good boy," Ray said. "Let's go home."

"You didn't mention the pictures of Treasure," I said as we roared through the dark back to Baird.

Ray shrugged and shifted gears, taking a cutback on what felt like two wheels. I hung on to the roll bar. "Didn't seem right. Girl goes off to the big city when she's young. Hillbilly girl. No education to speak of. She gets into some stuff that's kinda sleazy but she works her way out. Now she's got a respectable job and she's made somethin' of herself."

"What are you going to do with them?" I asked.

"Burn 'em, I reckon. I don't know."

We drove on in silence. Then, after a few minutes, he said, "She's a beautiful woman. Always was."

"LeRoy Whiteker says he dated both of them," I said.

Ray smiled. "LeRoy dated ever'one in the school at one time or another. He was quite a Lothario."

"What about Ray Junior?" I asked. "Did he know them?"

Ray nodded. He and May June rarely talked about their only son. The room I was using was a shrine to him . . . before he went off to Vietnam and the killing and the bombing . . . and the heroin. "Yeah, he did. He played football and was kinda popular, you know. He was kinda shy about girls though. Didn't date much."

I let the subject drop. "May June say what's for supper tonight?" It was well past the supper hour but May June usually kept back something from the diner's menu for us.

"Fried chicken and mashed potatoes, I think," he said, but he seemed distracted, uninterested in food, so I let that subject drop as well. We rode the rest of the way in silence. Fifteen minutes later we pulled to a stop in front of the Baird Diner.

"The light's out," Ray said, pointing to the streetlight outside the Volunteer Fire Department. He cut the engine and we stayed in the Jeep for a moment, letting our eyes adjust to the dark. There was light coming from around the curtains in the diner windows, but the only noise was the barking and crying of the beagle puppies from inside the diner.

Ray reached behind the driver's seat, flipped back a blanket, and came up with his shotgun. "You got that hog leg I gave you?" he asked. He didn't take his eyes off the front screen door of the diner.

I nodded.

"Bring it out. Keep it pointed at the ground and stay behind me. When we go through the door I'll go in standing up and to the right. You follow me in and go left and low, just like they do on television." He looked at me for a split second, then back at the door.

"You think—"

"I don't know," he said. "Just do it. Don't shoot anything you aren't sure of."

I brought the big pistol out of my shoulder holster and I stepped out of the Jeep. Ray looked at me and then started toward the door and I followed. He went up the three steps onto the porch, staying close to the ends of the steps so they wouldn't creak, and when he was beside the door, his back to the wall, I did the same.

When I was on the opposite side of the door, he held up three fingers and then began to count silently, moving his lips. One . . . two . . . three. On three he went through the door, bringing the shotgun up to his shoulder as he went. I followed, slamming the screen door all the way back so I could get past it. It hit the wall and bounced back faster than I expected, catching me on the heel, and I stumbled and skittered across the floor, into a table and down. I landed on my knees and elbows with the gun pointed straight ahead and managed not to shoot myself or Ray.

I looked across the room from where I lay on the floor, and Ray was crouched at the end of the counter, looking back at me. He made the okay sign with his left hand and I nodded. I looked around the edge of the overturned card table.

All the lights were on in the diner. The puppies were barking and crying back in Ray's office. Darnell Kody lay in the middle of the room with blood running from his head.

Ray must have seen him at the same time I did, because he came out from behind the counter at a run. I raised myself to my knees and leveled the pistol across the room, fanning it from one side to the other like they did on television. If someone had come running in from another room I probably would have shot him, good guy or bad. I was that nervous and that scared. Luckily no one came into the room.

I got up and stuck my head inside the store and the post office, then walked over to where Ray was kneeling over Darnell and fanned the gun around the room one more time, covering the door we had just come in.

"They're gone," Ray said. "You can relax."

I sighed and let my arms fall. The gun suddenly weighed a thousand pounds. I managed to lift it back into the shoulder holster. "Darnell?" I asked.

"Whacked him on the head. Looks like a couple o' times. He'll be okay, but he's gonna have a headache."

Ray got a towel from behind the counter, wetted it, and brought it back to Darnell, who had bled considerably from his head wounds. As Ray applied the towel, Darnell seemed to come around. He sputtered, coughed, and his eyes opened.

"Ray!"

"Hey, Darnell."

"They got May June."

"I know."

"I tried to stop 'em, Ray. Me and the pups come in. They was makin' her leave with 'em. We tried to stop 'em. I'm sorry, Ray."

Ray handed the rag to Darnell, who tried to sit up and decided against it. He placed the rag against his forehead and closed his eyes again. Ray said, "Ain't nothin' to be sorry about, Darnell. You done your best."

Darnell started to cry.

"Aw, now, don't be doin' that," Ray said. "Did they say anything? Leave me a message?"

"Your office," Darnell sniffled.

The pups poured out of the office when Ray went in. They spread out and explored the diner in about thirty seconds, found Darnell, and pounced on him, licking his face and climbing onto his stomach. He hugged and kissed them.

I left Darnell and the pups to their reunion and followed Ray into the office. It was jut a little bigger than the average bathroom with a metal desk, cheap swivel chair, and filing cabinet. My first day in Baird I had sat in the single wooden chair across the desk, sipped a beer, and told my life story to the big Kentuckian who would eventually adopt me as his "deputy constable." Ray was standing in the door and I had to brush past him to get into the office.

"They broke his neck," he said. "Just to show how mean they are."

"Oh, no," was all I could manage to say.

Gideon, the little runt puppy, lay on the desk, his head twisted around backward. A little string of blood and saliva ran from his mouth. Beneath his head was a note written in felt marker. "Bring the pictures and other stuff to the farm. Bring the preacher. No cops."

I fell into Ray's desk chair, afraid my legs wouldn't support me. A huge knot formed in my throat and I couldn't breathe. Somehow all the death and pain and misery that I had witnessed in the past week seemed to focus in the death of the puppy. I felt like my heart was breaking. That's the only way I can describe it. He was little and innocent and helpless, and they killed him for fun. I never really believed in the devil, a demigod with horns and a tail who tempted people to do bad things, but I believed in evil. The other cruelties the Gormans had perpetrated could be marked down to self preservation and the profit motive. Killing Gideon was just evil. I gasped and tried to keep from crying but I couldn't.

"They wanted to scare us," Ray said. "You scared?"

I nodded. I had never encountered anything so purely vile as this. I was really, really scared.

"I guess the point of all this is that they won't hesitate to kill May June. So I guess I'm scared, too." But I didn't hear fear in his voice. What I heard was an anger so deep, a hatred so dark that I was nearly afraid to turn around to look at him, certain that his face would have undergone some sort of transformation.

"Call Elias," I said. "Get help." Finally I looked at him. He was still the old Ray, except for his eyes. They were hooded, hardened, and impenetrable.

He shook his head. "Eli's a good cop but he'll insist on doin' it by the book. He'll go in there with sirens screamin' and guns blazin' and they'll kill her, Dan. And they'll laugh while they do it."

I didn't say anything. There was another possibility, one that was just too terrible to speak aloud.

As if reading my mind, he said, "They haven't killed her yet. They'll keep her alive as long as I have what they want. But the minute they get their hands on them pictures we're all dead."

I stood and took the gun out of the shoulder holster, checked the load once again. Then I leaned over the opened bottom drawer of Ray's desk. From it I took two boxes, one full of shotgun shells and one full of shells for the Python. I took a single shell from that box and slipped it into the empty chamber in the Python's cylinder which I had been keeping empty in case I dropped the gun. Another handful of shells went into each of my jacket pockets. I picked up the box of shotgun shells and handed it to Ray.

He slipped the entire box into the pocket of the gray windbreaker but his eyes never unfocused from the dead puppy on the desk. "I need a cup o' coffee. Keep me alert," he said. I went out to make a pot of coffee and he came out, got a couple of towels, and went back in to wrap the puppy in them. Back at the counter he poured himself a mug of coffee and began his cigarette ritual. When the cigarette was lit he sat down on a stool and sipped from his mug, looking straight ahead, thinking. I poured myself a mug and sat down next to him. Darnell and the pups were still playing on the floor.

When Ray's Camel was about an inch long he looked at it and said, "I bet you never had a church in the city where you had to carry a gun."

I shook my head. "Biggest fight I ever had was over whether to replace the roof or patch it."

He took a drag from his cigarette and looked at me as he blew the smoke out. "Well, I reckon you'll get your thing back tonight. Ain't that what Naomi called it? Your *thing?*"

I didn't answer. Let my eyes ask my own question of him.

"I aim to kill them boys," Ray said. "No way their daddy's gonna lawyer them outta this."

"That's why you don't want to call Elias," I said. It wasn't a question.

Ray didn't answer.

"There's three of them, Ray. And there's only two of us. And they have May June and we're going into a blind situation." I could feel my heart thumping in my chest. My hands were trembling so badly I could barely hold my coffee mug without sloshing coffee on myself.

Ray just nodded again. "They think they're dealin' with hill people. Think us hicks can't possibly know what to do."

"I *don't* know what to do, Ray!" I felt like yelling but I didn't for fear of scaring Darnell.

Ray finished his coffee in a gulp and turned to face me. "You keep that hog in your hand and you stay on my right. If we get in a tight situation you turn your back to mine and we cover each other. If I shoot, you shoot. Don't hesitate, don't question, don't think. Just point that big mother at the biggest target and start pullin' that trigger and don't stop until it's empty. Then get behind somethin' solid, reload, and do it again."

I took a deep breath. "Okay."

Ray smiled at me and patted my leg. "Let's go get May June and bring her home."

"Where you goin'?" Darnell asked as we headed for the door.

Ray stopped and looked back at the big retarded man sitting on the floor with a lap full of puppies. "We're gonna go get May June and bring her back, Darnell. Okay?"

"Okay."

"After we been gone a bit, you get on the phone and call Deputy Knowly. You know who he is?"

Darnell nodded.

"Tell him to get out here but don't tell him nothin' about what happened here. When he gets here you tell him the whole story, okay?"

"Okay."

Ray walked back to the counter and went behind it to the cash register. He found a notepad and a pen and began writing. "Here's the number to call. Then call this-here number and talk to Treasure and Blessing Haines and tell them to come on out here." He looked at me. "Anything else?"

"Yeah," I said. "Call Naomi and tell her . . . tell her I love her."

Ray wrote Naomi's number in Perry on the pad. "You got all that, Darnell?"

Darnell nodded. "Call Deputy Knowly. Call Ms. Haines and Ms. Haines. Call Naomi."

"Darnell?"

"Yessir?"

"You done good tonight. Thankya."

Darnell shrugged. He didn't look up from the pups.

Ray nodded toward the door and we left.

It took about fifty minutes to drive through the dark to Cut-Through Valley. Ray took it at a careful, sane speed, driving like he had drunk his coffee before we left. In the normal course of events he usually crashed and banged his way through things, slowing down only when he used his cigarette ritual to think. Now he was doing everything like it was part of the ritual—slowly, deliberately, methodically—thinking about everything before and as he did it.

He pulled off the road into an almost invisible cutback on Tread-water Trace about a half mile before the Cut-Through Valley turnoff. He cut the lights and killed the motor.

"We'll walk from here," he said. "They probably got someone watchin' the road. We follow this cutback about five hundred yards and then cut through the woods we'll come up behind the barn. I think."

"You think?"

He shrugged. "These old cutbacks is all loggin' roads. Used 'em to haul out logs back in the forties. They're all growed up now except for the ones the county keeps clear for firebreaks. Couple o' years back I helped clear some of these up here."

"This is one of the ones you cleared?"

He nodded. "Yeah, I think so."

I climbed out of the Jeep and checked the Python one more time. Checked for the extra shells in my pockets. Everything was intact. Ray stood next to me and lit a cigarette. We both sighed simultaneously.

"Well, let's go," Ray said.

CHAPTER 20

IT WAS JUST AFTER MIDNIGHT when we left the Jeep, and the dew was already forming on the grass and weeds. The undergrowth on the fire lane was nearly a foot high, and by the time we walked a hundred feet my pant legs and basketball shoes were soaked through. The moon was about three-quarters full and we could see well enough with Ray's penlight shining at his feet. He took the lead and I followed.

Small animals ran through the woods on both sides of us and I jumped every time something made a noise. Ray didn't even seem to notice. To the left, the ground angled up at about twenty degrees to a ridge thirty or forty feet above our heads. To our right the forest leveled out and probably went on over the rolling hills all the way to Baird, except you could see only about forty yards into it before the cover became a thick wall of vines and thorns.

After about fifteen minutes Ray stopped and turned off his penlight. We stood for a couple of minutes as he got his bearings. He pointed to a big tree at the top of the ridge on the left and nodded. One of its limbs had fallen off and was lying on the ground beside it. The fallen limb was a couple of feet thick.

"This should be about right," he whispered. "We'll climb up behind that tree and have a look around. We should be about to the chicken coop. Try to be quiet."

I nodded and Ray started up the hill. He placed each foot carefully, testing each step for sound. A couple of times he grabbed a sapling and used it to pull himself up. When he was about a dozen feet in front of me I followed.

Walking carefully and trying to be quiet, we took about twenty minutes to reach the top of the ridge, but it felt like an hour. I crawled up next to Ray and peeked over the top of the log while I caught my breath. We had gone a little past the chicken coop but it was still visible, about a hundred feet out and to the left. There were lights on in the house and someone was sitting on the front porch.

I ducked back down behind the log. "What now?" I asked.

Ray reached into his back pocket and pulled out a small packet of Beech-Nut chewing tobacco. He opened it, took out a small pinch and placed it in his cheek, and returned the pouch to his pocket. "Now we find May June," he said. "Any ideas?"

I shrugged. "The house, I guess. It looks like they've moved in."

Ray nodded. "Then that's where we'll check last. You take the chicken coop. I'll take the barn and the toolshed. We'll do the smokehouse together. Wait for me behind the coop."

He rolled over, picked up his shotgun, and was gone, running Indian style through the woods, along the top of the ridge. In a moment I couldn't see him.

I did as he said, working my way slowly along the edge of the woods to the chicken coop. The door creaked a little when I opened it and I froze for a full minute, waiting for someone from the house to shout or move. Then I realized that the red paint on the building rendered it nearly invisible from the house. Ray and I had been looking at it from the woods, against the open barnyard. From the house, the outbuildings were all silhouetted against the dark woods. Only the white trim on each building would be visible— and that only if you were really looking for it.

The chicken coop still smelled of chickens and mold and feed, but other than that it was empty. I felt the urge to sneeze and went back outside. I went behind the building and lay down so I could peek around the corner and wait for Ray. Whoever it was on the porch of the house stood up, said something, walked back and forth, and sat back down.

"She's in the house," Ray said in my ear. I had not heard him coming up on me and I nearly screamed.

"Damn, Ray!" I whispered as loudly as I dared.

"You gotta stay more alert, you're gonna be a night fighter," he said.

"Is she okay?"

"Sleepin'," he said. "On the couch in the livin' room. They musta give her the same stuff they shot into you. She's breathin' though."

"What about the Gormans?" I asked.

"From your description of 'em, Lewis and the big one is up there." He nodded at the house. "Bobby's somewhere out here. Lewis is talkin' to him on a walkie-talkie."

"That's Lewis on the porch?"

He nodded. "Frank's inside. Readin' a magazine and eatin' everything we didn't eat the other day. He's sittin' in that wing chair right next to May June."

"Okay, so what do we do now?"

He spit. "Well, I think and you pray."

So we sat there, leaning against the back of the chicken coop and he thought. It was hard to think about anything but May June.

I tried thinking about Naomi, then I tried to think about Treasure, but mostly what I thought about was how afraid I was. So I prayed.

Funny, when we were walking and climbing and skulking around in the woods I hadn't felt afraid at all. Now, sitting there in the dark doing nothing, it was like the fear I had left on that fire trail back by the Jeep had caught up with me and was making a head-on assault. I started seeing a mental picture of Gideon lying on Ray's desk.

I was getting that fluttering feeling in my stomach, and my hands were starting to sweat, when Ray finally spoke. "I got it," he said.

"What?"

"We don't go to them. We make them come to us."

"What about May June? They'll kill her if we—"

He shook his head. "They want all three of us. They want them pictures and documents I got. They won't do anything until they got 'em."

I looked around. "Where are those pictures and documents, Ray?"

"In the Jeep," he said. "They're safe." He looked at the barn. "Come on."

We wove our way along the woods and then ran across a hundred feet of open ground to the barn. When we were inside Ray went up into one of the lofts and started throwing down hay. Several bales hit the floor and broke with a quiet "whompf." Ray climbed halfway down the ladder and jumped to the floor.

"You got your lighter?" he asked.

I dug into my pocket and came out with my Zippo.

"All right. Give me five minutes and then light this-here pile o' hay." He threw some rags and papers from other parts of the barn onto the pile, using his penlight to find the trash. "Then open those big doors, yell 'Fire,' and haul ass over to the chicken coop." Pull off a couple o' shots if you want. Shoot in the air, though. I'll be up at the house comin' in the back door and I don't want you shootin' me."

"Won't this burn down the whole barn?" I asked, looking at the big pile of hay.

"Maybe. Probably not, though. The floor's dirt. Hay burns pretty fast and cool. Won't have time to spread to the wood. Probably."

"What if it does? What if the whole barn goes up, Ray?"

He looked around the barn then at me. "The hell with it."

I sighed.

"Remember," he said. "Wait five minutes. Light the fire, let it get rollin'. Yell, then fire a couple rounds. I'll be comin' in the back door while you're raisin' hell out here. When you get to the chicken coop, drop and reload."

I nodded and he patted me on the shoulder. "They don't teach ass kickin' in seminary, do they?" He handed me his penlight and then he was gone, out the back of the barn. For just a moment I wondered if I would ever see him alive again. I didn't want to do this man's funeral. I knew that I would remember his name forever, if I did.

I used the penlight to watch my wristwatch, checking it every half minute and looking out a knothole in the barn wall between time checks. Lewis was still sitting on the porch in Calvin Haines's rocking chair. I was closer to him now and could make out the walkie-talkie in his hand. He was talking into it almost constantly.

I decided to give Ray an extra thirty seconds, waited exactly five minutes from when he had left, and then walked to the pile of hay. I picked up a couple of rags from the pile, sparked my Zippo, and the fabric went up so fast they nearly singed my hand. I flung them down on the pile and the hay ignited like tissue paper.

The barn doors were heavier than I remembered, but they slid back against the pressure of my shoulder, first the right and then the left. I looked at the porch long enough to see Lewis stand up, then I pulled the Python from under my arm, stepped beside the door, screamed "Fire!" and fired four shots into the air.

Lewis disappeared and I hauled ass to the chicken coop, clearing the distance before I could get out of breath from the sprint. I dove behind it to the spot where Ray and I had sat, and my breath got there just as I did. I panted and tried to reload the Python at the same time, just dumping all the shells, spent and not, onto the ground and reaching into my pocket for some more, groping, feeling my way along in the dark, sliding them into the empty chambers one at a time.

"Hi, Dan."

Her voice startled me. I nearly dropped the gun as I looked up. Treasure Haines was standing before me in jeans and a T-shirt with CINCINNATI scrawled across the distinctive skyline on her chest. She was holding a gun, pointing it at me. It wasn't a big gun compared to the Python, but it was big enough.

"Put the gun down," she said. "Over here by my feet."

"Oh, no. Treasure." Images of the past few days started spiraling through my brain. Treasure standing by the graves of the dogs, Treasure in front of her father's refrigerator, Treasure at the cemetery, Treasure tied to the chair . . . behind me, where I couldn't see her. "Oh, damn."

"Such language," she said. "And you a minister." She shrugged. "It's a long, complicated story, Dan. Don't blame yourself."

"I use stories in my sermons. Can I use this one?"

"Oh, I don't think there'll be a next sermon," she said. "I tried, Dan. I really did try. But you and Ray just kept comin', didn't you?"

"Your own father?"

"I didn't have nothin' . . . anything to do with that. Those butt-head Gormans have screwed this thing up grandly. Now I have to fix it for them. Daddy was right. No one ever takes care of your things the way you do." She waggled her pistol at me. "The gun."

I reached out and put it between her feet and she stooped to pick it up, never taking her eyes off me. She put it in her belt.

"I guess we better go now," she said. She sighed. "Look at the barn. Damn. Bless is gonna be pissed." As I had feared, the barn was burning. She waggled the gun again. "Get up."

I got to my feet. "Ray has May June safe by now," I said. "He went in the back door while I was coming across the yard."

She shrugged. "Just a trade. Now we have you. We still have to have the pictures and documents and what-have-you. He'll give them up for you."

I shook my head. "No, he won't. He knows you'll kill us once you have the pictures."

"Then he'll try another heroic rescue and we'll get him then." She motioned toward the house. "Go on."

I walked toward the house, trying to keep the light from the barn fire out of my field of vision. I looked everywhere for Ray but he was staying out of sight. I wanted to do something brave, like scream out to him to run, take the stuff, and go to the sheriff. But fear and confusion have a way of confounding the brain. No thought or ideas would stay in my head long enough to get a foothold. Just walking toward the house took all of my concentration.

About halfway across the yard Lewis and Frank came running up to us from the direction of the barn. They were covered with soot and smoke.

"Damn, Treasure," Lewis said. "They set the barn on fire."

Frank nodded, panting and coughing.

Treasure prodded me in the back with the gun and I kept walking. They fell in step with her behind me. "What are you two doing here?" she asked. "Where's the old lady?"

Frank spoke, his voice gravelly. "She's sleepin' over in the house. We gave her—" he paused. "Son of a bitch!" He and Lewis ran off toward the house. From inside, they both swore at the same time.

"That would be their discovery that May June is no longer in their custody," I said. "They're not exactly rocket scientists, are they?"

"Shut up," Treasure said. She stopped and so did I. We were

standing about twenty feet from the porch. The barn was completely engulfed in flames, throwing orange light onto the whole area. She yelled. "Lewis! You and Frank get out here and bring your guns. Bring the walkie-talkie, too."

Franklin and Lewis came tumbling out of the house with guns in their hands. Lewis had the same cannon he had carried at my house. Franklin carried something that looked like the pictures I'd seen of an Uzi. Lewis stopped on the porch and picked up the walkie-talkie, came into the yard, and handed it to Treasure.

She pushed the button and spoke into it. "Bobby, get up here. We got a situation." There was a soft, static buzz on the radio while she waited for a reply. She keyed it again. "Bobby, you hear me?"

"Bobby's not here," a voice said from the walkie-talkie. It was Ray and I felt like crying and laughing at the same time.

Lewis grabbed the radio from Treasure and screamed into it. "Where's my brother? You better not have hurt him, you son of a bitch."

She grabbed the radio back from Lewis and gave him a look. He was nearly hyperventilating. Frank was impassive. "We just need to have those papers and pictures that you have, Mr. Hall. Then we're going to blow up the mine and be on our way. All the evidence will be gone and we'll all live happily ever after. Okay?" She waited, listening.

"I don't think so," Ray said.

Treasure stamped her foot. "Why not, damn it?"

"Because you didn't say anything about the money. You want the money, too. But you didn't say anything about it. Which means you're lying."

"I'm . . . not . . . lying, damn it!" She didn't use the walkie-talkie. She just screamed it. She shot another look at Lewis and Frank and they spread out, looking around them into the darkness as they moved.

"Treasure, honey, you been lyin' since you got here."

She threw the walkie-talkie on the ground and kicked it and then shot it twice. "All right," she screamed. "You've got one minute to bring that stuff up here or I'm gonna kill your preacher friend!" She aimed the gun at my forehead and I felt my knees weaken. I wanted to shut my eyes but I couldn't unglue them from the gun she was holding. It was little, probably a twenty-two like the one my uncle let me shoot, but the barrel was shorter. The bullet from that gun would be only about a half inch long and maybe a quarter inch wide and it would kill me as dead as if it were a cannonball.

Incredibly, it was Calvin Haines's favorite scripture passage that leapt into my brain. *Consider my affliction and my trouble, and for-*

give all my sins. Consider how many are my enemies, and how they hate me with cruel hatred. O guard my life, and deliver me; do not let me be put to shame, for I take refuge in you.

"Don't do nothin' stupid now that you're gonna regret later, Treasure," Ray shouted from the darkness near the driveway.

Treasure laughed without humor. "I already done that a thousand times over," she shouted. "Whataya call them pictures you found?" Her accent was coming back.

"Call 'em a mistake," Ray said. "Call 'em a young girl's foolishness but nothin' can't be understood. Had to be hard on you, goin' off to the city by yourself, nothin' but a little girl."

"Little girl," Treasure said so softly only I could hear her. She yelled at Ray. "You got thirty seconds! She cocked the pistol and I held my breath. Frank and Lewis were trying to zero in on Ray's voice but he kept moving around, out in the darkness.

"Now listen, Treasure," Ray shouted. "Ain't nothin' happened here with you that we can't work out. But you gotta put that gun down and let the preacher walk over here."

"Fifteen seconds!" The barn was burning out of control and she had to scream just to hear herself over the roar of the flames.

"No! Now you stop that right now." I could barely hear Ray. "I ain't never lied to you, have I? Now listen to me and—"

All hell broke loose.

Something big and white flashed by the corner of my eyes. There was a deep, growling sound and a scream, and I heard Frank hit the ground. In the same instant, there was a small explosion and Treasure Haines screamed, twirled violently to her left, and fell. Blood flew from her shoulder and arm as she fell, some of it spraying onto my jacket.

I heard a third scream and looked at Lewis. He wasn't looking at me. He was looking at the ground where his brother had been standing and now lay, writhing and gagging, trying to get the pit bull away from his throat. He was failing. As I watched, his hands dropped from the dog, his legs twitched, and he died. The dog continued to growl and chew.

I looked back at Lewis just as he looked at me and raised his gun and fired. The bullet buzzed past my ear as I dove to the ground next to where Treasure lay, groaning, trying to hold her arm together. Someone, not Ray, yelled from the edge of the woods and Lewis turned and ran toward the house. I pulled the Python from Treasure's belt and followed him. Someone, maybe Ray, yelled my name.

They had trashed the house. Food wrappers and papers and furniture were thrown everywhere. The only two upright pieces were the couch where May June had been lying and the chair Frank had been sitting in. Lewis was not in the living room or the dining room.

I walked into the kitchen, gun first like on television, but he wasn't in there, either. Something crashed upstairs and I took the steps two at a time, trying to hug the wall, sweeping the Python in front of me as I went. Someone crashed through the front door just as I got to the top of the stairs.

"Dan?" It was Ray.

"Up here," I called down. "Lewis is up here and he's got a gun."

I heard Ray talk to someone then he said, "Dan, get down here. We'll take it now."

Something seized up inside me. What was I doing? Ray was right. I was a minister, not some Wyatt Earp tracking outlaws through Calvin Haines's house. I started to turn back down the stairs and stopped.

No, I couldn't do it. I wouldn't. Something like rage boiled in me. The Python felt good in my hand. Really good. It was power and fire and death and I controlled it. I wasn't afraid. I had seen the look of terror in Lewis Gorman's eyes as he watched his brother die and I had reveled in the power that it gave me. I wanted to see it again, I wanted to be the cause of it.

I moved on down the hall.

Ray mumbled, "Damn it, Dan."

The bedroom doors were all open so I only had to look in, peeking around the corner, listening for a noise to find Lewis. He was in Victory's room, huddled in the corner with his knees drawn up to his face. His left arm was across his head and his right hand held his gun. He was pointing it out into the room, waving it around, but his eyes were buried in his knees. He was weeping.

I ignored his gun, walked straight up to him, raised the Python, and pointed it at the top of his head. Rage like molasses, sweet and hot, poured down my spine and warmed me. "Look at me."

His eyes peeked up from his knees and he let the gun drop to the floor. "Please. Don't kill me," he whimpered. "It was her idea."

"Treasure," I said.

He nodded, squeezing his eyes shut again.

I pulled the hammer back on the Python and Lewis screamed. He tried to crawl completely under his arms. He wet his pants.

Ray's hand clamped around mine, his palm holding the hammer back in case I pulled the trigger. "You got your thing back now?"

"How's May June?" I said. I was still looking at Lewis. I felt like my body weighed a thousand pounds. I let go of the gun and he took it, let the hammer down easy and put it in his jacket pocket.

"She's fine. Sleepin' out yonder in the smokehouse. She'll have a headache like you did but that's probably all. Gil and Gay Carmack are on their way with the unit."

"Conrad Foley?"

Ray nodded. "I called him from the office while you were makin' coffee. Took his time gettin' here, didn't he? He brought Hank and Loretta and that dog o' Hank's."

"Breaker," I said.

"Yeah."

I nodded at Lewis. "You gonna kill him?"

Ray sighed. "I reckon not. I guess I got a belly full o' killin."

He turned and walked slowly out of the room and down the stairs. I followed him.

CHAPTER 21

ELIAS KNOWLY ARRIVED WITH THE CARMACK TWINS, who came in the Volunteer Fire Department ambulance. Elias came in his official Sheriff's Department cruiser as Ray had predicted, with siren blaring and lights flashing. His guns were not blazing but his eyes were.

"Well, the one named Bobby's got two concussions," Eli said. "How the hell do you get two concussions? Will someone tell me that?"

"Musta hit his head twice," Ray said. "I think Gilbert and Gaylord mean he's got one real bad concussion from two whacks on the head."

Eli wasn't listening. "That big 'un yonder's dead. Lord, what happened to him? Looks like somethin' tore out his whole throat."

Ray shrugged and kept an eye on me. "Don't know, Eli. Heard him scream and saw him go down. Then I heard somethin' tear off into the woods. Maybe a painter or a wolf. Maybe just a wild dog."

Painter was how hill people pronounced *panther*, which was how they referred to the mountain lions that had roamed these hills a hundred years ago. No sober person had seen one in fifty years.

Eli snorted. "Malarkey. Ain't been a painter or a wolf in these hills since my daddy and you was wearin' short pants. And the only wild dogs around these parts is the ones fight in the pits and a few coyotes that are afraid of their own shadow. You sure you two was the only ones come up here?"

Ray and I nodded vigorously.

Elias shook his head and spit as more deputies arrived. "One dead, one with his head caved in, one pissin' in his pants and cryin' outta control. Treasure Haines with a bullet hole in her and you tellin' me to put her under arrest. The barn burnt to smithereens. Some kinda poison crap in the mine. You two been on a regular tear up here, ain't ya?"

Ray shrugged and lit a cigarette. "Just fightin' crime and upholdin' the law, Eli. Just doin' my job."

We were sitting on the porch of the house and Eli was standing at the foot of the steps. He turned and looked at the cruisers coming up the lane. Before he left he said, "Ray, I ain't a child an' I ain't a moron. You two wanna sit here and lie to me, well, okay. I guess you got good reasons and I'm willin' to trust ya. But don't patronize me, okay?"

Ray nodded. "Sorry, Elias. And thanks."

Eli stepped off the porch and started across the yard. "Yeah, yeah. Painter my ass."

We had given preliminary statements to Elias as soon as he arrived and agreed to meet him at his office at nine o'clock to write them down. As Eli was giving instructions to his people, Gil and Gay Carmack announced that they had somehow managed to get May June, Treasure Haines, Bobby Gorman, and Lewis Gorman all in the unit, with the two Gorman brothers tied and cuffed securely. They were ready to go to the Durel County Memorial Hospital.

"They're all sleepin' so they don't know how crowded they are," Gay said.

"Couldn't fit big 'un in there," Gil said.

"Don't figure he'll mind much. We put him in the house so the critters can't get to 'im," Gay said.

"We'll come back for 'im later," Gil said.

"What there is of 'im," Gay said.

"Painter, you say?" Gil said.

Ray nodded.

The Carmacks nodded.

I nodded and looked at Ray, and as the twins closed the back end of the unit, he winked at me. It was 1:35 a.m.

We followed the unit in Ray's Jeep and arrived at the hospital at 2:15.

At 4:00 Doctor Louise Markle told us that Treasure Haines could talk to us but she was full of drugs and may not be too coherent. Ray said that it was four in the damn morning and we were full of coffee and not too coherent ourselves, so it would probably be a swell party. Louise smiled beautifully and bowed us into the room where Treasure was handcuffed to her hospital bed.

I guess what followed was what the police call a Q and A. Questions and Answers. Ray and I sat in chairs on either side of her bed and Treasure lay in the bed with the head cranked up to about a forty-degree angle. There wasn't a stenographer or tape recorder, but Ray took some notes in his little notebook. Treasure stared straight ahead at the wall in front of her and spoke in clear precise English without even a hint of an accent. If there was any sign of drugs it was in her complete lack of emotion or hesitancy. Ray did all the questioning and I listened to the two of them, trying my best to unravel what had been going on in the past week in and around Durel County.

"You feel like talkin', Tiger Lady?"

She nodded, shrugged. "Why not?"

"We're kind of confused about some things. Wonder if you could put it all together for us." Ray lit a cigarette and I winced, expecting a doctor or nurse to come bursting in the door. None did.

She let the corners of her mouth turn up just a millimeter. "Tiger Lady. You knew all along?"

"I sorta figured," Ray said. "Had the preacher go over that scene in the parsonage several times and every time it came out the same. They come bustin' in. Order you around. Call you 'Tiger Lady.' Make you take your clothes off."

"Jerks."

"They are that," Ray agreed. "That little cat tattoo on your fanny isn't a kitten or a lion, is it? It's a tiger. But them boys hadn't seen the tattoo yet. You still had your clothes on when they called you that. So they musta seen it somewheres else."

Treasure shook her head. "Jerks, jerks, jerks."

"What'd you do, set that whole scene up? Scare the preacher but don't hurt him. Let them pretend to slap you around instead. Put a couple o' bruises on you, maybe make your nose bleed, but don't do nothin' too bad? With skin as white as yours I bet you bruise real easy."

"I liked him. I didn't want him to get hurt. That pig, Frank, got carried away."

"Maybe if you started from the beginnin'," Ray said.

Treasure Haines sighed. When she finally started talking it was in a monotone. No inflection, no emotion, just a rote rendering of the facts of her life.

She went to Cincinnati right out of high school. She had no skills, no money, no friends. She had an accent that placed her as a hillbilly, so high school diploma or no, everyone just figured she was an ignorant hick. She couldn't get a job doing anything but waiting tables or ringing a cash register at the local supermarket. That paid for the rent at a run-down flat in Over-The-Rhine, but it wouldn't pay college tuition.

One day she answered an ad in the classified section of the paper. Go-Go dancers. No experience necessary. Will train. Cash paid nightly. She started that night at a place in the industrial valley of the city. It was called the Kitten Caboodle and she made good money dancing in a string bikini, teasing the shot and beer guys, hustling drinks, leaning against the scotch drinkers and letting them cop a feel now and then.

The Kitten Caboodle was owned by a man named Cletus Gorman, brother of Artus. Cletus, who was about the same size as his obese brother and a couple of years older, took an immediate liking to Treasure and offered her a job where she could make some "real money."

It seemed that Cletus had a brother who owned a place over in Newport, Kentucky, across the river from Cincinnati. This place was called the Cherry Bomb Cabaret. At the Cherry Bomb the costumes were briefer. Pasties and a G-string or nothing at all, depending on the mood of the county prosecutor in any given week. She could work as much or as little as she wanted. She could start the night shift immediately, where the money was the best, and she would make enough to put some aside for college. She took the job.

In less than a year she was turning tricks for Artus Gorman.

"I was freebasing all day and hooking all night," she said to the wall. "I was that way for three years."

No fool, Artus, he realized that he was killing the goose that could lay the golden egg. He got her into rehab, dried her out, and got her back on the dance floor, turning the occasional trick only for "special friends and clients."

On her twenty-fifth birthday she told Artus Gorman she was through with him. She had saved enough money to put herself through school and that was what she was going to do.

Artus just laughed.

He showed her the pictures.

"There were a bunch of them. You saw two of the more modest ones. The others were. . . ." she swallowed. "The others were more intimate. There was a different man in each one. He took them at one of his after-hours parties when I was smoking base. I still can't remember anything about that night."

Artus said, sure, she was free to go. She was getting a little long in the tooth for his taste anyway. But she would go quietly. She wouldn't talk to any police or any reporters or anyone at all, or the pictures would go public. And from time to time he would maybe need a favor from her and when he did she would be nice and polite and do as he asked. He fanned the pictures out like a huge poker hand and waved them in her face.

"He called about once or twice a year for a while," she said. "Usually he was throwing a party and needed a special girl for a special client. Someone with my look, I suppose. I'd drive to Louisville or Lexington and do what he wanted and he'd pay me some ridiculous huge amount and I'd go home and pretend it never happened." She sipped some water from a plastic cup.

Then he didn't call for a couple of years. She graduated from college, went to graduate school, got her master's degree. She took a job working for the Hamilton County public library and did okay. She went back to school and took classes in computers and library application, and when the job at the college came along she took it.

She had made it. She was educated, respectable and respected. She had scratched, clawed, crawled, and dug her way out of Appalachia. Then, after a nine-year hiatus, Artus Gorman called again.

"He needed a moonshine source. Said he'd pay a finder's fee if I could set him up with one. See, with Artus it was once a hillbilly, always a hillbilly. I didn't even have to think about it. I set him up with the Foley family." Just a hint of amusement winked in her eyes and then went out.

"You were his inside source in the hills," Ray said. "I wondered how a city yahoo like Gorman managed to link up with Conrad Foley."

"Conrad never knew it was me who gave him his bona fides," she said. "Anyway, it didn't work out."

A year or so went by with nothing from the Gormans and then another call from Artus. He said she had to drop everything and meet him at the Cherry Bomb that afternoon.

"I put on a disguise," she said. "I didn't want to take even a chance of anyone seeing me going in that place. I looked like a spy. Trench coat, floppy hat, scarf. It was August, for crying out loud."

Artus had his sons with him. She had met them before and she was not impressed, but she heard Artus out.

"He had managed to get a contract with the state government to dispose of the paraquat they were cleaning up. There were lots of state and federal regulations but, of course, he was going to stiff everyone and dump it. But he didn't have anyplace to put it. He wanted me to find him a place up in the hills. It was a big deal and he was desperate. So I decided to try and use it to make a clean break."

Artus had three shipments of thirty barrels each. He would pay her $500 a barrel, $45,000. But that wasn't enough for her. She wanted the Polaroids. Artus was not happy about the price, but he reluctantly agreed. He would give her a third of the pictures each time he delivered a load. Now, where was he going to dump the poison?

"Your daddy's coal mine," Ray said.

She nodded.

No one had used the mine since her brother-in-law, Bert, had died in it. It was just a big hole in the ground. They would fill it with poison and cover it over by sealing it up. The only problem was getting Calvin to go along.

For that task Treasure employed the simplest and most powerful weapon she had at her disposal: the truth. She paid a visit to her father and she told him the whole story. The dancing, the drugs, the prostitution, the parties. She wept, she cried, she begged his forgiveness, and, of course, he took her into his arms and he forgave her.

Then she told him about the pictures and the only way she knew to get them back.

Calvin didn't like it. He was afraid of paraquat and he was afraid of these rich city slickers. But he loved his daughter and he would do whatever he had to do to save her. He agreed.

The first shipment was delivered in January and the payment was made with a big bonus because Calvin and Crazy George helped unload the barrels and "Lewis forgot to bring the pictures with him. Said he'd mail the pictures to me. Of course, he never did."

The next shipment was supposed to be delivered in May, but by April the barrels in the mine had already begun to deteriorate and Calvin was having second thoughts.

"He read up on paraquat," Ray said. He looked at me and back at Treasure. "We don't have computers in our library yet. We still have to sign the books out the old-fashioned way. I had our librarian look up everything she had on paraquat for me and she noticed that Calvin Haines had been the last person to check it out. All of it."

Calvin panicked. He called Artus Gorman and told him the deal was off. Gorman said a deal was a deal. Calvin called back the next day and said he'd give the money back and keep the barrels that had been delivered if Gorman would give him the pictures and find somewhere else to dump the rest of his barrels. Artus Gorman told Calvin to go screw himself.

On the Wednesday before Easter, Calvin called his daughter and told her his plan to get them both off the hook. If blackmail was good enough for the Gormans, he said, it was good enough for the Haineses. He would go down into the mine and take some pictures and use them the way Artus Gorman was using his pictures of Treasure. Treasure tried to talk him out of it. He was dealing with something different than he had ever come across. He was in way over his head. She begged and pleaded but his mind was made up.

On Thursday the Gorman brothers arrived.

At first they used intimidation. They did their best to scare Calvin. They broke some things and waved their guns around but no one got hurt. They gave him two pictures of his daughter and told him they would give the rest to the newspapers in Perry and

Cincinnati if he didn't do as they told him. Then they left.

By Friday morning Calvin had overcome his fear and was mad. He took his little Instamatic camera into the mine and took all the pictures left on the roll. He drove into Perry and had them developed at the one-hour place out by the highway and then he drove back to his house and called Conrad Foley, the leader of the toughest family he knew.

Conrad Foley told him to back away from the Gormans. He said to call him if they gave him any more trouble, but they didn't come back. When, on Saturday, nothing happened, Calvin must have felt vindicated. He called his daughter on Sunday morning and told her that he had fixed everything. Then he went outside and found his dog, Erasmus Wishbone, kicked to death in his front yard.

"Damn stupid old hillbilly," Treasure said. "He was gonna ruin my life and get himself killed over some barrels in an old coal mine that nobody cared about or knew about." There was some anger creeping into her voice now but her eyes were glistening with moisture. For her father or herself, I didn't know. "I guess you know the rest," she said.

Ray lit another cigarette and nodded his head. "You decided to come down and fix things yourself, but before you could, Blessing called and told you about your daddy."

"They killed him for the pictures he took," she said. "I told them, 'Kill the dogs. He loves those dogs. He'll do anything for them.' But he was so damn hardheaded and those stupid bastards don't know anything but muscle and blood. He must have died before he could tell them where the pictures were."

"Probably would have killed him anyway. They knew about George because he helped unload the barrels." Ray poured himself a cup of water from the pitcher and held it up to me. I shook my head. "They tried to scare the preacher and me off by callin' on the phone, and fiddlin' with my brakes and the bell in the church."

Treasure shook her head. "They didn't do the church bell. I don't know how that happened." She looked at me. "Maybe you got enemies you don't know about."

"So you orchestrated everything from then on?" Ray asked.

Her jaw clenched. "Those idiots were screwing up everything. All I wanted was those pictures and my money. I earned that money, damn it! I earned everything I have and nobody had the right to take it from me. Not Daddy and not Artus Freaking Gorman!"

"How'd you get out of the diner with a deputy keepin' an eye on you?" Ray asked.

"Lewis gave me some stuff to put in his coffee. He's a junkie, you know. Lewis, not the deputy. He's got more stuff than a pharmacy and knows more about drugs than most doctors. When the deputy nodded off I just slipped out the back door. I called Lewis on his cell phone and he told me where to meet him."

"Bless didn't find out you were gone until Darnell called," Ray said. "She was in a near panic. She's on her way over now."

Treasure sagged in the bed. "Oh, no. Do I have to see her?"

"Not if you don't want to," Ray said. "But you better see a lawyer. I can give you the name o' one if you want."

For the first time a real feeling seemed to impress itself on her face. She looked at me and then at Ray. "I need a lawyer?"

Ray nodded.

"Why? I told you what happened. They were blackmailing me. I was just trying to protect myself. You can't be serious."

Ray flipped a couple of pages in his notebook and started writing again. "Nothin' you've said to me or the preacher here can be used against you, hon. But directly, Deputy Knowly is gonna come in here and arrest you for a whole bunch o' stuff. He'll tell you your rights, but I suggest you call this-here man before Elias gets here." He tore a page from the notebook and gave it to her. "Percy's an old man. But don't let that fool ya. He's sharp as a tack and if he can't represent you he'll know someone who can and will do a good job of it."

She looked at the paper with something like confusion. Then the confusion turned to pain and the pain to anger. "Damn it, no! I didn't do anything wrong! I was just trying to protect everything I worked for. Don't you see?" She wadded the paper and threw it at Ray. "Get out of here, both of you. Get out!"

Ray stood and walked to the door. "Suit yourself."

CHAPTER 22

RAY AND NAOMI WERE SITTING at the counter in the diner when I came out of Ray's office. May June was standing on the other side, leaning over.

"So what'd they say?" May June asked.

"They asked if I was all right," I said. I told them that someone broke into the house and stole my new stereo. I didn't want to upset them with all of the details."

"And?"

"And then they asked if I had insurance."

"The church does, don't they?" Ray asked.

I nodded. "My daughter said, 'So no problem. Get a new one.'" I tried to imitate her California teenager accent. "She wasn't even upset."

"I guess she knows what's really important," May June said.

I sat down and May June poured a mug of coffee and put it in front of me with a packet of Sweet'n Low. "Where's Darnell?" I asked.

Ray looked over his shoulder. "Went home. Said it was time to exercise the pups. Blessing says he can keep 'em, sell 'em, whatever he wants."

I thought about Gideon. "I think he'll keep them," I said. They all nodded. "Did you and Elias open Calvin's safe deposit box?"

Ray nodded. "It was one of those little ones. Onliest thing in there was one of those spiral notebooks like secretaries use. He'd wrote the whole thing down. Musta put it in there when he came to town to have the pictures developed. It was signed and dated the Friday before he died."

"Good Friday," I said.

Ray noted the irony and nodded.

There was a long, comfortable silence then Naomi said, "Ray was tellin' us about what happened up at the farm last night."

I just nodded, not knowing how much he had told them and not wanting to damage his story if he had left out the Foley family with them as he had with Elias.

"So," she said, leaning into my arm. "Would you have shot Lewis?"

I thought about it for a moment. "I don't know," I said.

"He wouldn't have," Ray said.

I shook my head. "Maybe. Maybe not. I just don't know. I was so mad. I hated him so much. But he was so pitiful."

"You wouldn'ta shot him," Ray said.

I looked at him. "I appreciate your confidence, Ray. But I'm not so sure."

He smiled at Naomi. "His gun wasn't loaded," he said to her. He looked at me and shrugged.

I didn't know whether he was telling the truth or not. When I thought about it I realized that Treasure had interrupted me while I was trying to reload. It had been dark and I had been fumbling with the bullets, my hand shaking, dropping some. I thought some went into the chambers in the cylinder, but did they really? I finished my coffee and looked at my watch. "I need some sleep," I said.

Naomi tugged at my arm. "Come on, I'll tuck you in. You all take care now, y'hear?" Ray and May June nodded and smiled at her. No one could talk to Naomi Taylor without smiling.

Outside, the sun was bright and warm. Birds sang. Coal trucks banged back and forth on Route 42. It was midafternoon and the world was going on with its business as though nothing had happened. It didn't seem right and at the same time it seemed exactly as it should be. There was comfort in it. Life was going on.

We walked arm in arm down to the parsonage and waved at the Rudepohler brothers as they continued to work on the steeple. I would never find out about the cut bell bar. Maybe the Gormans had done it without telling Treasure. Maybe she had done it. Maybe someone had done it years ago, trying to fix the thing and then given up. Maybe I had enemies I wasn't aware of.

"So the whole thing was a charade," Naomi said. "You were never in any real danger that night when they came here, and neither was she."

"She was running the show," I said. "What happened to her in the city? What made her like that?"

Naomi shrugged. "Probably nothin' she didn't want to happen. The city just provided fertile ground for whatever was in her to grow. No one put a gun to her head and made her dance naked or smoke dope or turn tricks."

We went up the steps onto the porch of the parsonage. We turned to watch the guys standing on the scaffolding around the front of the church. I thought of Calvin Haines. "Consider how many are my enemies, and how they hate me with cruel hatred," I said. "She was one of his enemies and he didn't even know it. His own daughter."

Naomi took my hand in hers. "She came to him and told him the truth and she used it against him, to manipulate him. He could have been her Reverend Mayhew and she turned her back on him."

We stood and watched the workers in silence.

"So," she said, after a few moments. "How you doin'?"

"Okay, I guess."

"You get your thing back, out there at the farm, pointin' that gun at Lewis?"

I thought about it. "I don't know. As it turns out, he wasn't even the one who stole my . . . thing . . . as you call it. Maybe it was never stolen at all. Maybe it was Treasure who stole it."

"And you and Ray faced them down and now they're both in jail," she said. "And you didn't have to shoot anyone."

"I'm glad of that," I said.

"Me, too. I'm glad you didn't pull that trigger, bullets or not." She squeezed my hand.

I really was glad, too. Pulling the trigger on that gun would have changed my life forever and I don't think it would have been a good change. I'm glad I didn't have to find out. Bullets, no bullets. It didn't matter. Pulling the trigger was what mattered. And I didn't pull it.

Something made a sound at the door of the parsonage—scratching, squealing. Naomi and I looked at the door and then at each other. She was just about to say something when another sound came from the other side of the door. It was a dog barking.

We went to the door and opened it and a beagle puppy came bounding out. He ran between my legs, tumbled down the stairs into the grass strip below the porch, and squatted to pee. Then he came running back up the stairs, climbing laboriously up each one, ran to my leg, took the cuff of my blue jeans in his mouth and tried to drag me across the porch and down the stairs.

Naomi giggled and bent down to pick him up. He tried to bite her hands as she took the note that was pinned to a string around his neck. She read it, smiled, and handed it to me. "It's from Darnell," she said.

The spelling was Darnell's usual homemade, phonetic variety and the handwriting was that of a third grader, but it was easily readable:

"Reverent Dan. I am sorry about what happened to poor Gideon. Ray said you liked him. This-here pup ain't afraid of nothing. I call him David like in the Bible. You can have him if you want. Darnell."

I took David from Naomi and held him up to look into his face. He had the Wishbone/Trueblood mark on his nose and for a moment he stopped fighting and biting and tilted his head to look back at me. There was a little bit of Gideon in those eyes and I wondered for a moment if his feisty nature was because he was afraid of nothing or everything.

I pulled him up under my chin and held him there and felt his heart beating rapidly against my throat. He made a half grab for my shirt collar but his heart wasn't really in it. The fatigue seemed to hit me then and I sat down on the porch swing with the little beagle tucked to my chest. Naomi sat down beside me and laid her hand on my knee. I stopped fighting it and let the tears come, silent and easy.

Naomi called it my "thing." Something deep inside a person that can be stolen with violence and cruelty and can only be replaced with love. I still didn't know what it was, but I knew mine was coming back.